CAROL HIGGINS CLARK

POPPED

A Regan Reilly Mystery

DOUBLEDAY LARGE PRINT HOME LIBRARY EDITION
SCRIBNER
New York London Toronto Sydney Singapore

This Large Print Edition, prepared especially for
Doubleday Large Print Home Library, contains
the complete, unabridged text of the original
Publisher's Edition.

SCRIBNER
1230 Avenue of the Americas
New York, NY 10020

SCRIBNER and design are trademarks of
Macmillan Library Reference USA, Inc. used under license
by Simon & Schuster, the publisher of this work.

Manufactured in the United States of America

ISBN 0-7394-3793-3

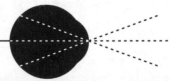

This Large Print Book carries the
Seal of Approval of N.A.V.H.

Acknowledgments

Up, up and away! I would like to thank the following people who helped me along the way as I wrote this book—from the original concept to the final liftoff.

Gratitude to my editor, Roz Lippel, who always has such wonderful suggestions and advice. Thanks also to her assistant Laura Petermann. Praise to Michael Korda and Chuck Adams for their comments and encouragement.

Many thanks to my agent, Sam Pinkus, and publicist, Lisl Cade, for their continuing guidance.

Kudos to art director John Fulbrook and associate director of copy-editing Gypsy da Silva. Thanks to photographer Herman Estevez.

Long time balloonist Ruth Lind introduced me to the world of hot air ballooning—thanks Ruth! I'm also grateful to Tom Rutherford who was so helpful to me at the Albuquerque Balloon Fiesta. I appreciate the time James Hamilton, aka "Chicken Jack," took to come down from the Imus Ranch for kids with cancer to show me around the Fiesta. And John Kugler, thanks for taking me up in your balloon. It was a fun landing!

Finally, thanks to my family and friends, especially my mother, Mary Higgins Clark, and my stepfather, John Conheeney, who are always there to encourage me.

You're all the best!

For Elaine Kaufman
of
Elaine's
who has welcomed writers into her legendary
New York City establishment for forty years now.
Happy Anniversary!
With love.

BALLOONISTS' PRAYER

The Winds have welcomed you with softness.
The Sun has blessed you with his warm hands.
You have flown so high and so well,
    that God has joined you in your laughter.
And He has set you gently back again
    into the loving arms of Mother Earth.

POPPED

Monday, October 6

1

Regan Reilly sat down at the scarred oak desk in her cozy office on Hollywood Boulevard in Los Angeles. Developers were dying to take a wrecking ball to the ancient structure, but so far the building managed to remain standing, which made Regan very happy. A private investigator who worked alone, Regan loved everything about her work, except the fact that it kept her three thousand miles from her boyfriend of ten months, Jack Reilly. Jack was the head of the major case squad in New York City. He was coming out to spend the weekend with her, but that was still four more days away.

Monday mornings, Regan thought, as she took a sip of coffee. They're the pits even if you like your job. There's just something about them. For one thing, they certainly put a damper on Sunday nights. I shouldn't complain, though, Regan mused. This Monday morning brings me one day closer to seeing Jack.

The quiet of the early October morning was broken by the ring of the phone.

"Regan Reilly."

"Wow. Am I talking to Regan Reilly after all these years?" a male voice asked.

"You're talking to Regan Reilly," she assured the caller. "Who's this?"

"You don't remember me?"

Here we go, Regan thought. It's not even nine o'clock on a Monday morning, and the weirdos are already on the horn. Don't these people ever give it a rest? "I have no idea who you are," Regan answered simply as she turned on her computer.

"I'll give you three guesses. But only three."

All this before my first cup of coffee, Regan thought. "Why don't you call back later," she suggested. "I'm sure you'll have your identity figured out by then. Bye." She started to put down the phone when she heard a shout from the other end.

"Wait! Regan, it's Danny Madley. The tree boy!"

Regan's hand froze in midair. Her mind raced back in time. The tree boy. No, it couldn't be. She pulled the phone back to her ear. "Tree Boy?"

"Yes!" he replied triumphantly.

"Danny Madley." Regan laughed. "I guess you haven't changed a bit." She pictured the gangly boy from her grammar school days in New Jersey. Danny was the class clown, the one who always had a scheme going. In second grade the teacher refused to give him a speaking part in the school production of *The Wizard of Oz* because he'd been such a nudge. She cast him as one of the trees. But, of course, trees talk in *The Wizard of Oz,* and Danny managed to blurt out a few lines he'd written especially for the occasion. He even stuffed apples in his pockets to throw at poor lost Dorothy, a scene the teacher had deliberately omitted from the official version of the play. The kids always called him Tree Boy after that. That is, after he'd spent a week in solitary confinement in a corner of the principal's office.

"You can tell that I haven't grown up?"

"That can be a good thing," Regan replied. "So, Danny, to what do I owe the honor of this phone call?"

"For one thing, I know you're a private investigator."

"You know that, huh?"

"Yes. You're always mentioned in the articles about your mother and her books, and I read something recently about when your father was kidnapped. Your new boyfriend's name is Reilly. Very cute."

Regan's mind wandered back to Christmastime when her father had been kidnapped in New York City. It was when she met Jack. He had been in charge of the investigation and had worked day and night to get Luke back. Jack always joked that it helped to get on the good side of a girl's family from the beginning. And Luke always said he'd do anything to contribute to his child's happiness—even if it meant getting kidnapped. Regan's mother, Nora, the suspense writer, was just thrilled that Regan finally had a decent boyfriend, however they happened to meet. Regan now smiled and informed Danny, "Jack Reilly is a great guy."

"I'm sure he is. Regan, I looked you up on Our Lady of Good Counsel's website and saw that you were registered. That's how I got your phone number."

"Those school websites are kind of fun, so I figured why not?" Regan said, leaning back in her chair. "It's great to hear from old friends, and it's a good way to network."

"That's why I'm calling. Regan, I really need your help."

Oh, God, Regan thought. Knowing Danny, what can he be up to now? "What's the matter?" she asked.

"I live in Las Vegas and work in television. I was asked to produce a reality show. There's a competition to see if my show will get on the air . . ."

Just what the world needs, Regan thought. Another reality show.

"A guy named Roscoe Parker who's been out here for years owns a local cable station called the Balloon Channel, also known as Hot Air Cable. That's because he also owns a hot air ballooning company. Anyway, he has a ton of dough. He gave me money to produce a reality show and is backing somebody else who is producing a sitcom. Both shows involve hot air balloons. This week we're putting together pilots to show

Roscoe on Friday afternoon. The one he likes best he'll put on the air Friday night."

"That's competition for you," Regan commented.

"You're not kidding. Roscoe's station is small but it's growing. This is a big chance for me. If my show is chosen, I'll have a regular slot on the Balloon Channel lineup. But things have been going wrong on the set lately. Yesterday one of our cameras was stolen. Then I was filming an introduction to the show at the hot air balloon field and the platform I was standing on collapsed under me. I think someone is trying to sabotage my operation. What I was wondering is, could you come to Vegas for a few days and help me out?"

Regan was afraid to ask but somehow she managed. "What is your show about?"

"It's called *Love Above Sea Level. Calamine lotion for the proverbial seven-year itch.*"

"Excuse me?"

"I wanted to create a show for married couples. So many reality shows are about singles looking for love. How about one for people who have found love and now need a little help to keep it going? We have three couples who no longer consider themselves honeymooners, to say the least, spending the week in Vegas recapturing the love they once knew. At the end of the week the advice columnists Aunt Agony and Uncle Heartburn will decide which couple truly deserves to renew their vows. We're flying to the Albuquerque Hot Air Balloon Fiesta on Roscoe's private plane. We'll all go up in a hot air balloon shaped like a wedding cake as soon as the sun rises on Friday morning. With a camera, of course. The winning couple will be announced up in the air. Then they'll renew their vows and come back down to earth with a million bucks."

I have not words, Regan thought.

"Regan, are you there?" Danny asked anxiously.

"Indeed." Regan cleared her throat. "Just out of curiosity, where did you find these couples?"

"Roscoe's people found them. I guess they had plenty of folks to choose from. We wanted couples who needed our help and could benefit from a little excitement in their relationship. I see this as the only reality show that is a real positive contribution to society. If we can get just one couple to rekindle that lost spark, then we've done our job."

The thought of a million dollars would make any couple do a lot of rekindling, Regan mused. "So you want me to come to Vegas?"

"I know I can trust you."

"Really?"

"Anyone you survived grammar school with you should be able to trust. There's got to be a permanent bond between two people who sat together in the same class for eight years."

"That's true." Regan laughed. "But I have to tell you: I know at least one person from our class has served time. Credit card theft. I'd never ask him to hold my purse no matter how many years we sat together."

"Let me guess. Bobby Hastings."

"Bingo."

"Well I'm afraid there's at least one Bobby Hastings kind of character hanging around my show. And I'm afraid whoever it is is going to cause more trouble."

Regan opened the drawer of her desk and pulled out her trusty legal pad. This is what I get for signing up for that classmates website, she realized. What was the old expression . . . be careful what you pray for? She picked up a pen. "Okay, Danny. Let me ask you a few more questions. Then I'll call the airlines. I'm sure I can catch a plane to Vegas this afternoon. But I have to be back Friday night."

"Don't worry, Regan. By Friday the show will be finished. One way or the other."

———◆———

2

Roscoe Parker banged his fist on the massive mahogany desk and chuckled. He was looking up at one of the sixteen video screens mounted on a wall of his private office. Behind Parker hung a large logo of his Balloon Channel. The photo of a multicolored hot air balloon dreamily floating off into the heavens filled most of the wall behind the desk. A plaque inscribed with the "Balloonists' Prayer" was mounted nearby. This room was Roscoe Parker's inner sanctum. Only his most trusted advisers were allowed inside. Not that they advised him much. They did everything he told them to do. The job paid very well.

Roscoe saw himself as a combination of Howard Hughes and Merv Griffin. But unlike

Howard Hughes, Roscoe liked to get out of bed and socialize. No holing up in a hotel suite for years, trying to take over Las Vegas without seeing anyone. No eating the same boring food all the time with the drapes permanently drawn. Roscoe wanted to get out in the limelight and have fun as he made his mark. Like Howard Hughes, he wanted to make a difference in Las Vegas. And like Merv Griffin, he wanted to build an empire. He didn't own a big hotel like Merv yet, but he did have a hot air balloon business and a cable station that he envisioned as the next HBO. It bothered him that, unlike Merv, he hadn't thought of an original idea for a successful game show. The ever popular *Jeopardy* and *Wheel of Fortune* were Merv's creations, and they showed no signs of wearing out. What Roscoe did dream up was a competition pitting a reality show against a sitcom to see which one would have the most appeal.

These days it was all about reality shows versus scripted television. Which was more entertaining? What was the future of television? It was driving a lot of people in the entertainment business crazy. But Roscoe loved the frenzy. His motto was "Competition is what makes America great."

Roscoe watched as the video screens depicted the goings-on at *Love Above Sea Level* and the sitcom *Take Me Higher.* Both groups were agitated, which delighted Roscoe to no end.

"Survival of the fittest," he cried, banging his riding crop against the desk. Roscoe wasn't a horseback rider. He was actually afraid of horses but liked the effect. Roscoe did most things for effect. Recently he'd taken to buying studded cowboy boots and chunky jewelry. The jewelry was for himself, much to the dismay of his long-suffering, ever-present girlfriend Kitty who was curled up on the red leather couch reading a romance novel and chewing gum. In her fifties, Kitty knew that it was impossible to find a man who was perfect. She had been with Roscoe almost a year, and even though he could be eccentric and obsessed, she stuck it out with him. She listened to his ramblings with one ear because most of the time he could be fun, and God knows he was rich. Lately it was bugging her, though, the way this TV project had taken over his life. And she did think it was just a little macabre the way he got such pleasure out of other people's misery. Worst of all, he'd just bought himself another gold chain.

Roscoe was a sixty-four-year-old average-looking guy, slightly paunchy, with a receding hairline that he dyed every three weeks whether it needed it or not. He had made millions over the years in various ventures. Recently he inherited a nifty sum from a long-lost uncle who he was glad reached out to him from the hereafter, and he'd even managed to win a million in the lottery back when a million actually meant something. Two years ago, after a health scare, Roscoe had a revelation. He decided to have more fun with his money as he tried to take over the town, even if it meant putting his money at risk.

In other words, he stopped being cheap.

Now his two trusted advisers, the top executives at Hot Air Cable, sat in the red ultrasuede chairs facing his desk.

"What have we got going?" Roscoe asked the man and woman sitting in front of him. Erene, in her late twenties, was a sharp-featured, no-nonsense kind of gal who had taken lots of business courses in college and liked to quote surveys and studies. Her light brown hair came to her shoulders, and she always dressed in nondescript business suits. She was a practical numbers kind of person who had fire in her eyes. Leo was a stocky redheaded guy in his mid-thirties. He'd had several jobs in advertising, dressed in Hawaiian shirts, and considered himself the creative force at Hot Air Cable.

"Well, sir—" Erene began.

"Well what?" Roscoe queried, tapping the desk with his riding crop. "What are our plans to pump up the competition so Hot Air Cable ends up with a hit?"

In the corner, Kitty rolled her eyes as she turned the page of her book.

Erene cleared her throat and began again. "We have come up with a number of ideas that we hope you will find satisfactory. . . ."

3

———◆———

Regan made a reservation on an afternoon flight to Las Vegas, closed up her office, and drove home to her apartment in the Hollywood Hills. She unlocked the door, stepped inside, and felt that sense of peace she always experienced when returning to her abode. The two-bedroom apartment, nestled in the Hills, had a soothing quality.

Except when Regan opened the front hall closet.

The closet was where she kept her suitcases and a host of other assorted items, including athletic gear, Christmas decorations, umbrellas, and two old tape players that she would probably never use again but couldn't throw away. Everybody has a closet like this, Regan told herself as she pulled a medium-sized suitcase with wheels from the top shelf and dragged it into the bedroom. She set it on the bed, sat down, and called Jack.

"You're going to Vegas? Maybe I should meet you there for the weekend," he suggested.

"Let's see how this goes," Regan answered. "I might want to escape from the bright lights by then." She looked at the picture by her bed of the two of them. Jack had sandy hair and strong, even features, and was six feet two inches tall. Regan had inherited the black Irish looks from the Reilly side of the family: raven hair, blue eyes, and light skin. Jack was thirty-four; she was thirty-one. People often remarked that they complemented each other perfectly.

"You know this guy from grammar school?" asked Jack. "I hope you don't rekindle any old crushes."

"Believe me," Regan said with a laugh. "I remember him as being a cute kid, but he's not my type."

"Well, Regan, I'm glad you'll be keeping the world safe for reality shows. Be careful, would you please?"

"I'll do my best."

"I can't wait until this weekend. Call me when you get to Vegas."

"I will." She hung up and tried her parents. She always liked to let them know when she was going out of town.

"How's Jack?" her mother inquired within two seconds of Regan saying hello. These days it was always her first question.

"Fine, Mom." Regan smiled and told her about her trip to Vegas.

"Dad and I are heading out to Santa Fe tomorrow."

"I forgot about that," Regan admitted.

"I'm speaking at a writer's conference."

Nora was a best-selling suspense writer and often spoke to groups of aspiring and established writers. Luke owned three funeral homes. They had been happily married for thirty-five years.

"We're staying a few extra days with the Rosenbergs at their house out there. Harry loves those hot air balloons. He wants to take us to the hot air balloon festival in Albuquerque later in the week. One of the days they have a parade of 'special shapes' balloons which is supposed to be quite a sight. Balloons that look like everything from beer cans to cartoon characters. Harry said it's a great event." Harry Rosenberg was Nora's longtime literary agent and dear friend. His wife, Linda Ashby, was a painter.

"That's funny," Regan said. "The guy who is sponsoring Danny's reality show is big into hot air balloons. The winning couple is going to renew their vows in a balloon at that fiesta," Regan explained. "So I'll be there on Friday. We'll have to hook up."

"Are you going up in that balloon?" Nora asked with concern.

"To tell you the truth, I don't know. Danny will fill me in on everything when I see him. I'd better go, Mom. I have to pack."

"Well keep in touch. I'll have my cell phone with me. I must say the thought of you going up in a balloon doesn't thrill me."

"Mom, don't worry. Everything will be fine. Anyway, I've heard it's the safest form of air travel."

"You can get caught in telephone wires. And the one time I went up in a balloon with your father, we had a pretty hard landing. I'm telling you, that basket hit the ground three times before it came to a stop and we climbed out."

"I hope the champagne bottles didn't break," Regan said.

"They were in the cooler in the chase vehicle. We had a nice toast on terra firma."

"That's good. Mom, I really have to pack."

"Well, keep in touch."

"I'll talk to you during the week. Love to Dad."

Regan quickly opened the top drawer of her dresser and smiled to herself, wondering if she should get the shin and elbow guards out of the closet. They were remnants of her rollerblading days, days that had turned out to be few in number. An old boyfriend who she was convinced had a sadistic streak talked her into buying all the paraphernalia for the sport. After her third fall on the pavement within ten minutes, she gave up. The hall closet welcomed several more items that would have no other purpose than to gather dust.

Thank God for Jack, she thought. He, on the other hand, was always trying to protect her. I'll get through this week in Vegas and then have a great weekend with him.

I hope. Who knows who Danny Madley got himself involved with? Regan was convinced there had to be more than one shady character in the bunch.

———◆———

4

In a cramped, dingy apartment a few miles from the Strip, Honey's alarm went off. It was 11:30 A.M. Honey rolled over and groaned. It's amazing how fast eight hours can pass, she thought sleepily. No matter how tired she was, she made herself get out of bed before noon every day. It made her feel good about herself.

A showgirl, she rarely arrived home before one in the morning. Then she needed time to wind down. Sometimes she'd watch an old movie until her eyes felt droopy. Sometimes she'd play computer games. Sometimes she felt like talking on the phone, but the time zone she lived in didn't make that easy. Everybody on the East Coast was in bed, and she didn't know anybody in

Hawaii. But no matter how she tried to distract herself, Danny was always in the back of her mind.

With a small burst of energy, Honey thrust herself from the bed. She wrapped a flowered silk robe around her twenty-eight-year-old dancer's body, went into the tiny kitchenette, and turned on the kettle. That done, she felt a sense of accomplishment, went to the living room, and plopped on the couch. As if in a trance, she picked up the remote control and flicked on the television. It was tuned to the Balloon Channel.

"Be sure to watch on Friday night when Roscoe Parker will choose between Danny Madley's *Love Above Sea Level* and Bubbles Ferndale's *Take Me Higher.* Only in Las Vegas!!"

Honey started to cry. "Danny!" she whined. "I'm sorry I dumped you. It was a terrible mistake." She pulled a tissue from the box she kept next to her couch for when she watched sad movies. It was all too much for her. Her head had been turned by a high roller who came into town and had the big bucks, the really big bucks. He'd wined and dined her, sent her a dozen roses, bought her a reflexology and pedicure series to relieve her aching feet, and she was hooked. She dumped Danny Madley without a second thought. The next day her high roller left town, never to be heard from again.

Not even one email.

Then the rumors started. He was married. Married! Some nerve, that guy. Some nerve. If she had his real address, she'd drop in and show him just how good her feet looked.

Now Danny was gone from her life forever, and he was going to be a big shot. He wouldn't take her calls and returned her letters unopened. It had been five months since Danny had made her laugh. Five months since he picked her up in his crazy car and drove her out to Hoover Dam for a little fresh air. Five months since he told her that he thought his luck was finally about to change, that things were going to happen.

"And now they are happening for you!" she cried as she blew her nose and wiped her eyes. Honey opened the drawer of the table next to the couch and pulled out her diary. It was covered in pink polka dots and had a yellow felt daisy glued on the front cover. She turned to a blank page and started to write.

Dear Diary,
   Today I feel so sad I just can't stand it. I would do anything to get Danny back. I pine and pine and pine for him. Maybe I should start my own reality show about the world's biggest dummies. Starring me.
   I heard once that some girl had blown off George Washington and then saw him in a parade when he was president. She fainted dead away from a broken heart. Two hundred years later, I can identify. I wish she were alive so I could talk to her. Or how about Scarlett O'Hara when she treated Rhett Butler like garbage? She vowed to get him back but was going to think about it tomorrow.
   I can't wait till tomorrow! I have to act now! The more famous Danny gets, the more out of my reach. I have to get him back.
   Oh—the kettle's whistling, diary. I have to go. I'll keep you posted about my battle plan to GET DANNY.

Honey got up from the saggy couch, pleased with herself. She caught her reflection in the hallway mirror as she went into the kitchenette. Curly honey-colored hair, a baby doll face, wide blue eyes, cute pug nose, generous lips. A perpetual pout except when she was dancing onstage or when Danny was around to keep her smiling.

Honey poured her tea and thought about what that married louse had told her: "Honey, I'm successful because I always have a plan. I have goals. Where do I want to be five years from now? Did you ever think about that? Where do you want to be five years from now?"

She'd wanted to answer, "With you," but her instincts told her that wasn't a smart answer. So she said, "I don't know." Mr. Big Shot wasn't impressed. She could tell.

"Well, now I have a plan!" she declared to the empty room. "I'm not going to stop till I'm with Danny. And nobody's going to get in my way." Honey stirred sugar into her tea with great gusto and flung the spoon into the sink. It chipped the wineglass she'd meant to wash the night before. Was that an omen? she wondered.

5

---◆---

Regan gazed out the window as the plane descended toward Las Vegas. The City of Sin, famous for its nightlife, gambling, and flashing neon lights, actually looked quite normal from the air. Regan knew that the amusement park for grown-ups was also a great place for golfing, shopping, and sight-seeing. There were a lot of "faux" attractions along the famous strip of hotels. In a single stroll you could encounter a look-alike Statue of Liberty, a replica of the Eiffel Tower, pirate ships, a recreation of Venice, Italy, water fountains that dance and play music at scheduled intervals, and, of course, the proverbial Brooklyn Bridge.

Las Vegas was a mythic city of cash and flash, glamour and kitsch. In the 1990s the town fathers had tried to turn it into a family destination but soon realized you don't make much money off little people who fall asleep before the night gets going. The idea flopped, and now the town was concentrating on attracting adults who would park themselves at craps tables and slot machines. And here I am, Regan reflected, to work on a reality show in the land of unreality.

After stepping off the plane and walking into the airport, the first thing that caught her eye were the slot machines. The one-armed bandits were ready and waiting. The fun was just beginning. Win money before you collect your bags, they seemed to say. Don't waste a minute. Here we go, she thought with a smile.

As any visitor to Las Vegas would soon discover, slot machines were everywhere. Every time you turned around, you bumped into a slot machine. The city definitely made it easy for people to gamble.

Danny had told Regan that he'd meet her at the baggage claim area. He'd also said that his blond hair was no longer a crew cut. "And my braces are gone."

As Regan walked down the corridor and

stepped onto the escalator, she was once again surprised at the cavernous feeling of the baggage claim area. Huge billboards advertised the shows that were currently playing. And, of course, the ubiquitous slot machines beckoned. She was staring up at an ad for Siegfried and Roy when she heard her name being called. Regan looked around.

Her former classmate was hurrying toward her. He now sported shaggy blond hair and was dressed in blue jeans and a white button-down shirt with the sleeves rolled up to his elbows. Tinted aviator glasses completed the look. He still had the same impish quality, with his crooked smile and freckles, but he was now over six feet tall. And he still looked as if he was capable of the pranks he'd carried out in grammar school, but at the same time there was a sweetness about him.

"Danny!" she greeted him as he gave her a hug.

"I'm telling you, I'm so glad you're here." He led Regan to the luggage carousel to retrieve her bag. "You were one of the smartest kids in our class."

Regan laughed. "Well, shucks."

"That's okay. I know you can't return the compliment. I barely got by."

"That's not true," Regan protested. "You had your mind on other things, that's all." She didn't know why, but all of a sudden she felt like he was her little brother.

He shook his head. "Regan, I'm a wreck. This show has to work for me. But things are getting worse."

"What now?"

He pulled an envelope out of his pocket. "I just found this on my desk at the studio." He handed it to Regan.

The envelope had Danny's name on it. No address. No postmark. She pulled out the white sheet of paper inside and unfolded it. It was handwritten in red lettering, and its message was right to the point.

Danny,
    You'd better halt production of your show! Something terrible is going to happen if you don't! And you'll be responsible! Mark my words!!!!

Regan stared at it for a minute. The letter certainly looked as if someone who was angry had written it, someone who was fond of exclamation points.

"What do you think?" Danny asked.

"This could just be an idle threat," Regan reasoned. "Do you have any enemies?"

"None that I know of."

"Have you shown this to anyone else?"

"No. I just opened it before I left for the airport."

Regan sighed. "It's certainly not what you'd call a friendly letter."

Danny leaned over her shoulder. "I'd say all those exclamation points are a sign of agitation."

Regan furrowed her brow. "Say, Danny, that reminds me. Didn't you used to wear a pair of lime green socks with question marks on them when we were in seventh grade?" she asked as she spotted her suitcase and reached over to grab it.

"That's correct. But they've gone the way of my braces, thank God."

Ten minutes later they were tooling into town in Danny's old Volkswagen with the flower power decals. They were headed to a small hotel, just off the Strip and its famous hotels, where the cast and crew of *Love*

Above Sea Level was ensconced for the week.

"You know, Danny, this could just be a note from someone who wants to put you on edge."

"Well, they're succeeding."

"Maybe you should call the police."

Danny shook his head. "I don't want to involve the police. What are they going to do anyway? They've got enough to worry about. Besides, I don't want bad publicity for our show. You're right—it's probably just somebody who wants to make me crazy." He turned to her. "That's why you're here, Regan."

"To make you crazy?" she teased as they passed the Paris Hotel with its steel replica of a hot air balloon in the driveway and the faux Eiffel Tower in the background.

Danny laughed. "No, Regan. It's to keep the wolves at bay—to deter whoever is trying to sabotage my show." He turned down a side street and pulled into the parking lot of the Fuzzy Dice Hotel. It was a modest three-story building that hopefully had seen better days.

What will they think of next? Regan wondered as she looked up at a huge pair of fuzzy-looking dice attached to the hotel's roof like a weather vane.

Danny parked the car near the door. "I know this isn't the Bellagio. But it's where old Roscoe decided we should stay. Let's take your bags to your room and then head over to the studio. That's where the whole group should be now. Oh, Regan, I don't want anyone to know that you're a private investigator. I'll introduce you as a friend from home who is interested in producing a reality show and is helping me out."

"Sounds good to me."

The hotel's dingy front entrance was uninspiring. Clearly this was one of the more inexpensive hotels in Vegas. And the owner seemed to like dice. Dice patterns were everywhere, in a variety of colors. The carpeting. The wallpaper. The lampshades. The effect was only broken by the pillows on the couch and loveseat in the seating area. Their theme was playing cards.

Regan felt dizzy. Staying here would test any marriage, she thought, reality show or no reality show. *I'd rather be stranded on a hot sweaty island and forced to eat bugs.*

Six slot machines were lined up against the wall.

"Welcome!" a young woman behind the reception desk said cheerily to Regan. Her jewelry was all dice—necklace, earrings, bracelet, and rings. Her name tag read Delaney Ann Fell.

"Hi, Laney," Danny greeted her. "My friend Regan Reilly is checking in."

"You're in room six and six," Laney told Regan with a big smile. "I guess it's your lucky day."

"We'll see." Regan laughed.

Danny carried Regan's suitcase up to her room on the second floor, which was the temporary home for everyone from *Love Above Sea Level.* Not surprisingly, the dice on the bedspread and on the curtains all had six dots.

"Regan, why don't I meet you in the lobby in about ten minutes?" Danny suggested as his cell phone began to ring. He quickly answered it. "Danny Madley. Yes, Victor. What's wrong? . . . Oh, that's just great," Danny said sarcastically. "We'll be right over."

"What's the matter?"

"One of the contestants just fell, and they think he broke his arm. We'll meet them at the hospital."

6

Danny's mother, Madeline Madley, loved Scottsdale like there was no tomorrow. She'd grown up at the Jersey shore and had always loved the Garden State, but when her family moved west after Danny's grammar school graduation, her health had gone from okay to positively robust. Taking less time to sneeze gave her more energy to meddle in other people's affairs. "Mad Madley," as she was nicknamed by her friends when she got engaged to Shep Madley all those years ago, always said, "I'm a gal with devotion to two states in the Union, New Jersey and Arizona, although I do love to travel. I always meet such interesting people."

Madeline had a large map of the world on

the wall in her den. Colored dots indicated the cities she and Shep had visited. Green meant they had a good time, yellow meant it was so-so, and red meant forget about it.

Sixty-three years old, Mad Madley was fit and trim, although her face more than hinted at the hours and hours she had spent out by the pool in Arizona and on the sands of the Jersey shore. She was an attractive woman with a permanent tan and seemingly permanent blond hair, a woman who always looked good in white tennis outfits, though she had never hit a tennis ball in her life. She liked to wear her whites to go grocery shopping.

Mad had the heart of a showgirl. She'd always dreamed of seeing her name in lights, but she'd never really gone for it. She fed her need to entertain by standing around the piano at parties and bars and singing her heart out. She'd even learned three songs she could play when given the opportunity. "Heart and Soul" was her favorite.

Madeline couldn't stand Danny's ex-girlfriend Honey. Although Honey wasn't on Broadway, she was living Mad's dream. Mad couldn't admit it even to herself, but she was jealous of Honey for pursuing the career that Mad really wanted. So she blamed Honey for everything wrong in Danny's life, before and after the breakup. "How could he possibly make it in this world when he's involved with a flake like her?" she'd ask Shep during pillow talk on the water bed she'd purchased in the 60s. "How can he possibly get ahead with her in the picture?" Danny's father would shrug and raise his bushy eyebrows up and down several times as the bed rippled around them.

Shep was in his early seventies and happily retired. He'd owned a pet store in New Jersey, which meant Madeline could never visit him at the office. Some people thought that was his intent. Mad's allergies precluded any pets from being brought home, so Danny used to go to the pet store after school to play with the dogs and cats that were on sale. Sometimes Danny blamed his inability to form a permanent relationship on the fact that animals he had loved were there one day and gone the next. The two shrinks he had confided this to had basically told him to get a life.

But they all loved each other, thank God.

"We've all had a few bumps along the

way," Mad would say to anyone who would listen. "But we get through."

The Madleys' daughter, Regina, was very different from her parents and brother. Not only wasn't she interested in reality shows, but she didn't own a television. She taught biology at a prep school in Maine and spent all her days off in the laboratory doing research or tending to her garden. The bright lights of Broadway didn't interest her at all, a fact that constantly dismayed her mother. But her not caring at all about jewelry was even worse! Regina had always been her own person. It was Danny who inherited his mother's love for offbeat living.

But they all loved each other, thank God.

When Danny called his mother to tell her that there were a few problems with his show and that Regan Reilly was going to work for him for the rest of the shoot, she was thrilled. She remembered the Reilly family fondly. Years ago the grammar school parents had put on a show to raise money, and Mad had been in a skit that Nora wrote. Mad read all of Nora's books. She was disappointed to learn from Danny that Regan had a boyfriend; she had secretly hoped that being with Danny in Vegas would spark something between them. Who was this guy Regan was with anyway? she wondered. He couldn't be as interesting as Danny.

Shep and Maddy were hoping Danny's new reality show would bring him success and the opportunity to settle down. It never occurred to them that their eccentricities might have had an influence on his lifestyle choices.

In her beige bedroom in the condo, Mad put on her swimsuit and patted her tummy as she looked in the mirror. "Keep going with the situps, girl," she said aloud. "Fighting nature ain't easy."

The phone rang. Mad took one final approving glance, walked across the beige carpeting, and sat down on the beige beanbag chair next to the bed. The water bed was too much trouble to get up and down from if this was a short conversation.

She hurriedly lifted the receiver, always wanting to sound on the run. "Hello."

"Mad?"

"Yes."

"It's me. Jacqueline De Tour."

Mad smiled. Jacqueline was in her bridge club and was a bigger busybody than Mad was. She couldn't wait to hear whose misfortune Jacqueline was about to unload.

"You know my son Alfie is a computer whiz," Jacqueline began.

Here we go, Madeline thought. "Yes, that's wonderful."

"Well, he was surfing the net, as they say, just a little while ago. I said to him, 'Why don't you look up Danny Madley's show? See what they're saying about it.' "

"Yes?" Madeline replied somewhat nervously.

"Boy, those contestants of his sound like a bunch of deadbeats. You must be so disappointed. I mean, after all, you'd been so happy that this was working out for Danny and—"

"Jacqueline, I have an appointment I must run to," Mad Madeline announced firmly. "Talk to you soon." She hung up the phone, her heart racing. She jumped up like a shot from the beanbag chair and ran to the den where Shep was reading the paper.

"Shep, Danny needs us."

"What are you talking about?"

"He's having problems with the show. I think we should head up to Las Vegas in his hour of need."

Shep looked at her quizzically. "I don't know whether he'd appreciate our company at this time. I mean he's busy and . . ."

But Madeline had already dashed out of the room.

Shep stood and looked at the map on the wall. Las Vegas had a green dot on it. Why do I think that pretty soon there will be a red one on top if it? he wondered.

———◆———

7

Bubbles Ferndale was at her wit's end. She was seated at the head of a long conference table in the sitcom's studio of Roscoe Parker's television headquarters. Her writers and actors were reading the pilot script they would be taping Friday morning. The script wasn't so bad, but one of the actors who had been cast couldn't have gotten a laugh out of a hyena. Parky, as Bubbles called the studio head, had insisted on casting the actors himself. Bubbles was the type who added a *y* at the end of everyone's name who didn't already have one.

Bubbles met Parky when he came to see the variety show she was in at a flea-bitten theater off the Strip. Parky loved to see every spectacle Vegas had to offer, big or small. "Make a spectacle of yourself," he advised people both in and out of show business. "It's the way to get ahead in life. Sitting in the corner just doesn't cut it."

Bubbles knew that the theater she was working in was a pathetic venue, but it gave her a chance to hone her stand-up act. The curtain went up at three in the afternoon, usually to a lot of empty seats. Bubbles felt encouraged the day not too long ago that Parky and his girlfriend were in the audience. He laughed at all her jokes. What really impressed him, though, was her bio in the program. It was obviously a pack of lies—well, if not exactly lies, certainly exaggerations of the truth. Who had ever heard of some of the comedy awards she supposedly won? And if they were worth anything, what was she doing here?

Parky felt that Bubbles was a girl after his own heart. He went backstage after the show to say hello. It was her thirtieth birthday, and she was in a very bad mood. Her gig at the theater was almost up, and she'd have to hit the road again on the comedy circuit, doomed to performing in joints worse than this. She was weary and felt long in the tooth.

Parky invited her to join him and Kitty for champagne and dessert. When he toasted Bubbles's birthday, he offered her the job of producing, directing, and acting in a sitcom for possible airing on his cable channel.

"My channel is growing by leaps and bounds. I plan to make my mark in the world of television. And you can help me do it."

Bubbles leaped over the table and kissed him. It made turning thirty almost bearable.

Now Bubbles sat at the conference table chewing on her thumb, knowing that she had only four days to whip the show into shape. Her name belied her temperament. She was as tough as nails.

Besides personally hiring the actors, the other provision Parky had made was that the sitcom had to use hot air balloons in the story line. He was doing everything he could to promote Hot Air Cable.

Bubbles felt a headache coming on. She ran her hands through her long red hair. She was tall and lanky, attractive in a don't-mess-with-me kind of way.

"Let's try that line again," she urged

James Volmer, the unfunniest actor on the planet. He was playing her brother-in-law.

James, a soft-spoken guy with a brown and gray goatee and a serious expression, looked at her and blinked. "Why? I liked that line reading."

"There was only one problem with it," Bubbles snarled through clenched teeth. "It wasn't funny!"

"I beg to differ." James stood and placed his hand on his stomach as though to protect himself from further blows. "I've had enough. This atmosphere isn't good for my health. I quit!"

Bubbles jumped from her seat the same way she had when Parky offered her the job. "No! Please! You have to stay!" Bubbles hugged him fiercely. "You're a wonderful actor, and I'm so proud of you."

The actors and writers waited for this latest eruption to calm itself. Bubbles was high-strung, to say the least. But it was only because she cared so much.

Peter Daystone was the actor playing Bubbles's husband, a lovable wiseguy who thought it was funny to trick friends who were afraid of heights into riding in his hot air balloon. Peter had gotten lots of jobs acting in pilots that never made it to the air, thereby earning him the nickname "Pilot Pete." In his early thirties, Pete had been playing the Hollywood game since he was eighteen, always coming close to the big break but never being able to grab the brass ring. When his agent sent him to audition for *Take Me Higher,* he was convinced that this show would change everything. He would become a big success, and he'd finally get his swimming pool.

But as he sat at the table and put up with this guy who played his brother, Pete's frustration was mounting. James Volmer stunk up the whole show. Pilot Pete could tell that Bubbles was doing her best not to crack. From where he sat he could see the vein in her temple throbbing. When we take a break, I'll talk to her, he thought. We'll figure out how to rectify this situation.

I really want my swimming pool.

Meanwhile, up in his office, his feet on his desk, Parky was watching the proceedings with glee. "I never thought it was going to turn out this good!" he exclaimed to Kitty.

She looked up from her book. "You're going to be sorry. Somebody's going to end up killing somebody."

"It's all in fun," he cried as he clapped his hands.

Kitty shrugged and tapped her bookmark against the page. "I wouldn't be so sure."

8

At the local hospital near the studio, which was a couple of miles outside of town, Danny and Regan ran into the small emergency room. The camera crew was recording the actions of the famous Aunt Agony and Uncle Heartburn as they interviewed the afflicted contestant, Barney Schmidt, and his wife, Elsa. Barney was a big, beefy guy with a dark handlebar mustache. He was holding his injured arm, and tears were rolling down his face. Elsa was small but solid. Her hairdo made her look like Buster Brown. They were probably in their thirties.

"Do you think this experience is bringing you closer as a couple?" Aunt Agony asked sweetly. Agony looked as if she was straight out of central casting: white hair in a bun, granny glasses, petite.

"Is it strengthening your relationship?" Uncle Heartburn added. The sight of him reminded Regan not to squeeze the Charmin. Half glasses that slid down his nose, a receding hairline, a little mustache.

Barney and Elsa looked at each other.

"She never used to like it when I cried," Barney said softly.

"I do now," Elsa insisted.

Of course, Regan thought. Anything for a chance at a million bucks.

"Men who cry are in touch with their inner selves," Uncle Heartburn said gently. "And a man who can cry in public like Barney is doing, with the cameras going, well, I call that a man who's not afraid."

"Oh, he cries everywhere," Elsa said emphatically.

That must have been what drove her crazy, Regan thought.

The swinging doors to the treatment room swung open. "Barney Schmidt," a doctor called.

"Here!" Barney answered in a shaky voice, his lip trembling.

The camera zoomed in on Elsa's worried

face as she watched him go off for X-rays. After a few seconds the cameraman ended the shot. A burly young guy with dark gelled hair emerged from the bathroom behind where the scene had taken place. It was obvious he hadn't wanted to get in the shot.

"Boss!" he cried out to Danny.

Danny introduced Regan to his assistant, Victor.

"Nice to meet you." Victor shook Regan's hand. He was a hometown Vegas boy who had worked as a bouncer at one of the bars in town. As a matter of fact, he'd had a lot of jobs. He and Danny had met at a black-jack table when Danny was putting together the plans for the reality show. Victor begged him for a job. Danny, who found it hard to say no to anyone, took him on as his assistant. So far it seemed to be working out.

"What happened to Schmidt?" Danny asked.

Victor rolled his eyes and waved his hands around.

"Well?" Danny asked a trifle impatiently.

"Boss, we're running into problem after problem," Victor began importantly. It always took him a while to get to the point, which is why he lost his job as a bouncer.

Victor's former boss told him he spent too much time talking instead of throwing people out the door. "Maybe we should talk outside."

Danny and Regan followed Victor into the parking lot.

"Okay," Victor said. "I'm not quite sure how it happened. He just slipped on the floor."

"That's it?"

Victor looked at him and blinked. "Yeah."

"You took us outside to tell us that?"

"There's more."

"Okay, then. What?" Danny prodded.

Victor pointed self-consciously at Regan.

"Regan's a friend of mine from childhood. I trust her like a sister. She's interested in producing her own reality show, and I promised to include her in on everything."

"That's cool," Victor said with a trace of skepticism. "Regan will be interested in what I have to say then."

"I'm sure I will."

"My girlfriend went online and found a website called Blowing the Lid Off that is focusing on our show. They're saying that one of the couples is phony. Never been married. Aren't even boyfriend and girlfriend.

The two heard about the show and wanted to make money. So they got a forged marriage license. The website is encouraging anyone and everyone to write in about the other couples. They want the dirt." Victor turned thoughtful for a moment. "I guess it's one of those websites that specializes in gossip about reality show contestants."

"But we haven't even been on the air yet."

"The power of the Internet. They posted all the contestants' pictures."

"How did they get the pictures?" Danny asked.

"Beats me. Another rumor is that one of the contestants has violent tendencies."

"Violent tendencies? But Roscoe did background checks, didn't he?"

"I heard they filled out forms."

"Forms?" Danny screeched.

"You have to admit that things have been rushed. Besides, everyone has a past."

"Not a past that includes violent tendencies! This show won't fly if these three couples aren't legitimate! They didn't say who it was?"

"Of course not. Everybody's afraid of getting sued."

"I know someone who can do some more

thorough background checks," Regan offered. "But if you have to eliminate a couple,
will you be able to replace them?"

"Only if we can get the replacements here
by tomorrow," Danny said. "That gives
enough time for them to participate fully in
the show. Regan, let's go back to my office
and get started. Victor, we'll meet you back
there. But first I want to see how Barney is
doing."

As they stepped inside, the treatment
room doors swung open, and Barney
emerged with the doctor.

"It's not broken," Barney reported joy-
ously as Elsa ran over to give him a hug.
"Just a little sprain."

The cameras recorded the tearful reunion
between husband and wife.

"Where's Aunt Agony?" Regan whispered
to Danny.

"She went out back for a smoke," one of
the assistants answered.

Regan glanced over at the doctor. He
looked properly serious. When his eye met
Regan's, he looked at her questioningly. "Are
you one of the producers?" he mouthed.

Regan shook her head and tapped Danny
on the shoulder. She steered him over to the

hallway where the doctor was standing. "Danny Madley is the producer," Regan said to the doctor in a low voice.

"Mr. Madley, I thought you might be interested in knowing that Schmidt tried to bribe me into putting on a fake cast."

Oh, boy, Regan thought. I'd better get started on those background checks.

———◆———

9

The headquarters of Hot Air Cable was a collection of low buildings in the middle of the desert, surrounded by acres and acres of undeveloped land that Roscoe had bought for a song. The snowcapped mountains beckoned in the distance. The complex felt as if it was in the middle of nowhere, but in no time Roscoe could be in downtown Vegas at a show or sitting at the craps table. For Roscoe it was the best of both worlds.

Roscoe's hot air balloon business was housed on the property, and his private plane was parked on his very own runway. He loved the thought of taking off into the wild blue yonder almost whenever he wanted.

Roscoe built an elaborate television studio, with a dozen satellite dishes, state-of-the-art equipment, and a huge office for himself. He also constructed three extra high-tech studios to be used for future productions. *Love Above Sea Level* and *Take Me Higher* had set up shop in two of the studios.

He planned to create an empire. A tour long ago of the Paramount Pictures lot in Hollywood had stuck in the back of Roscoe's mind. He loved the beehive of activity, people going back and forth between the studios and the offices and all the different departments. And Roscoe, being the control freak that he was, wanted to be at the helm of his own operation. He knew that Hot Air Cable had a long way to go, but he also knew that by Friday night he'd have a decent show to put over the airwaves. One way or another.

"Come on, Kitty," he said to his paramour as he got up from his desk. "It's three o'clock. Time to go for a swim and a little workout."

Roscoe hated the middle of the afternoon. It was the only time of day he felt a slump in his energy. That was why he went to some of the dreadful afternoon shows. No matter how bad the acts were, in the darkened theater he felt renewed. But if there was no show or movie he wanted to see, he used that time to exercise. By four-thirty or five o'clock he was as fresh as a daisy, ready to take on the evening.

Kitty sighed. She hated to exercise, but she knew Roscoe wanted her with him. She was happy about his devotion but some-times wondered if the joys of constant com-panionship weren't highly overrated. Es-pecially lately when he was distracted by these new shows. They were together, but Roscoe wasn't really paying attention to her.

Kitty and Roscoe left the studio through the back door that was Roscoe's private en-trance. The sun was bright and all was quiet. They walked to Roscoe's gleaming silver Jaguar arm in arm. Roscoe had a state-of-the-art gym set up in the mansion that he was renting near the studios. The mansion's previous owner had been a well-polished fraud who bilked unassuming in-vestors out of millions. Before him, a drug dealer had called the fifteen rooms home. Now the joint belonged to the bank. Most sane people wouldn't sleep there alone if their life depended on it. Who knew who might return in the middle of the night to seek revenge, unaware that ownership had changed hands?

Roscoe pointed his key chain at the Jaguar and unlocked the doors. Behind him he heard a car pulling into the complex. He turned and saw Danny Madley steering his Volkswagen into a nearby parking space. Danny got out of the car accompanied by an attractive young woman.

"Danny!" Roscoe called. "Come over and say hello."

"Sure, boss."

Roscoe reached out to shake Danny's hand and turned his attention to the young woman. "And who do we have here?" Roscoe asked.

"This is my friend Regan Reilly. Regan, this is Roscoe Parker."

"Nice to meet you." Roscoe pointed his thumb behind him. "And this is my girlfriend Kitty."

Kitty gave a little wave.

"Hello," Regan called over.

"You live here in town?" Roscoe asked.

"No. Los Angeles," Regan replied.

"What brings you here?" Roscoe asked quickly.

"I am interested in reality shows," Regan answered honestly.

"She's thinking of producing one," Danny jumped in, a little too quickly. "We're old friends, and I told her she could come and help me on *Love Above Sea Level.* Get a feeling for it."

"Uh-huh." Roscoe didn't sound convinced. "How are things going?"

"Terrific," Danny practically croaked. "By Friday we're going to have one great show."

"I hope so," Roscoe grunted as he turned around, opened his car door, and slid into the driver's seat. "I certainly hope so." He backed the Jag out of his VIP space.

Kitty filed the nail on one of her pinkies. "She has no more interest in producing a reality show than I do."

"I know it," Roscoe agreed. "We'll have to find out exactly who she is."

10

"I don't think he believed us," Regan said under her breath as they waved good-bye to Kitty and Roscoe.

"I just want to keep him happy," Danny answered. "He gave me the money to produce a good show. It's up to me to deliver one."

Regan took a breath and looked around the complex. "Looks like a nice setup."

Danny shrugged. "Come on. Our studio is around the back."

They walked around the main building. Regan followed Danny to the back studio. A sign, LOVE ABOVE SEA LEVEL, was posted on the front door. Inside there was a tiny reception area on the left and a hallway straight ahead with a glass wall at one end.

Regan could see a control room at the far end of the corridor.

"The studio itself is around the corner," Danny explained. "The contestants are right here." He led her into a small waiting room off the hall. A table was filled with an assortment of snacks and drinks that would keep a sugar freak happy for weeks. A large screened television was tuned to the Balloon Channel where an on-air team was demonstrating how to inflate a hot air balloon.

There was an immediate chorus of "How's Barney?"

"He's fine," Danny answered quickly. "Just a sprain. I want to introduce you to my friend Regan Reilly."

Regan said hello to the four people in the room.

"These are our two other couples," Danny said. "Chip and Vicky, and Bill and Suzette."

There was a general nodding in Regan's direction.

"Regan's an old friend who's interested in producing a reality show, so she'll be with us this week to learn the ropes. I've also asked her to act as our trouble shooter. Feel free to talk to her if you need anything.

Regan's a great listener. But first we need to talk to you about something that has come to our attention."

They all waited.

"We were told that there's an Internet site that is encouraging people to dish the dirt on you people."

A collective gasp went up in the room.

"The dirt?" Suzette whined. She was middle-aged with a broad face, blond hair in a flip held off her face by a plaid headband, and a sturdy look about her. She blinked her eyes several times. Her husband, Bill, was a tall, skinny redhead with freckles and a permanently befuddled look. Regan quickly realized that Suzette was the boss in that relationship.

"I value my privacy," Suzette cried indignantly.

And you're on a reality show? Regan thought. I wonder if she and Bill are the unmarried ones.

The other couple, Chip and Vicky, were both extremely tall with dark hair, dark eyes, and olive skin. He was about six feet seven, and she had to be six feet two. They looked as if they could be brother and sister, except Chip's eyes were beady and Vicky's were huge almond-shaped saucers. They both stared quietly at Regan, and she assumed they were shy. Of course, she was about to be proven wrong.

"We're back!"

Everyone turned to see Barney and Elsa in the doorway. Barney had an Ace bandage around his arm and was smiling coura-geously. Aunt Agony, Uncle Heartburn, and Victor were right behind them.

"Come in, please," Danny urged them. "Take a seat." Regan stood beside him.

"For those of you who just joined us, I was telling the others that it has come to our at-tention that there is an Internet website that is looking into all your backgrounds."

"Digging up the dirt!" Suzette said em-phatically.

Barney looked at her, and his eyes started to fill with tears. Elsa pulled on his arm. "Get a grip," she whispered.

"We all want to be on the air Friday night," Danny continued. "And we wouldn't want anything that people say about you to ruin our show. We all have a stake in this. Al-though only one couple will renew their vows, the exposure this show gets could open up lots of opportunities for the rest of you."

Aunt Agony jumped up. "And best of all you will have rediscovered your love for each other!"

Oh, sure, Regan thought. Something told her that the two couples who lost would be running in opposite directions from each other the minute the winning couple was announced.

"Did you ever find out who stole the camera?" Chip asked suddenly, staring intently at Danny.

"No," Danny replied.

Chip doesn't look as if he says much, but he gets right to the point, Regan thought. To her he seemed a little sinister. His beady eyes didn't have much expression.

"We should consider ourselves a unit," Danny urged. "Now Regan wants to say a few words to you."

Regan looked at him, surprised. They'd talked in the car about how to handle this but hadn't really reached a conclusion. She cleared her throat. "As Danny has stated, we all want the show to proceed without delay. We do have to address the Internet rumors. Now, uh, I know that you all consider yourselves married, but is it at all possible that a couple here has not formally gotten married?"

Chip laughed, two short staccato noises emanating from his throat. Vicky looked annoyed, but then the rest of the group seemed to find the concept of being single funny as well.

Bill shook his head and pointed at Suzette. "We met in high school when I played basketball and she was a cheerleader. She still practices her cheers. Especially when she's doing housework. 'Go team go!' It drives me nuts, but"—he turned to Aunt Agony and Uncle Heartburn—"I'm working on it. Miss Reilly, I can assure you that without a doubt we've been married for twenty years. I'm married to a forty-two-year-old cheerleader."

"Excuse me," Suzette interrupted. "But did you notice he said 'when she's doing housework'? Maybe if he helped out once in a while and picked his socks up off the floor, I wouldn't have to cheerlead so much. For me it's a release. Some people go to the gym, I do my cheers around the house. It makes my work a little bit of fun."

"Did you need to do a cartwheel and

knock over the lamp my mother gave us for our wedding?" Bill demanded. "Mom got really upset that you broke it." He turned to Regan. "Every other day there's something new that she breaks. I come home to find a million pieces of glass and ceramic on the floor. It's been years since I dared to walk barefoot in our house."

Aunt Agony and Uncle Heartburn were scribbling furiously in their notebooks.

"I can promise you we're married," Elsa chimed in. "We've been together so long, Barney has cried a river in front of me. The Mississippi River. I loved it when we were first dating. He cried at sad movies. He cried when he first told me he loved me. He cried when we got engaged. I thought I had finally found a sensitive man. But as the saying goes, be careful what you pray for . . ."

I was just thinking that this morning, Regan mused.

Tears rolled down Barney's cheeks.

"But Barney is doing his best to gain some control over his runaway emotions, and I am striving to be more understanding. The last time I cried was six months ago when I stubbed my toe. Boy, did that hurt.

Now that was a good reason to cry," Elsa declared, pointing her stubby finger with deliberation.

This is unbelievable, Regan thought. This has got to beat the sitcom. Now what proof does couple number three, Chip and Vicky, have that they've been torturing each other for years? she wondered. She looked at them hopefully, as if to egg them on to confess something, even though that was probably Aunt Agony's job.

"He never wants to eat at the table!" Vicky blurted, as if on cue.

"We never did before we were married," Chip reminded her.

"Oh, sure. All he liked to do was take me on picnics. It seemed so romantic. Picnics on the beach, in the forest, in the car, in the living room. Did I know we'd never sit down to the table like normal human beings? I've barely used any of the good dishes we got as wedding presents. He insists on eating off paper plates on the floor in front of the television. He says it's an adventure. Our rug is threadbare from the number of times I've had to vacuum over the years."

"I wanted to buy a dog," Chip continued. "But noooooo."

"What do you do when you go out to dinner?" Regan inquired.

"Drive-thru. He only likes drive-thru."

"That's not true," Chip disagreed. "I've taken you to plenty of nice restaurants."

"With peanut shells all over the floor. Or sawdust. They're the only places we can go where he doesn't have the urge to sit on the ground."

"But we're working on it," they said in unison.

"It's hard when you're so tall," Chip said beseechingly. "I like to be able to stretch out my legs. I'm an outdoorsman. A hunter. A gatherer. The cavemen didn't have furniture. Why should we? It's unnatural."

"I bought him a La-Z-Boy recliner for his birthday," Vicky said sadly, "but he still prefers the floor."

"I'm trying to get used to it," Chip said. "But my feet hang over the edge."

Aunt Agony and Uncle Heartburn looked on approvingly.

"You all sound as though you've been married for a long time," Regan acknowledged. "Now if there's anything embarrassing that might show up on the website that you don't want to talk about in front of the group, please see me privately. That way we can head off any little problems before they become big problems."

They all nodded in agreement.

Fat chance any of them would admit anything, Regan thought. None of them want to be disqualified, and they all want to win the money. "Good. Now I think Danny wants to say a few words."

"If any of you have any wedding photos that your family can forward to us, they would be great to use at the beginning of the show."

They all shook their heads.

"Our house is all locked up," Elsa explained. "I wouldn't give anybody a spare key—not even my mother. You never know what can happen."

"We don't live near any family," Chip said.

"Our wedding pictures were destroyed in a fire," Bill lamented.

"Okay, then." Danny tried to laugh. "No problem. Why don't you have something cold to drink and relax? In five minutes we'll be heading into the studio for an Agony and Heartburn session."

What would you call what we just had?

Regan wondered. "Excuse me," she said to Danny. "I'll be right back." She really wanted to call Jack. She just needed to hear his comforting, sane voice.

———◆———

11

"Do I like to eat on the floor?" Jack repeated. "Regan, what are you talking about?"

Regan laughed. She was standing outside the studio with her cell phone and started to walk toward the open field. It felt good to be outside. It felt great to hear Jack's voice. "Jack, you wouldn't believe these people."

"Yes, I would. It's a reality show, isn't it?"

"I know, but my God!"

"Is there anything I can do to help you?"

"Well, we're a little worried that the contestants might not be legitimate in one way or another. Like they might not even be married, and the basis of this show is saving married couples from getting a divorce. The goal is to figure out who stands the best chance of sticking it out even though they were all about to call it quits."

"See what information you can get on them, and I'll run some checks. Get their Social Security numbers."

"I'll try. You know I briefly met the guy who is in charge of this whole operation. Roscoe Parker is his name. He's financing both shows. I'm at his cable station now—the Balloon Channel. He also has a hot air ballooning business. I have a feeling it would be interesting to find out a little about his background."

"He should be easier to look into. If he lives in Vegas and has that much money, he must be known. Call me back when you have the other names and numbers, and I'll do what I can for you."

"Thanks, Jack. I'd better get back inside. We're about to have a session with Aunt Agony and Uncle Heartburn."

"Aunt Agony and Uncle Heartburn?"

"They're advice columnists in this part of the world. Turns out that for the past forty years they've had a small cafe on a two-lane road in the desert. Humanity in all its forms would come in there for breakfast, lunch, and dinner. Agony has such a sweet face that people would end up telling her all their problems—truckers, travelers, businessmen. She'd dole out advice while her husband made his famous four-alarm chili. Sometimes she'd ask him what he thought of a certain problem. One day about five years ago a local newspaper publisher offered them a column. Now they're trying to break out and go national."

"I guess the Heartburn refers to his chili."

"You got it. With all the cable stations on the air now, they want to give advice on television. They still work at the cafe. They sort through their letters at a table in the restaurant. Apparently it's not too far from Las Vegas."

"One day we can have a column together answering people's questions about how to investigate crime," Jack suggested.

Regan smiled. "We can call it 'How to Be a Buttinsky.' "

"That's it. Okay, call me later."

After hanging up, Regan hurried back to the door of the *Love Above Sea Level* studio, glancing at the parking lot. There are enough cars here, she thought, but everything is so quiet. Eerily quiet. Where is everybody? she wondered. Danny had filled her in on the layout of the place when they pulled in the driveway. The sitcom was in the studio on the other side of the main building. Each unit seemed to be self-sufficient.

Regan went back inside and walked down the hall. The greenroom was empty. She followed the hallway around the corner and pulled open the studio door. Spotlights were focused on a raised platform where there were eight seats. The couples were standing around, getting miked. Regan took two steps inside and slipped on the floor. She started to fall but managed to catch herself. Her heart was beating wildly.

"Are you okay?" the cameramen called out to her. "That's exactly the spot where Barney slipped!"

Regan reached down and touched the floor with her finger. Terrific, she thought. There was a thin coat of oil that she was sure had been planted on the floor.

———◆———

12

"Drive faster, Shep," Mad Madley urged.

"I'm already over the speed limit."

The two of them were on the open road, heading from Scottsdale to Las Vegas. It was a trip they normally enjoyed at a leisurely pace. Three hundred miles of fun, Madeline called it. They'd listen to the radio, books on tape, and stop for a little lunch along the route. If Shep wasn't in the mood for much conversation, Madeline would check in with friends on her cell phone to see if she'd missed anything yet. She drove Shep crazy by repeating her entire conversation to him, word for word, the second she hung up. He'd already heard half the dialogue and could have guessed the rest.

"I don't know who would want to hurt

Danny," Madeline declared. "It's just down-right mean. Why do people have such a need to spread bad things about others?"

Shep looked away from the road and glanced at Madeline quickly. "I can't imag-ine."

"I mean, sure, I like to know what's going on in people's lives, but that's just a healthy interest." She turned around and leaned back into the cooler that had a permanent place in their backseat. "Water, Shep, dear?"

"Snapple."

She poured the Snapple into paper cups that had a picture of Madeline and Shep in their old Mustang convertible with the top down. The caption read TRUCKIN' WITH SHEP AND MAD. Friends had the cups specially made for the couple's last anniversary.

"Thanks," Shep said as Mad lovingly handed him his cup.

"You're welcome, dear. Now I've been thinking, I wouldn't put it past that ex-girl-friend of Danny's to cause trouble. He told me that Honey has been trying to get in touch with him, but he has no interest in rekindling the spark. And I say thank God for that. I don't need a floozy for a daughter-in-law."

Shep stared ahead at the seemingly endless highway, bathed in bright sunlight. He'd heard this all many times before.

"I would really like to see Danny and Regan Reilly get together. I think they would make an adorable couple, don't you?"

Shep shrugged. "How would I know? I haven't seen her in twenty years."

"Well, she comes from a lovely family."

"Didn't you say she had a boyfriend?"

"What does that have to do with it?" She looked at him coquettishly. "I had boyfriends before I met you."

"And I had girlfriends. My last girlfriend before you was really cute although—"

"Shep!" Madeline interrupted. She couldn't stand to hear about any other woman who had been in his life. She didn't like to think it was possible. He was her Shep. She was his Maddy. Truckin' down the road of life.

Shep laughed, reached over, and squeezed Maddy's hand. He loved the fact that she still got jealous after thirty-five years of togetherness. "By the way, where are we staying?" he asked. Maddy always chose the hotels when they traveled. She was a master bargain hunter if there ever was one.

"Well, the big hotels are all full. There are so many conventions in town this week. There's a little hotel called 7's Heaven that sent us a coupon. It doesn't look like a luxury palace, but I'm sure it'll do. We'll really just be sleeping there anyway."

"How long are we staying?"

"All week. We will see it through till the end with our son."

Shep nodded.

They rode along for hours, listening to talk radio. It seemed everybody had problems.

Shep finally spoke. "I'm hungry. I can't wait till we get to Vegas."

"The Heartburn cafe isn't too far from here. Why don't we stop there for a bite to eat?"

"Aren't Agony and Heartburn in Las Vegas with Danny?"

"Yes. But that doesn't mean the cafe is closed. I wouldn't mind some of their famous chili."

Maddy and Shep had stopped at the cafe many times on their way to Vegas. It was Maddy's suggestion that Danny use them on the show.

A half hour later they were pulling into the dirt parking lot outside the cafe. The little establishment looked as if it had been dropped from the sky in the middle of nowhere. There was nothing in the distance but cactus and scrub brush. A big dog barked halfheartedly when Maddy and Shep got out of the car. After a final low growl, the dog wandered off and there was dead silence.

"That's a good boy," Madeline cooed to the departing canine. She turned to Shep. "Chow time, honey."

They walked onto the creaky porch and stepped inside the cafe. It felt good to get out of the blazing sun. The small room had a counter, stools, and a cash register along the wall, and a handful of rickety wooden tables placed willy-nilly around the room. Some might have called it homey. A blackboard listed the day's specials, and a large piece of cork on another wall was covered with business cards that customers had been tacking up for years. Many of them were curled and yellowing. A large fan revolved slowly overhead and seemed to have minimal effect on the temperature in the room. No other customers were present.

"Howdy," the lone waitress greeted them. "Sit where you like."

"We're Danny Madley's parents," Maddy announced.

"You can still sit where you like."

"Danny is producing the reality show that Aunt Agony and Uncle Heartburn are appearing on," Maddy explained with a touch of impatience. Clearly she expected better recognition. But this waitress had been here for more years than she cared to remember, and nothing much impressed her. One day just rolled into the next.

"Let's sit here," Shep stated matter-of-factly. They took seats at a table for four in the middle of the room.

The waitress grabbed a couple of menus and walked over to the table. "Danny's a nice boy."

The remark softened Maddy's expression. "It was my idea for Danny to use Aunt Agony and Uncle Heartburn on the show. We're headed to Las Vegas now."

"Oh, really. Would you mind bringing Agony and Heartburn their mail? I got a whole sack here, and I know Agony likes to keep up with it. She doesn't sleep much, so she reads letters in bed."

Maddy was thrilled. Now she had a good reason for barging in on Danny. "We'd love to."

They quickly ordered two Cokes and the infamous chili. Heartburn had cooked up a big batch before he left for the bright lights of Vegas and stashed it in individual containers in the freezer. Thank God for the microwave oven, he'd noted. The waitress retreated to the kitchen, where the freezer was the size of a vault. "Be right back," she promised.

Maddy got up to use the ladies' room and stopped to read the wall of business cards. They always intrigued her. One card in particular caught her eye. The logo was a sketch of Elvis Presley and the famous theatrical masks—one happy face, one sad. "Ah, showbiz," she said wistfully.

"Here we are," the waitress announced as she emerged from the kitchen with the chili. "Don't let me forget to give you that mail when you leave. Agony will be in ecstasy." The waitress chuckled.

"Don't you worry." Maddy dashed through a little side room that had every trinket imaginable for sale. Most of it was junk and covered with dust. She sneezed but didn't even get annoyed. "Don't you worry," Maddy repeated to herself as she pushed open the warped wooden door marked DAMES. "I'd forget my own name before leaving here without Agony's mail."

13

At 5 P.M. sharp a deafening whistle blew on the grounds of Hot Air Cable.

"What was that?" Pilot Pete cried. The sit-com actors were in the middle of their first rehearsal on the actual set. He, like Bubbles, was about to have a meltdown. His swimming pool was becoming more and more of a pipe dream.

The whistle blew again, three long, sharp, loud blasts.

"It sounds like the beginning of a musical," James murmured. "Like dancers are going to appear from offstage."

"Or a choo choo train with an impatient conductor," Bubbles muttered.

There were seven people on the set of *Take Me Higher*. They'd just begun putting the show on its feet, so to speak. James's acting hadn't improved at all since the morning, and the woman named Loretta, who was playing Grandma, was equally terrible.

The two young male sitcom writers whom Bubbles had recruited from Hollywood were sitting in director's chairs facing the set, taking notes after every line of dialogue. The writers were brothers. They looked alike and were "Irish twins," born within a year. Neil and Noel both had light brown hair and freckles, and were frustrated that reality shows were cutting into their livelihood. They'd been in Hollywood less than a year when the reality craze hit the airwaves. They were working for Bubbles at a cut rate, just like the actors.

Bubbles, Pilot Pete, James, Loretta, and Hal, the actor who played Grandma's new boyfriend, were all rehearsing a scene set in the kitchen of Bubbles and Pete's home. Grandma was breaking the news that she was going on a three-day ballooning trip with her new beau. Just the two of them. James wasn't crazy about Hal. He was warning her that she might catch a cold being up in the air for seventy-two hours and suggesting they take a Greyhound bus to the Grand Canyon instead. But Grandma didn't think that sounded nearly as thrilling. She assured James that her new boyfriend was very experienced with balloons. She wanted a more exciting life, and it was going to start now.

The scene wasn't working. It had been a trying day.

The whistle sounded again.

"Where is that coming from?" Bubbles growled.

James shrugged, stretched his arms overhead, and yawned as if he didn't have a care in the world, actions that annoyed Bubbles no end. "I think it's coming from outside," he noted.

When the exasperating whistle sounded again, Bubbles ran out of the room, down the hallway, and out the door of the studio. Her gang was close behind. The group from the reality show was also hurrying out of their studio. In the parking lot Roscoe had a large speaker set up next to his Jaguar, with the volume turned full blast. It was a sight to behold.

"It is five o'clock," Roscoe declared as he shut off the stereo. "Time to go back to your hotels. The vans will depart in five minutes. The studios are closed."

"What?" rang the collective cry.

"It's part of the challenge. We all face obstacles in our work—like having limited time to do what we must get done. You must leave. You may not remain on the property. You have five minutes to collect your belongings. Now get out! And have a nice night! You are free to return at nine A.M. tomorrow morning." Roscoe turned up the volume on the loudspeaker, and the whistle sounded again.

Bubbles put her hands over her ears and hurried back inside the studio. "Parky's a nut," she cried as she stuffed her script into her handbag.

"Let's rehearse back at the hotel," James suggested. "Perhaps we could all rest and meet after dinner." The sitcom group, like the reality show, was staying together in a small dumpy hotel off the Strip, 7's Heaven. "You can all come to my room if you'd like."

The twins looked at each other. Noel, the son born on Christmas day, turned to Bubbles. "We have some rewrites to do on the script tonight."

Bubbles wore many hats on this produc-

tion—director, producer, star, cowriter. Her
word was law. "The three of us will work on
this together, till three in the morning if need
be. The rest of you have the night off. Noel
and Neil, I'll see you back at the hotel in an
hour." She picked up her bag and stormed
out. Pilot Pete hurried after her.

"Bubbles," Pilot Pete called as he ran to
catch up with her. She didn't stop. He kept
pace with her as she strode out the studio
door and back into the parking lot where her
car was parked. Only Bubbles and Danny
were allowed to drive onto the lot. Everyone
else was shuttled around in the Balloon
Channel vans. Roscoe wanted his logo to
be seen everywhere. "Bubbles," Pilot Pete
repeated, "I have an idea for our show. Can
I ride with you back to the hotel?"

Bubbles turned toward him. "It depends
on what the idea is."

He stared into her eyes. "Believe me,
you're going to like it."

Bubbles was desperate. She welcomed
any suggestions. She stared back at him.
"Get in the car."

14

Regan followed Danny into his office. They were in a hurry to get out of there as quickly as possible. Danny pulled the files he had on the contestants out of his top drawer. Regan wanted to see if there was any information there that would help with background checks.

It had been an interesting afternoon. After she nearly slipped on the floor, the microphones on the set stopped working. They had finally gotten started with the Agony and Heartburn session when the whistle blew and everyone had to leave. Danny was not happy.

"Roscoe is one eccentric guy," Danny commented as he handed Regan the files and took a final glance around the room.

"It seems he likes to be in charge," Regan observed. "But why would he kick everyone out if he wants two good shows to choose from?"

"It beats me."

Regan paused. "Danny, I don't think that oil on the floor where I slipped was spilled accidentally. It was such a very thin coat that it's almost like someone deliberately applied it with a small paintbrush."

A tap at the door startled them both. Victor was standing there with Sam, a handsome guy in his mid-thirties with long, streaky blond hair and a laid-back surfer boy manner. He was wearing flowered board shorts and a T-shirt. His pale blue eyes were playful and crinkled when he smiled. He was the cameraman who had come to Regan's aid when she nearly hit the floor. As a matter of fact, he was the only cameraman. Danny had a very small crew.

"Everybody's ready to go," Victor announced. "They're in the vans."

"Okay. Tell them we'll have cocktails at seven in the recreation room," Danny instructed. "We'll pick up with the Agony and Heartburn session in the morning. Everything okay with you, Sam?"

"Sure, man. You want me to resume taping at the cocktail party, right?"

"Right."

"Oh, Danny, what happened when the camera disappeared?" Regan asked quickly. "I never got the details about that."

Sam looked a little sheepish. He shifted from one sneakered foot to the other. "Yesterday we were doing background shots of Las Vegas. The hotels, the fountains at the Bellagio, that kind of thing. I spilled some coffee on my shirt, so I took one of the vans back to the Fuzzy Dice Hotel and ran upstairs to change my shirt. When I came back down, the camera was gone."

"From that little parking lot in front of the hotel?"

"Yes."

Regan hated to ask but did anyway. "Were the doors locked?"

"I thought they were, but I'd never driven the van before. I hit a button on the key chain and it chirped, so I thought that meant everything was locked. I was in such a hurry . . ."

Regan watched Sam closely as he spoke. He seemed a little spacey, but it probably meant he was creative.

In contrast, Victor impatiently ran his hands through his gelled hair. "Those cameras are expensive. We're lucky we have another one."

"Another one?" Regan repeated. "But there are at least two cameras set up in the studio—"

"Those are for use only in the studio. They don't leave the premises," Victor explained.

"Who owns the camera you use when you go out?"

"Roscoe."

"And he owned the one that was stolen?"

"Yes," Danny said quickly.

"Does he know yet?"

"Yes. I told him yesterday."

"What did he say?"

"That we had to make do with one."

Regan raised her eyebrows. "He wasn't upset?"

"No. He took it remarkably well."

The whistle blew again, a long, strident assault to the ears.

"I guess we'd better get out of here," Regan advised.

"We'd better," Danny agreed as they hurried out.

Roscoe was standing by the speaker,

grinning broadly. The first Balloon Channel van was pulling out of the parking lot. He waved at them as they walked by. "Have a good evening," he called.

"Good evening," they murmured in unison.

Ten minutes after Regan and the others departed, Roscoe was still standing outside the studio. A limousine full of his stealth employees pulled into the parking lot. He clapped his hands and lovingly greeted his "night owls."

15

Pilot Pete and Bubbles stopped at Jason's, a popular local bar on the outskirts of town. Jason's had a Western theme—cowboy hats hung on the walls, and mournful country tunes played on the jukebox. It was dimly lit, the way a lot of folks like their bars, but there was hardly anyone there. Apparently the bar attracted more of a late-night crowd of the raucous variety, at least according to the commercials on local radio.

"I'll have a draft beer," Bubbles told the bartender as she plopped herself on a stool.

"You got it!" the bartender replied with enthusiasm. "How about you, sir?" he asked Pilot Pete.

"The same."

"You got it!" He reached for two mugs, filled them to the brim, and placed the foam-covered brews in front of his two newest customers. "You want to run a tab?"

"Yes," Bubbles answered testily. She picked up her beer, took a long, cold chuga-lug, wiped her mouth, and then turned to Pete. "So what did you want to discuss with me?" Before he could answer, she picked up her glass again and noisily gulped down the beer.

"I think we should kill James."

Bubbles started to cough. Beer came out of her nose. "What?" she gasped as she grabbed the little square paper napkin, which was supposed to serve as a coaster, and dabbed at her eyes and nose. "Are you crazy?"

Pilot Pete began to laugh. "I'm just kidding, Bubbles. For God's sake, can't you tell when someone's joking? Maybe I'm too good an actor. I had you convinced, didn't I?"

Bubbles looked at him cautiously. "Yes, you did."

"What I mean is, can we kill off James's character?"

"The show is supposed to be a comedy."

"Okay. Then how about if we send James

off on a balloon race at the beginning of the show? By the time he gets back, the episode will be over. Give him two lines and get him out of there."

"It doesn't work with our story line. As it is, Grandma and her lecherous boyfriend are taking off on a balloon ride. We'd have to give Grandma more lines, and she's no Lucille Ball."

Pilot Pete stared into his beer. The tune "I'm So Miserable Without You, It's Like You Never Left" was playing softly in the background. Pete's hands were wrapped tightly around the beer mug. His knuckles were white. He turned to Bubbles. She looked wary. Pete laughed and tried to put her at ease. "Let's just hope that the reality show is *really* bad."

"A real stinker." Bubbles nodded in agreement and took another sip of her beer. "You've been in this business for a while?"

"Fifteen years. This show has got to work for me."

"How do you think I feel?" Bubbles asked.

Pete looked at her with steel in his eyes. He grabbed her arm tightly. "How can we make it work? What can we do to make this work?"

Bubbles raised her arm so he'd let go of her and shrugged. "I don't know." All of a sudden she felt uneasy. All of a sudden she realized that he might not be joking about James. He had a crazy look on his face. And to think his agent boasted that he was the perfect all-American dad. A chill ran through her. "We should pay the check," she suggested.

"Allow me."

They drove back into town in silence. Pilot Pete stared straight ahead. Bubbles was sure he didn't blink once. When they got to the hotel, Bubbles hurried to her room. She called her boyfriend. "Please be there," she prayed aloud. But he didn't answer. "You're not going to believe this," she cried hysterically when his voice mail picked up. "Pilot Pete was talking about murdering James. And I wouldn't put it past him! *Call me back! As soon as you can!*"

———◆———

16

Victor rode to the hotel with Regan and Danny. He wanted a chance to talk to Danny without interruption.

Regan sat in the backseat.

"Boss, I got bad news."

"Now what?"

"On my own initiative I contacted the three backup couples for the show—to see if they might be able to step in, you know, like Miss America's runner-up. 'If you know any reason she can't complete her reign, blah blah blah.' "

"What's the bad news, Victor?" Danny asked.

"It turns out that none of them want to do it."

"What? I thought they were all dying to be on our show."

"Not now, thanks to that website. They know they'll be scrutinized."

"They all have something to hide?" Danny asked, his voice squeaking.

"I told you, everybody's got something to hide." Victor turned around and smiled at Regan. "Even you. I bet you've got a secret."

"I've never been arrested," Regan said matter-of-factly.

Victor laughed. "That's good. Being on a reality show is like running for office. Someone'll find out all your vices. It's amazing the way these shows have captured America's imagination."

"So what we're saying here," Danny realized, "is that we're stuck with these couples no matter what they've done. Whether they're married or not. Whether they're criminals or not. Whether . . ."

"Boss, it's not our fault if they lied. We just have to put on a show that's entertaining. It's a one shot deal. If Roscoe likes us, our next show will be about something else. Look at it this way—if we find out after the fact that the couple that wins is not really married, then Roscoe doesn't have to pay the million bucks prize money. Who knows? It might provide more publicity for his station."

If Roscoe's paying the million bucks himself, Regan thought, he must have money to burn.

"Well we don't have a show without these couples," Danny concluded. "So we've got to work with them."

Victor nodded. "Unlike the website, we've got to keep the lid on any problems. As they say, 'The show must go on.' "

Regan leaned forward. "Danny, what about the background checks I was going to look into for you? When can you get me more information?"

Victor turned to her. "I wouldn't go asking them too many questions because any one of the contestants might get cold feet and bail out. Then we're stuck. After all, they were just minding their own business when Roscoe's people intruded in their lives. You know what I mean, Regan?"

"Roscoe cast the sitcom, and he provided us with a choice of six couples. The rest was up to us. We interviewed them to see which couples would be most interesting," Danny added.

"Interesting you got," Regan noted. "But why would he give you a choice of contestants? If he cast the sitcom, you'd think he would want to control this show as well."

Victor shrugged. "Who knows with him?"

Regan sat back. Something tells me that Roscoe is the one who could be up to no good, she thought. But he was providing a lot of people with work, and that was good. She looked out the window. It was nearly five-thirty, and the lights of Vegas were coming on. The night was beginning.

When Danny pulled into the parking lot of the Fuzzy Dice Hotel, one of the young production assistants came running out to the car. "Elsa just won $412,000 at a slot machine! She says she's outta here!"

Oh, my God, what next? Regan wondered.

Danny threw the car into park and dashed inside.

Regan and Victor hurried after him. Regan couldn't believe her eyes. Little Elsa was rolling around on the floor, in a catfight with another woman. Aunt Agony and Uncle Heartburn were trying to break them up.

And Sam was capturing it all on tape.

17

Uncle Heartburn's chili lived up to its name.

"Wow," Shep exclaimed as he scraped the bottom of the bowl with his spoon. "This stuff will wake you up."

But Maddy didn't need any chili to come alive. Ever since the waitress asked her to deliver Aunt Agony's mail, she had been electrified. She downed only two mouthfuls, and it almost sent her over the edge. Maddy could barely contain herself. The minute Shep put down his spoon, she stood up. "Shep, dear, we'd better get moving."

"Where's the fire?" he asked rhetorically as he drained his glass of Coke.

The waitress appeared from the back room, dragging a large cloth sack. It was marked U.S. MAIL—AUNT AGONY. "Here it is," she announced. "A big pile of cares and woes. All packed up and ready to go."

Shep raised his eyebrows. "That's a lot of agony."

"I don't know how she does it," the waitress replied, "but she reads every single one of them. Me, I'd get depressed."

Maddy tried to pick up the bag, but Shep stopped her. "That's too heavy, dear. I'll carry it."

They paid the check, said their goodbyes, and stepped out into the late-day sunshine. The dog was asleep in his basket next to the porch and didn't even flinch when the screen door slammed behind them.

"Why don't you put the sack in the backseat?" Maddy suggested.

"Don't you think it would be easier to just stick it in the trunk?"

"No."

"Okay."

Shep opened the back door of the car, placed the bag on the floor, and got into the driver's seat. Maddy got into the passenger seat and turned to wave at the waitress who had stepped out onto the porch. Shep started up the car, pulled out slowly onto the lonely two-lane road, and off they went. As soon as the restaurant was out of sight, Maddy climbed into the backseat.

"What are you doing?" Shep asked in dismay as her foot grazed his shoulder.

"Just drive, honey." Maddy pulled her body into a sitting position. She reached down for the thermos of hot water she kept in a container next to the cooler on the floor of the car. Maddy liked to make tea on their road trips. She unscrewed the thermos lid, and little circles of steam rose from the container. "That'll do just fine," she purred. "Just fine." She closed the thermos and then practically dove into Aunt Agony's sack.

"It's a federal offense to tamper with other people's mail," Shep cautioned from the front seat.

"This isn't tampering. Like I said before, I just have a healthy interest in other people's lives."

Shep shook his head and reached to turn on the radio. "I'll be sure to visit you in jail."

18

"That was my slot machine!" the stocky disheveled woman on the ground with Elsa shrieked. If someone had told Regan the woman was a lady wrestler, she wouldn't have been surprised. Elsa's opponent was of an indeterminate age and had broad shoulders, long bleached blond hair, thick black eyeliner, and enough pancake makeup to sink a ship.

Aunt Agony and Uncle Heartburn offered advice about people needing to talk out their problems as the two women rolled around the floor beneath the one-armed bandits.

"Look out!" Regan yelled with authority. Aunt Agony and Uncle Heartburn quickly moved out of the way as Regan leaned down and got a grip on Elsa. Danny grabbed the lady wrestler, moved her away from Elsa, and held her in an armlock.

"What happened?" Danny demanded.

"I won fair and square," Elsa cried. "We got back from the studio, and I decided to throw a couple of quarters in one of the slot machines. I win, and this broad comes out of the ladies' room and goes nuts!"

"I was using that machine for the last three hours. It's my favorite. I only left it to go to the bathroom. I knew I should have peed before I left the house!" Her voice cracked, and she started to cry. "I really need the money," she wailed. "I really need it." Her ample chest started to heave up and down as she sobbed uncontrollably.

Elsa inspires a lot of tears, Regan thought.

The manager of the hotel came over and put his arm around the large woman. "I'm sorry. Lady Luck wasn't with you today. But, you know, this is Vegas."

The woman sobbed even more loudly.

Regan noticed that not only was Sam recording the proceedings, but behind the desk, the young receptionist with all the dice jewelry had her video camera going as well. Do they plan to use this in some sort of promotion for the hotel? Regan wondered.

"Elsa, can we go upstairs and talk?" Danny asked quietly.

"I want to tell Barney that I won."

"Where is he?"

"He went to the room to rest. His arm hurts."

"Are you all right?" Aunt Agony asked Elsa with concern. "It's a shame that such a joyous occasion as winning big money has to be spoiled by jealousy."

Spoiled by jealousy, Regan thought. That woman could have killed Elsa. And now the manager was escorting her outside.

"I'm fine," Elsa assured everyone. "It feels so good to win. It feels so good to know that Barney and I can go out and have a great time spending this money as a couple."

Uncle Heartburn nodded approvingly.

We're back in the game, Regan thought. Flush from her victory, Elsa is concentrating on the next prize. Even bigger money. The bonus round.

One million dollars.

Clearly, Danny has nothing to worry about. Elsa isn't going to leave. She came to her senses and realized that if she puts in a few more days, it just might be worth it.

"Danny," Regan said quietly. "I'm going to go upstairs and get freshened up. How about if I stop by your room at about quarter to seven? There are a couple of things I want to talk to you about in private."

"No problem, Regan. I have the suite at the opposite end of the hall from you."

"Great. See you in a little while." Regan headed for the staircase, the contestant files under her arm. She wanted to take a quick look at them and then call Jack. Everything had happened so fast. It was hard to believe she had started the day in her office in Los Angeles.

She laughed to herself. If the next four days are like today, I'll be loony by Friday night. Jack will have to restore my sanity.

Regan started to take the steps two at a time. She had less than an hour before the next gathering, and she could only imagine what tonight might bring.

———◆———

19

Roscoe had summoned Erene and Leo to a meeting in the backyard of his mansion. There was a gazebo at the end of the property, which had probably been used for all sorts of illegal activities by the previous owners. Roscoe liked to have a drink in the fresh air when the sun was setting. The sky looked so pretty as it changed from one color to another. Tonight it was streaked with gold. At this hour Roscoe often went for a balloon ride.

"That whistle blowing really got them, didn't it?" Roscoe asked as he took a sip of his fine single malt scotch.

Erene leaned forward. "It was wonderful. Studies show that when people are forced to work under pressure, they often become more creative. Now both 'teams' realize they can't waste a minute when they're on the grounds of Hot Air Cable."

"Bubbles looked as if she was going to split a gut," Leo offered. "As it is, she's having trouble with a couple of those actors."

Roscoe laughed and slapped the side of the gazebo with his riding crop. "It's all so marvelous—"

"But Roscoe," Erene interrupted. "There are some issues we must address."

"Yes, ma'am." He liked to call her ma'am. It sounded so dopey for him to call her that that it made him laugh.

"There's something sinister going on at the reality show that we have nothing to do with."

"The case of the slippery floor."

"Yes."

"We could be sued if someone gets hurt."

"Who greased the floor?" Roscoe asked.

"We don't know. The hidden camera covering that area of the studio was broken."

"Is it fixed?"

"They're working on it now."

"So there's someone who's causing a problem at *Love Above Sea Level,* and we don't know who it is."

"Correct," Erene answered.

Roscoe banged the table. "Not acceptable. Leo, are you asleep?"

"No, sir. I'm doing some thinking."

"You should have done that on the way over here."

"Yes, sir. But I think you'll enjoy my latest thought."

"Spit it out."

"To create more drama, if you will, I was thinking that we should have a dinner party for both groups in your lovely home here tomorrow night."

Roscoe's eyes widened. "Both teams are out to get each other!"

"Wouldn't it make for an interesting evening? We can really check everyone out, then compare notes. And, Roscoe, you can give one of your wonderful inspirational speeches. After all, we can't let someone ruin *Love Above Sea Level* now, can we?"

Roscoe started to laugh. "Let's have a barbecue," he said enthusiastically.

Kitty emerged from the house and hurried to the gazebo. "I knew her name sounded familiar!"

"What are you talking about, sweetie pie?" Roscoe asked.

"Regan Reilly."

Roscoe explained to the others: "Danny has a friend with him who supposedly wants to produce a reality show."

Kitty held up one of Nora Regan Reilly's books. "I just got this in the mail from my book club. I decided to try reading suspense even though I'm kind of a scaredy-cat." She opened the book to the acknowledgments page. "Look! 'I want to thank my daughter, private investigator Regan Reilly, who was so helpful . . .' "

"She's a private investigator!" Roscoe cried. "We don't need her nosying around."

"We certainly don't," Erene agreed. "Studies show that if—"

"Forget the studies!" Roscoe ordered. "She could ruin everything for us!"

Leo shook his head and pursed his lips. "Let's have that party tomorrow night, boss. We can keep an eye on her—and everybody else for that matter."

Undeterred, Erene pointed her index finger in the air. "There was a survey that said people who dine together are much more likely to—"

"Call the caterer!" Roscoe interrupted. He was getting sick of her surveys and studies.

Next thing you know, she'd be pulling out graphs and charts. Roscoe wanted to have fun and get a good show that would put Hot Air Cable on the map. He didn't care about statistics. "We'll grill hot dogs and hamburgers and marshmallows. Let's set up a campfire in the backyard here. Just like *Survivor!*"

Leo smiled smugly. He knew it would be an interesting party.

20

Honey spent the day getting beautified. She was waxed, tinted, highlighted, polished, exfoliated, and massaged. I need it, she rationalized. When I run into Danny, and I will run into him, I don't want to have one chipped nail, one hair out of place, or one piece of dead skin on my body. She returned home exhausted, turned on the six o'clock news, and heard the anchor announce that they had a breaking story.

"Reality show contestant ends up in a tussle with fellow gambler at the Fuzzy Dice Hotel," he reported excitedly.

Honey watched in pain as Danny dove right in to break up the fight. Her heart just about broke. Danny was so strong, so fair, so good to people. She watched as the large woman with the bad dye job screamed that she needed the money. Honey felt sorry for her. *What she really needs is the name of a good hairdresser. No woman should go around looking like that.*

That's it! Honey realized. *I will show Danny what a good, caring person I am. I will go to the aid of people in need. I will find people on the street who desperately need makeovers. God knows there are enough of them walking around Las Vegas. Help them with their self-esteem.* Honey was elated about the limitless possibilities of becoming a twenty-first-century Florence Nightingale. But her spirits sank quickly.

In practical terms, she thought, *how will this work? And how will Danny learn about all my good deeds?*

Take action now, she thought. She pulled the Las Vegas phone book out from under her couch and looked up the number of the Fuzzy Dice Hotel. She said the number aloud, reached for the phone and dialed.

"Pauly's Pawn Shop," a male voice answered gruffly.

"This isn't the Fuzzy Dice Hotel?" Honey asked anxiously.

"Nope." Click.

Honey picked up the phone book again. "I knew I should have written it down," she said to herself as she looked up the number again, repeated it twice, and redialed.

"Fuzzy Dice Hotel."

"Yes, hello. I was just watching television and saw the little skirmish in your lobby there—"

"We had a big winner!" a young woman said proudly.

"My congratulations to her. I understand she's one of the reality show contestants."

"Yes. The whole gang is staying here for the week. Lots of excitement. We have a couple of rooms left. Do you want to make a reservation?"

"Actually, I was wondering if you could give me the name of the woman who didn't win the money. I need to contact her."

"Lady, we threw her out. We don't need customers like her. And we don't give out our guests' names. Besides, why would you want to contact her? She's crazy."

"I do makeovers. I felt sorry for her and wanted to offer my help."

"Well, I will admit she was a good candidate for a makeover, but I can assure you that our manager escorted her out and made sure she never darkens our door again. You know, you ought to do makeovers on the contestants. Just between us, the woman who won the money could use some help. Her haircut reminds me of Buster Brown. She has no style at all."

"You're right. What a great idea!" Honey breathed.

"Just a thought. After all, the couple who wins will renew their vows in a hot air balloon. They should look their best, shouldn't they?"

"They most certainly should! And I'm the person who can make that happen! Could you ring Danny Madley's room for me?"

"You know Danny?" The woman didn't wait for an answer. She connected Honey to his suite.

Honey's heart practically stopped as the phone began to ring. The adrenaline flowing through her body could have powered the dancing fountains at the Bellagio.

"Hello." Danny sounded rushed.

"Danny, this is Honey," she began in her most cheerful and confident tone.

"Honey, I'm really busy now. I can't talk. Maybe another time."

Honey's lip started to tremble as the dial

tone buzzed in her ear. She sat frozen for several seconds, listening to an irritating recording play, "If you'd like to make a call, please hang up and dial again. If you need help, hang up and dial your operator. If you'd like to make a call . . ."

Honey pressed the off button and slammed the phone down on her coffee table dejectedly. I can't sit here, she thought. I'll go crazy staring at these four walls tonight. I'm going out on the town. She picked up the phone and called her best friend, Lucille, a dealer in one of the casinos who luckily had the same nights off as Honey.

"Lucille, we're going out!"

"Where are we going?" Lucille always got to the point. She was the original no-nonsense kind of girl. At the casino she swept up the losers' chips faster than any dealer in Vegas.

"Out on the town. I got some things to do."

Lucille laughed. "Like hunting down Danny?"

"Lucille!" Honey protested.

"That means yes. I'll pick you up in my car. Danny won't recognize it, and you can duck under the seat if the need arises."

"I'll be ready in five minutes," Honey announced. After the day she had, there was not much more grooming her body could take.

"That's nice," Lucille replied. "I'll be there in an hour."

Honey hung up the phone feeling a little bit better. I'm going to get him back, she thought. He knows we were meant for each other. No matter what that rotten mother of his said about me.

———◆———

21

"My, my, my." Madeline pulled a handful of letters from the sack. "I don't know where to begin."

In the front seat Shep shook his head and unconsciously pushed his foot farther down on the gas. "This is not a good idea," he warned. "Why don't you just call one of your girlfriends if you want gossip?"

Mad ignored him. "Look at these return addresses. All from Arizona and Nevada. There must be someone we know who's written to Agony. Maddy placed the letters on the seat next to her and was about to reach back into the sack when she had an idea. She grabbed the sack and turned it upside down. The letters scattered over the floor of the car. "Now I can see them all."

Maddy shuffled the letters around trying to decide which one to open first. She finally spotted an intriguing return address on a business-sized envelope—Brenda Nickles, Attorney at Law. Mad grabbed the plain white envelope and opened the thermos bottle. She ran the letter back and forth over the tiny trickle of steam. The seal on the envelope started to give way. Gingerly, Mad gave it a little extra prodding with her index finger.

"There we go," she said, curling her tongue as she concentrated on her task. Ever so gently she tugged on the soggy envelope until it was completely open. "Not a rip or tear," she declared triumphantly. She pulled out the letter and started to unfold it.

"Oh, my God!" Shep cried. "Where did he come from?"

A state trooper was right behind them, lights flashing.

Maddy glanced around in a panic. "Shep, what did you do?"

"I wouldn't worry about what I did. You're the one reading someone else's mail," he growled as he steered the car to the side of the road.

Frantically, Maddy stuffed the lawyer's letter into a pouch in the backseat. Then she grabbed a fistful of the rest of the mail and jammed it back into the sack. Then another. Then another. She turned and saw the state trooper walking toward their car. "I feel like a criminal," she whimpered to Shep.

"You are. Now just sit still."

The trooper spotted Maddy in the backseat and approached the passenger side of the car with caution. Shep had rolled down the window.

"You're in a little bit of a hurry," the trooper observed.

"I'm sorry, sir. I didn't realize I was going over the limit."

"Where are you headed?"

"Las Vegas."

"License, registration, and insurance papers, please."

Shep reached into the glove compartment and procured the necessary documents. The trooper looked at Mad quizzically.

"I get carsick riding in the front," she offered quickly. "I always ride in the back. Always, always, always. It's so much more comfortable. I can stretch out if I want."

The trooper looked from Maddy to the

pair of ladies' shoes on the floor of the front seat. "Those your shoes up front?"

Maddy blinked. "Yes, officer. Those are my shoes up front. You see, what happened was, I thought I'd keep my husband company. But then, you know, my tummy started to hurt, so I—"

"I'll be right back," the trooper said curtly. He walked back to his car with Shep's papers.

Maddy stuffed the few remaining envelopes on the seat back into the sack of mail.

"Do me a favor, Maddy. Keep your mouth closed," Shep said wearily. "You're making yourself seem suspicious."

Maddy shifted down in her seat and tried to avoid the glances of people in the passing cars. She knew what they were thinking. It's what she always thought when she saw someone pulled over on the side of the road by the cops. Lawbreaker! Those flashing lights were downright embarrassing.

The trooper came back and handed Shep a hefty ticket for speeding. Twelve miles over the limit. "You go to Las Vegas a lot?" he asked.

"Yes. We love Las Vegas," Maddy answered. "Our son is producing a reality show up there."

"Can I take a look in your trunk?"

Shep nodded, pushed the button that popped the trunk, and got out of the car.

"Be careful, honey," Maddy cried.

The officer took a quick look at the luggage in the trunk, then walked back to Maddy's window as Shep got back in the car. "Mind if I take a look in that sack you got there?" he asked Maddy.

"The sack?" Maddy repeated.

"That's right, ma'am. A lot of people transport drugs on these roads. You wouldn't have anything illegal back here now, would you?"

Maddy just about fainted. "No, sir, not at all. Just a bunch of letters we're delivering to Aunt Agony."

"Aunt Agony?"

"The gossip columnist."

"Oh, yeah. My wife likes her." He opened the door of the car. Maddy slid out of the way and pushed the sack toward him. He started poking through it, just as Maddy had done minutes before. "I hope there isn't a letter in here from my wife," he joked.

Maddy laughed a little too hysterically. "I can check for you if you'd like."

He stared at her. "You shouldn't be going through this mail. What are those envelopes I see there on the seat?"

Maddy stopped laughing quickly and looked down to discover that she had ended up sitting on two letters. When she slid over, they were in plain view. "Officer, they must have slipped out of the bag somehow."

"Hand them to me, please."

Thank God I hadn't steamed those, she thought. Maddy handed the officer two flowery envelopes that were probably filled with heartbreak. He examined both sides, saw that they hadn't been disturbed in any way except for being sat on, and dropped them into the sack.

"What's the name of your son's reality show?" he inquired.

"*Love Above Sea Level.* We're hoping it will be on the Balloon Channel this Friday night. Do you get the Balloon Channel?" Maddy asked, coquettishly smiling up at him.

"I never heard of it." He tied the rope of the sack decisively, then double-knotted it.

He gave a slight wave and walked back to his car.

Shep pulled onto the highway. "I hope you learned your lesson."

Maddy nodded. Her heart was beating a million miles a minute. "I did, my dear. The only thing is, I have one letter in the pouch here. It looks very interesting."

———◆———

22

Regan shut the door of her room with a profound sense of relief. The quiet, empty room was a welcome change. Even the sight of all the dice designs on her bedspread didn't bother her. She kicked off her shoes, sat down on the bed, propped up the pillows, and leaned back. I would love to close my eyes, she thought, then take a nice soothing shower and go out for a relaxing dinner.

"No dice," Regan said aloud as she stared at the decor of her room. "So to speak." She opened the file on Barney and Elsa Schmidt. Boy, they had some day. Barney falls and hurts his arm, then Elsa hits the jackpot. Hey, Regan thought. I fell in that same spot. Maybe I should play the slots tonight.

After looking through the files on all three couples, Regan realized she didn't have much helpful information. All their addresses gave only the towns and P.O. boxes. No street addresses. No Social Security numbers were given. No occupations. There was lots of information about their likes and dislikes, why they wanted to be on the show, how the couples had met. Regan raised her eyebrows. These shows were primarily concerned with how the contestants come off on television. It's about whether they work for the concept of the show. Who cares if they have violent tendencies?

She picked up her cell phone and called Jack. He answered on the first ring.

"Regan, how's it going?"

"Only in Vegas." She laughed. "Since I talked to you a couple of hours ago, one of the wives won over $400,000 on a slot machine and threatened to quit the show."

"Can you blame her?"

"Well, she's decided to stay. Why not? In a few days she might bag another million."

"Do you want me to run some of those background checks?" he asked.

"I only have names and P.O. boxes. That's

all the information I could get so far. I'll see what else I can find out at tonight's cocktail party. But the fact of the matter is, Danny needs everyone to stay. Without them, he doesn't have a show."

"When you think of all the people who are dying to get on these reality shows . . ." Jack observed.

"I know. But it's too late to replace any-one. Roscoe Parker is the one I want to find out about. He's very eccentric. At five o'clock today he blasted a very loud whistle and threw everyone off the grounds of Hot Air Cable. He does this when both produc-tions need every minute to prepare for Friday."

"Are you kidding?"

"I wish I were. That was one shrill whistle. Roscoe said that no one could come back until nine o'clock tomorrow morning. Oh, and as long as we're on the subject of things that could be considered annoying, I slipped and almost fell in the studio today. In the exact same spot as the contestant who went to the emergency room. Some-body put oil on the floor. I'm sure of it."

"Regan," Jack said, his tone turning seri-ous. "I don't like the way this sounds. Be careful, would you? I'm going to call some of my contacts out there and see what I can find out about this Roscoe Parker. And I'll try to check out the contestants. What are their names?"

Regan relayed the information to him.

"Anything else?"

"Danny thinks someone working for him may be out to sabotage his show. I've met a couple of his employees, but I don't even know their last names yet."

"Call me as soon as you know more. I want you to be safe and sound on Friday night."

Regan smiled into the phone. "I will be."

"Regan, I do worry about you, you know."

"Jack, I'll be fine," Regan assured him, still smiling into the phone. "Danny wants me here as an extra pair of eyes and ears. I'll be careful. I just hope that his show is a success on Friday. Then I'll be happy."

"What do you know about the sitcom that's being produced?"

"Not much. I'll see what I can find out about that as well. If anyone has a motive for trying to ruin things for Danny, it's some-one from that camp."

"Again, just call if you have other names for me to check."

"You're so good to me," Regan teased.

"I know." Jack laughed. "There's something about you, Miss Reilly. I don't know what it is, but I can't wait to see you."

When she hung up, Regan jumped up from the bed. Talking to Jack always made her feel alive. She was invigorated and ready to face whatever the evening had to offer.

23

"How about adding more of a ballooning theme to the story line?" Noel suggested to Bubbles. "Roscoe is crazy about balloons."

Bubbles and the Irish twins had a hard night ahead of them, and to complicate things, Bubbles couldn't get her mind off Pilot Pete. She'd worked with some weird actors before, but he took the cake. Even the actor she'd rehearsed with for a class in L.A. who had wanted to hold a switchblade to Bubbles's neck instead of a prop knife so their acting would be more "believable" didn't seem as crazy. After one scene with that guy, Bubbles vowed to stick to comedy.

Noel, Neil, and Bubbles were sitting at a small corner table in the bar of the 7's

Heaven Hotel. Bubbles knew that 7's was on a par with the Fuzzy Dice, which was a slight consolation. The reality show group wasn't living in the lap of luxury, either.

"Our sitcom family already runs a ballooning company. What more do you want about ballooning?" Bubbles asked impatiently. These two were clearly no Laurel and Hardy.

"There are some funny facts we can incorporate. Neil and I went on the Internet and looked up the history of hot air ballooning."

I'm going to kill myself, Bubbles thought.

"Human beings have dreamed of balloons since the beginning of time. But I bet you don't know where hot air ballooning was actually invented."

"That's correct."

"In a kitchen in France. In the 1780s. Two brothers who were scientists discovered that they could float paper bags of hot air over their kitchen fire. Joseph and Jacques Montgolfier decided to build a larger air bag made out of fabric and paper. Under the balloon they hung a small cage. Hot air ballooning was born," Neil explained, smiling.

"How do you plan to incorporate that into the show?" Bubbles challenged.

It was Noel's turn to speak. He pointed his finger at Bubbles. "I bet you don't know who the first three passengers were on a Montgolfier balloon flight."

"I can't say that I do."

Noel cleared his throat. "France, 1783. A duck, a rooster, and a sheep were sent up in a balloon because the brothers didn't know whether a human could survive the flight."

"It's a good thing PETA wasn't around then," Bubbles observed.

"The flight lasted only about eight minutes. It was a safe landing, and the animals were in perfect shape. As a matter of fact, the sheep was found grazing in a field. They retired him to Marie Antoinette's private zoo."

"Well, cockadoodledo."

"Exactly," Neil cried. "Because most balloon flights take off at sunrise when the winds are calm, we were thinking we could have a resident rooster on the show. The rooster will be in the field at sunrise to greet not only the day but the hot air balloon passengers. We'll say he's a descendant of that very first rooster to fly in a balloon."

Bubbles stared at them in amazement.

"We're still trying to figure out what to do with a duck and a lamb," Noel admitted. "But we have a unique opening for the show that we can use every week. If the show is picked, that is."

"What is it?" Bubbles's voice was quieter with each word.

"With most balloon landings there's a good chance that the balloonists end up trespassing," Neil began.

"Right."

"Well, in eighteenth-century France the farmers were petrified by balloons descending from the sky onto their land. They'd never seen anything like it. So you know what they did?"

"No."

"They attacked them with pitchforks!"

"They did?"

"Yes!" Noel and Neil cried in unison.

Noel picked up the story. "So the balloonists figured out that if they carried champagne on board, they could present it to the farmers when they landed."

"Hopefully before they got poked with the pitchfork."

"That's right. Get the farmer drunk and happy. Seriously, that's how the traditional champagne ceremony at the end of balloon flights started."

"I thought it was to celebrate making it back to the ground in one piece."

"There might be a little of that, too," Noel agreed. "But we thought we could recreate a genuine eighteenth-century landing at the beginning, with you guys dressed in period clothing. Grandma and her beau will be the farmers, and you and James and Pilot Pete will land in the balloon. They'll come running at you with pitchforks, and you break out the champagne. Roscoe told us to feel free to use his balloon for the show."

"We're writing a funny theme song that will play during the scene," Neil added.

Bubbles closed her eyes and thought for a moment. "It could work. Let's try it. I'll ask Roscoe tomorrow if we can use his balloon on Wednesday or Thursday morning." She paused and then added under her breath, "Pilot Pete will probably like the idea."

"He loves it!" Noel assured her.

"When did you tell him?" Bubbles demanded, feeling slightly peeved.

"Before you got down here, he passed through the lobby with James."

"With James?"

"They were going out for a drink."

Bubbles's stomach did a somersault.

———◆———

24

At quarter to seven Regan knocked on Danny's door.

Victor opened it and greeted her. "We were just looking at that website Blowing the Lid Off."

Regan followed Victor into the living room of the small suite. Danny was on the couch bent over his computer. He looked up. "Hi. Have a seat."

Regan sat down next to Danny and dropped her purse on the floor. "Anything new?" she asked as Victor took a seat in the chair next to the couch. Regan had hoped she could talk to Danny alone.

Danny handed her the laptop computer. "Take a look."

Love Above Sea Level is the latest entry in the reality show craze. Three couples are presently competing to see who deserves to renew their vows in a hot air balloon shaped like a wedding cake and win a million dollars. None of these couples had been happily married. Now they must convince Aunt Agony and Uncle Heartburn, advice columnists from the Las Vegas region, that they are back in love and will live happily ever after. With their one-million-dollar prize, of course. Hey, we'd fake it for a million bucks. Wouldn't you? Hah.

We posted the happy couples' photos and names last week and asked for your comments. We're not naming names because we don't want to get in trouble, but we've heard repeatedly that one of the contestants is a real psycho, the type who could *snap* at any time. Has violent tendencies.

Makes the contest interesting, doesn't it? So, folks, please write in and give us your thoughts. Aunt Agony and Uncle Heartburn are the judges. Danny Madley is the executive producer. Most

of you have probably never heard of
him . . .

Danny was reading over Regan's shoulder. "I love that last sentence."

"You should be happy. You don't need
people criticizing you online."

"As my uncle always said," Victor proclaimed, "sometimes you have to walk
through the fire if you want to take on a
glow."

"Thank you, Victor. Listen, Vic, would you
head downstairs to the cocktail party?
Make sure everything is set up. Regan and I
will be down in a couple of minutes."

"Okay, boss." Victor looked disappointed.

Regan had the impression that Victor always wanted to be where Danny was. She
watched as Victor walked slowly out of the
room. "He's devoted, huh?" she asked
Danny when the door closed.

Danny rolled his eyes. "I think he's trying
to do his best."

"So this website keeps emphasizing that
one of the contestants is a psycho," Regan
observed.

"You know that people always write in
hateful messages on these things."

"I know that," Regan agreed. "But maybe one of the contestants wants to cause problems. Maybe one of them left that letter on your desk today. And put the oil on the floor."

"It's certainly possible."

"If it's not someone who works for you."

Danny threw up his hands. "I just don't know, Regan. I don't know what to think."

"What about Victor?" Regan asked frankly.

"He's been my right-hand man. It's hard to imagine . . ."

"The question is, why would someone want to ruin your show? I think they either want the sitcom to air on the Balloon Channel, or they have a personal vendetta against you. Do you know much about what's going on with the sitcom?"

"A comedian named Bubbles Ferndale is producing it. She has four actors working with her. The two guys writing the show are brothers."

"Where are they staying?"

"A hotel not far from here called 7's Heaven. It's on a par with this place. Fairly small and dumpy."

"After the cocktail party, I'll head over

there. Sit at the bar and have a drink. See if
I can learn anything."

"Someone might have seen you coming
out of the studio today when the whistle
sounded. You might be recognized."

Regan smiled. "I always come prepared. I
have a red wig and glasses and an outfit
Regan Reilly wouldn't be caught dead in
that I use for disguise."

"I'd feel better if I could go with you,"
Danny said.

"I'll be fine, just fine."

"I could never face your parents if something happened to you."

Regan laughed. "Don't worry, Danny. This
is what I do for a living, remember? Speaking of my parents, my mother's giving a talk
at a writer's conference in Santa Fe this
week. She and my father are spending a
few days with her agent. He loves hot air
ballooning and is taking them to the balloon
festival in Albuquerque. I promised to let
them know when we'd be arriving."

"We're flying down in Roscoe's private
plane early Friday morning. We'll go straight
to the balloon field. At sunrise when all the
special shapes balloons start ascending,
our group will go up in the wedding cake.

That's when we'll announce the winning couple. They renew their vows, we come back down, we have some champagne, and fly back to Vegas to do the final edits on the show. We present *Love Above Sea Level* to Roscoe at five o'clock Friday afternoon.

"It sounds great, Danny. Your show is going to be terrific," Regan assured him. "You've got to believe that you're going to win. What is it they say? Visualize yourself as the winner."

"I'll try. At the moment I'm visualizing what the next disaster might be. And I think it may have something to do with Elsa winning all that money. The other contestants are not going to be happy about it, I'm sure."

"They can't be as unhappy as that poor woman who gave up the slot machine to go to the bathroom. I bet she never has another glass of water as long as she lives," Regan joked. "Come on, Danny. Let's go downstairs and check out the scene."

25

Luke and Nora were packing their bags in New Jersey when the phone rang. Nora put down the beige silk slacks she'd been trying to decide whether to bring or not and picked up the cordless phone next to the bed.

"Hello."

"Nora, it's Harry."

"Hello there. Luke and I are packing as we speak."

"Tell Harry I'm finished," Luke noted as he tossed one last pair of socks into his suitcase. "How about a glass of wine?" he whispered to Nora.

"Ummmm," she murmured, her eyes brightening. "Harry, Luke asked me to tell you he's finished packing."

Harry laughed. "Glad to hear it. I just wanted to check in. Linda and I will pick you up at the airport tomorrow at two o'clock. We'll meet you in the baggage claim area."

"That sounds great. We're looking forward to relaxing at your beautiful digs."

"I'm telling you, Nora, we wish we could get out here more often. It's good to get away from the rat race."

"It sure is. Oh, Harry, I talked to Regan today. She's in Las Vegas doing some work for a reality show that a guy named Roscoe Parker is financing. Apparently he's big with the hot air balloons. You don't know him, do you?"

"Roscoe Parker? Are you kidding me?"

"Why?" Nora asked, dreading the answer.

"He's a little annoying."

Nora laughed, somewhat relieved. "What do you mean?"

"I really shouldn't say anything."

"Please, Harry. There's been some trouble with the show. I want to warn Regan if there's something she should know about Parker."

"Nothing serious. He's an old windbag

who could fly a balloon on his own hot air. He doesn't need any burners in his basket. That guy is always trying to grab attention for himself by being outrageous. A little Roscoe Parker goes a long way."

"Apparently he has his own cable station up in Vegas now."

"One of his many expensive toys. He's unbelievably wealthy. He shows up at these balloon festivals in his private plane and talks about himself to anyone who will listen."

"Awww," Nora said softly. "He sounds harmless. Maybe he didn't get enough attention growing up."

Luke came back into the bedroom and handed her a glass of pinot noir. "She can't say anything bad about anybody," he declared loud enough for Harry to hear.

"Tell Luke I'm very well aware of that," Harry said with a laugh.

"Well, at least this man is giving a lot of people work. A schoolmate of Regan's is producing the reality show. How bad can Parker be?"

"Not so bad, I guess," Harry said. "But I hope you get to meet him. You'll see what I mean. He keeps threatening to go around the world in a balloon. I know a lot of people who would gladly go to Roscoe Parker's send-off party."

26

I've been to many cocktail parties, Regan thought as she and Danny walked down the steps to the main floor of the hotel. Some bore you to tears with the endless small talk, others have an indefinable energy and buzz. But this cocktail party's sole purpose is to create more interesting footage for Danny's show. Drum up some soundbites. Provide some drama.

Regan paused at the door to the lounge. "Danny, I had better stay to the side. I don't want to be on camera."

"You won't," Danny assured her. "Sam is careful to shoot only the couples, Aunt Agony, Uncle Heartburn, and maybe me. He'll ask questions as he moves around with the camera. Besides, if you do end up on camera, we just won't use it. We'll have plenty of tape to choose from." Danny opened the door to the room that had, naturally, a dice motif and found everyone gathered around Elsa and Barney. The camera was rolling.

Elsa was beaming, and even Barney had a smile on his face.

"We're planning to give fifty percent of the money to charity," Elsa announced, looking directly at Agony and Heartburn.

"Fifty percent!" Suzette the cheerleader cried. "Wow!" She raised her fist and pumped it three times. "Go! Go! Go!"

"Planning" is the key word here, Regan thought. Let's see if it happens.

Vicky did not look happy at all. "I have something to say," she declared.

"What is it, dear?" Aunt Agony asked kindly.

"You want us to express our feelings, right?"

"Of course."

"The contest isn't fair anymore!"

"Why not, dear?"

"Barney and Elsa had two big things happen today that strengthened their relationship—Barney falling on his butt and Elsa winning the money. How are the rest of us supposed to compete? They're getting all the attention."

"My dear," Aunt Agony replied sagely, "today is only Monday. Who knows what else will happen this week? Life takes twists and turns that no one expects. Whoever is up today," she proclaimed, raising her arms above her head, "could be down tomorrow." Aunt Agony was now bent over.

Regan wanted to run over and catch her, but Agony quickly straightened up, smoothed her hair, and continued. "When I was a young girl and good things kept happening to other people, I always said to myself, 'Virginia—that's my real name—I'd say, Virginia, your turn will come. I just know it. And look at me now. I have Heartburn, I have an advice column, I am on this wonderful show. . . .'"

Come to think of it, Heartburn doesn't look too happy, Regan observed. He looked a little distracted.

"I was just wondering what your favorite charities are," Bill challenged Elsa and Barney. "Suzette and I have our own personal favorites that we give to every year, even if it's just a small amount."

Elsa got that deer-in-the-headlights look. "To t-t-tell you the truth," she stammered, "we haven't donated that much lately because times have been tough. Barney lost his job, we had to apply for loans, but now, thanks to our good fortune, we're going to make up for it."

Good recovery, Regan noted. She watched as the couples mixed and mingled. They were all doing their best to appear civil to one another. But there was an undeniable tension in the room. Sam never stopped moving around with the camera rolling. His long blond hair was pulled back in a ponytail, and a bright red baseball cap rested backward on his head. He approached Vicky and Chip and asked them each to relate something special about their spouse that they had never appreciated before.

"I never realized how pretty Vicky looks when she's asleep. She's like a little angel. I just want to protect her."

I bet her next present is a sleeping bag, Regan thought.

"Chip is so adventurous," Vicky responded. "He's not a run-of-the-mill kind of guy."

Definitely a sleeping bag, Regan concluded.

Sam turned the camera on Bill and
Suzette.

"Suzette takes such good care of herself.
I never appreciated how her exercising
around the house has kept her in great
shape. That is so important."

"Bill and I are going to sign up for a
couple's exercise class when we get home,"
Suzette smiled. "He adapts so well to any
situation."

"And now Elsa and Barney, what do you
have to say?" Sam asked them in his easy,
mellow manner.

"Barney is a wonderfully sensitive man
who I am lucky to spend my life with."

"Elsa, here . . ." Barney began quietly.

Don't cry, Regan pleaded silently. Please
don't cry.

"Elsa's strength has guided me through
good times and bad. I never understood
how important that was. She is the reason I
walk. She is the reason I talk. She is the reason I live."

Victor walked over to Danny and handed
him a piece of paper. Danny read it quickly
and moved into camera range. "I have an

announcement. Roscoe Parker has invited us to dine at his mansion tomorrow night with the sitcom group."

"Hobnobbing with the enemy," Aunt Agony joked.

I think that's what we're doing right now, Regan decided as she looked around the room. Who could it be? she wondered. Who could it be?

27

Shep and Maddy pulled up to the 7's Heaven Hotel. Maddy was still in the backseat, but she hadn't yet read the letter from the attorney. Shep had put his foot down.

"Maddy, I'm going to have a heart attack! Don't read that letter while I'm driving! You can do what you want when you get out of the car, but I'm not going to be considered part and parcel of your lawbreaking. What if we get stopped again?"

"Oh, all right." Maddy sighed.

Shep parked the car since there was no valet at the 7's. It was not that kind of hotel. They grabbed their bags because there was no bellman, either. Shep pulled out the sack of mail, and they walked inside to the reception desk.

"We have a reservation," Maddy announced in a loud voice. "Madley is the name. Shep and Madeline Madley." She looked around the lobby in her imperious way, not exactly thrilled with what she saw. There were the usual slot machines, but the place was kind of dingy. Well, Maddy always said she'd rather travel more and spend less.

The clerk tapped the keys of the computer. Then he tapped them some more. He grimaced and scowled and grunted.

"Madley," she repeated. *"Madley."*

"He heard you, honey," Shep said quietly.

"Here we go," the clerk finally said. "You have our last room. Could I have your credit card, please?"

Shep pulled a card out of his wallet. "You're pretty busy, huh?" he said conversationally.

"Yup. We have a few groups staying here this week. Some television people."

"Our son is producing a reality show," Maddy noted proudly as she wandered over to the bar area and looked around. Walking back to the desk, she suggested to Shep, "Why don't we drop our bags and then grab a drink at the bar?"

"What about Danny?"

"We'll call Danny later. When I talked to him this morning, he said he'd be busy until late tonight." Maddy hated the thought of turning over the sack of mail just yet.

The hotel room didn't invite lounging. It was strictly utilitarian. The bathroom light was dim, and the thin bedspread had a big "7" on it. Shep dropped the mailbag on the floor. "I could really use a beer. That chili keeps repeating on me."

"Thank you for sharing. Let's go." Maddy stuffed the letter into her purse and followed Shep to the elevator.

The bar area was small. There were six tables with groups of people crowded around them and a long Formica bar. Shep ordered a beer and a glass of red wine for Maddy. She decided to wait until they'd been served and Shep had a sip or two before pulling out the letter. Shep stared up at the television over the bar. It was tuned to a baseball game.

The letter was burning a hole in Maddy's bag. When the drinks arrived, she lifted her glass. "To Danny's show," she toasted.

Shep clinked his glass with hers, took a

swallow, and gazed back up at the television.

Maddy reached into her purse and pulled out the letter. She opened it up and spread it on the table so the light from the candle would illuminate the words. The bar was a little dark. Maddy read:

Dear Virginia and Sebastian,
Please contact my office immediately. Sebastian, your ex-wife Evelyn claims that you haven't paid alimony in months. She is threatening to go public and plans to reveal that your recipe for heartburn chili is really hers. All the hoopla about you experimenting in the cafe to find the perfect recipe is all a public relations scam.
Believe me, Evelyn's nose is out of joint and she's out for revenge. One of the tabloids has offered her a lot of money to tell her story. If she decides to talk, a lot of skeletons will come tumbling out of the closet. That's not good when you're supposed to be an up-and-coming advice man. I'd advise you to pay Evelyn before the tabloids do.

Call me now! I think your phone must be broken. It did nothing but ring. Your folksy image is getting on my nerves. Get an answering machine and a cell phone and a computer and a fax. Please!!!! I need to be able to communicate with you.

Evelyn said that if she doesn't hear from you by Tuesday of this week, then she'll give the tabloid interview. She plans to tell the world what a hypocrite you are. As she puts it, capital H.

I'm sorry to be the messenger. They're always the ones who get shot.

> *Sincerely,*
> *Brenda Nickles,*
> *Attorney at Law*

P.S. This is my first case, and I promised my client satisfaction.

"Oh, my God, Shep!" Maddy cried, knocking over her glass of red wine. Wine seeped all over the letter. "Oh, my God!" she cried again as she dabbed at the letter with her cocktail napkin. She jumped up and grabbed napkins off an empty table. It was hopeless. The white letter was now a deep shade of magenta.

"I knew something like this would happen," Shep declared testily. "Why can't you learn to mind your own business?"

"We've got to get that mail to Agony and Heartburn right away! They're in trouble, and it may ruin Danny's show!"

Shep downed his beer, got up, walked over to the bar, and signed for the check. They hurried out the door, took the elevator to the third floor, and raced to their room. "What did the letter say?" he asked as he unlocked the door.

Before she could answer, Maddy screamed. The sack of mail was gone.

———◆———

28

Honey and Lucille drove up and down the Strip. There was a lot of traffic. It was Vegas and things felt alive. The neon lights were flashing and the night was young.

"Where do you want to go now?" Lucille asked as she drove past the neon-lit casinos—Mandalay Bay, New York-New York, the Bellagio. It was not going to be an easy evening, she realized. But Honey was her friend, and this was what friends did for each other. Get them through their crazy times.

Honey stared out the window. Tears glistened in her eyes. She knew she looked adorable. It was one of those nights when Danny would have said, "Baby, you're the cutest girl in town. I love having you by my side."

"I don't know," she squeaked, blinking back tears.

Lucille made a quick right turn.

"Where are we going?" Honey asked.

"The Fuzzy Dice."

"But what will I do?" Honey implored.

"Listen, all Danny cares about right now is his show. I think the hotel receptionist you spoke to had a great idea. Go in and tell Danny you have a plan to make *Love Above Sea Level* a success. Explain that if these couples are promising to love each other forever, then they should look good. And they have to look *really* good if he expects anyone to watch his show. Tell him you'll get a hairdresser and a makeup artist in to make over the ladies this week and that it will add to the appeal of the show. That he'll like."

"You think so?"

"Definitely," Lucille lied. "They probably don't know what they're doing from day to day anyway. That's what these reality shows are like. They make everything up as they go along and hope something exciting will happen."

As they pulled up to the hotel, Honey got nervous. She had been so full of vim and vigor back at her apartment. But ever since Danny hung up on her, she felt deflated. Now her courage was waning.

"He'll think I'm a stalker," Honey protested.

"He probably does already," Lucille declared. "We'll go in and sit at the lobby bar and have a drink. We'll spot Danny. He has to pass through the lobby at some point."

Lucille parked the car, and they both opened their doors to get out. A car sped into the parking lot and zipped into a spot two spaces from Lucille's car.

"Come on, Shep, let's move," the woman emerging from the car yelled. "We've got to explain everything to Danny."

"How are we going to explain the fact that you read Agony and Heartburn's mail and then spilled wine all over it?" he growled in a loud voice. "I told you it's illegal."

"Well, the important thing is that Heartburn pay his ex-wife her alimony. He'd better not ruin this show for Danny. That's all I can say."

"If anybody finds out about this . . ." Shep

cautioned. "A lot of people will have big troubles."

It was the moment Honey had been waiting for ever since she had met Danny's mother. The woman was a viper, and Honey finally had the goods on her. Honey stepped out from the shadows as Shep and Maddy were about to pass Lucille's car. "Hello, Mrs. Madley. Hello, Mr. Madley. How on earth have you been?"

29

"Last call," Danny yelled jokingly as he prepared to address his crew.

"Make mine a double," Aunt Agony called out.

"You're cut off!"

Everyone laughed heartily. It seemed to Regan that the contestants were trying their best to put up a jovial front despite their competitiveness.

"Now, as you all know, this week was meant to be unpredictable," Danny began. "We told you that you wouldn't know what you'd be doing from one day to the next. Tonight two couples will have the evening free. One couple will accompany Heartburn and Agony on a special date."

"How do you decide who gets to go?"

Suzette interrupted in a confrontational tone.

Elsa and Barney's good fortune today is really getting to her, Regan decided.

"Hold your horses," Danny joked. "Let me explain. Tomorrow night we're going to Roscoe's for dinner. Wednesday and Thursday nights the two remaining couples will have their special evening with Agony and Heartburn. Right now we're going to pull one couple's name out of a hat."

"Drum roll, please," Victor quipped as he came forward with a baseball cap.

"Uncle Heartburn, please draw the lucky couple's name," Danny requested.

"Fine by me," Agony declared. "What's his is mine, and what's mine is his. It's the secret of a good relationship. We're soul mates, you know. We never go to bed angry. We make up first, then go into the bedroom and reach for the stars."

Way too much information, Regan thought. I think Agony copped a buzz. She wasn't kidding about that double.

Heartburn smiled at the group. "I'll close my eyes so no one can say I'm cheating." He squeezed his eyes shut and reached into the baseball cap. There were three pieces of paper in there. He picked up all three and let them drop back into the hat, in a dramatic gesture. He did it again. Then he pulled one piece of paper out. "Would you like me to reveal the name of the first couple?"

"Go ahead," Danny instructed.

Uncle Heartburn unfolded the paper and paused. "Vicky and Chip, are you ready to come on a dream date with us?"

"We are!" they exclaimed.

Thank God it wasn't Barney and Elsa, Regan thought, glancing around the room. She was anxious to get to the 7's Heaven Hotel. Then she'd catch up with Danny and the dream date crew. Something told her it was going to be a long night.

30

In the Fuzzy Dice Hotel parking lot, Maddy and Shep jumped back, startled, to say the least, by the sudden emergence of Danny's old friend.

"Missy!" Maddy exclaimed.

"My name is Honey."

"Of course. Honey."

"Let me introduce you to a dear friend of mine. Lucille, say hello to Danny's parents, Shep and Maddy Madley."

Lucille stepped around from the driver's side of the car. "I've heard so much about you from Honey."

Maddy looked at her suspiciously. She knew it couldn't have been good.

"I was surprised to hear you read Agony

and Heartburn's mail, Mrs. Madley," Lucille continued. "That is against the law, isn't it?"

"I don't know what you're talking about."

"And Heartburn owes his ex-wife money. Not good karma for an advice columnist. I'm sure the local press would love to hear about that and the story of Danny Madley's mother rifling through—"

"What do you want from me?" Maddy practically spat at her.

"Well, since you asked . . ." Lucille smiled at her. "My friend Honey here would really like to help Danny with his reality show. But because of a little mistake she made, which she now deeply regrets, he won't talk to her. I think you can intervene. What I want is for you to march in there and tell your son that Honey will arrange for makeovers for the contestants. Her hairdresser and makeup artist would love the publicity."

"Are you crazy?" Maddy looked at her, seething.

"Lucille," Honey fretted. "I don't know whether—"

"Honey," Lucille said with more determination than she felt, "either this woman helps you or I call the press. I've made up my mind." Lucille knew she was pushing things, but this was Honey's only chance. What the heck did Lucille care if this woman liked her or not? Maddy Madley was never going to be her mother-in-law, praise the Lord.

"To think," Shep muttered to himself, "this morning I was sitting peacefully in my den, reading the paper and minding my own business."

"Shep!" Maddy hissed. "You're not helping things."

"As they say in this town," Lucille challenged, "are you in or are you out?"

"I'm in!" Maddy yelled. "I'm in! I'm in! I'm in!"

"Good. Let's go talk to Danny. I warn you, I have my cell phone right here. The gossip columnists would just love to hear about this."

The foursome walked toward the front door of the Fuzzy Dice Hotel. Lucille turned and winked at Honey.

It's a dream come true, Honey thought. Holding a guillotine over your boyfriend's mother's neck. I can hardly stand it. I just hope Lucille's scheme works.

They asked at the reception desk where

Danny's group was and were directed down the hall to the recreation lounge.

"Mrs. Madley," Lucille said, "or may I call you Mad?"

"Maddy or Madeline," she replied curtly.

"I think it's best if Honey and I wait here in the reception area. We don't want to over-whelm Danny. Now be sure to stress all of Honey's good qualities to your beloved son."

Shep looked as if he wanted to go through the floor. Nonetheless, he led his wife down the hallway. They paused at the door to the lounge and peered through the window just as the cameraman turned his light off. Maddy knocked and waved. The expression on Danny's face when he saw her was utter disbelief. He rushed to the door and opened it. "Mom, Dad, what are you doing here?"

Maddy grabbed him and kissed both his cheeks. "Darling. I've been so worried about you."

"Why?"

"I just have."

Shep shook Danny's hand.

"Dad, what's going on? Is Regina okay?"

"She's fine, just fine."

"Good. I'm kind of busy at the moment. Can I call you later? Where are you staying?"

"We have to talk to you now."

"Now?"

"Yes. Right now."

"Okay." Danny turned around. "Hey, everybody. Those of you who are going to dinner—be in the lobby in fifteen minutes. The rest of you we'll see in the morning. Regan, come on over and say hello."

Maddy nearly died. To think that that floozy was waiting in the lobby and Danny was with Regan Reilly. It would be so wonderful if she and Danny fell in love.

"Hello, Mr. and Mrs. Madley," Regan said as Maddy grabbed her and kissed her.

"You look so wonderful, Regan," Maddy gushed. "Look at you. You're still single?"

"Yes, I am, but—"

"Mom," Danny interrupted.

"I'm sorry, dear. It's just I remember the two of you in school together."

"Hello, Regan. It's been a long time," Shep observed.

"That it has." Regan laughed. "Hard to believe how long."

"Mom, you're sweating. Are you all right?" Danny asked with concern.

"To tell you the truth, no. I need to talk to you, Danny. If you could excuse us, Regan. I hope we'll see you later."

"How long will you be around?" Regan asked.

"Several days."

"Then I'm sure I'll see you again. Danny, I'll take off now. I'll call your cell phone and catch up with you in an hour or two."

"That's great, Regan."

The three of them watched her walk down the hall.

"Such a lovely girl," Maddy noted sadly. She turned to Danny. "Where can we talk privately?"

"Come up to my suite."

They went up a back elevator and were soon seated in Danny's living room.

"You have me a little nervous," Danny admitted. "What's up?"

Shep and Maddy looked at each other. "It's your story," Shep sighed to his wife.

Maddy cleared her throat. "This morning Jackie De Tour called and told me her son Alfie looked up some website that had terrible things printed about your contestants."

"I know all about that, Mom." Danny interrupted impatiently.

"Well, I was worried and I said to your father that we should come up here and be with you."

Danny frowned. "Mom, that's nice, but I'm fine. Regan is here to help me out. We just have to keep moving forward with the show and—"

"I'm not finished."

"Uh-oh."

"Uh-oh is right," Shep muttered.

"So we got in the car and on the way we stopped at Aunt Agony and Uncle Heartburn's cafe."

"It's on the way," Danny affirmed.

"The waitress gave us a sack of their mail to deliver to them. Apparently, Agony has insomnia and likes to get stuff done at night."

"What happened?" Danny asked quickly.

"Well, we checked in to the 7's Heaven Hotel and went for a drink at the bar, and when we got back to the room, the sack of mail was gone."

"Are you kidding? Did you report it to hotel security?"

"Not yet."

"Not yet! Why not?"

"Your mother left out an important part of

the story," Shep remarked dryly. "Something that made her frantic when the sack of
mail was discovered missing."

"Mom, what did you leave out?"

Maddy closed her eyes and leaned her
head back as if in pain.

"Enough drama, Mom. What happened?"

"I had taken out one letter from a lawyer. I
read it in the bar and accidentally spilled
wine all over it."

"What?" Danny squealed.

"Now the rest of the mail is missing, and
we have a soggy letter that demands Uncle
Heartburn pay alimony to his ex-wife or else
she'll expose him as a fraud. The tabloids
are very interested," Shep finished.

Danny jumped out of his chair. "Mom,
how could you?"

"It'll never happen again," Maddy promised.

"Of course it won't happen again! How
could it?" Danny picked up the phone and
asked to be connected to Agony and Heartburn's room.

"What are you doing?" Maddy cried.

"We have to tell them."

'Ewwwww," Maddy wailed. "I'll never
gossip again."

Shep rolled his eyes. "Promises, promises."

"Agony, can you and Heartburn come up to my room, please? It's important. Thanks." He hung up. "Now, before they get here. Is there anything else I need to know?"

Maddy wiggled her index finger. "Just one little thing."

31

"I've got my car," Pilot Pete told James. "Why don't we take a drive?"

"A drive? Where to?"

"There have to be some good bars down the road. I feel like going to a quiet place, away from all the hubbub."

"Ohhh, I know what you mean," James acknowledged. "This has been one hectic day." He stroked his little goatee.

They got into Pete's Saab and drove off.

"How long have you been an actor?" James asked Pete.

"About fifteen years. And you?"

"I took my first acting class last year."

Pete almost lost control of the car. "Last year?"

James smiled. "I couldn't believe I got this job."

"It is unbelievable," Pete agreed.

"It's my first paid acting job."

He deserves to be killed, Pete decided. "Your first?"

James smiled. "Yup."

"Are you a member of the Screen Actor's Guild?"

"Now I am! Roscoe said that I was the only actor he could find who could play the part the way I could. So I got into SAG!"

"How did you get the audition in the first place?"

"My acting teacher told me about it."

"Who do you study with?"

"Darby Woodsloe."

"Never heard of him."

"Her."

"Her, then. Where is her class?"

"At her house in Venice Beach. Sometimes we just ran up and down the beach, at one with the waves."

Pete tightened his grip on the steering wheel. "Sounds great. Do you have a regular job?"

"Oh, yes. I just got the week off so I could

come here and do the show. If we get picked, I'll quit."

"What do you do?"

"I'm a dog walker every morning. Then I go to the mall and hand out pamphlets for the department stores. You'd be amazed at how many products are on sale these days. I get to meet a lot of interesting people. And I'm learning how to really observe all their different physicalities so I can be specific when I play all sorts of different characters. They say it's important to be specific when you're an actor. Did you know that?"

Pilot Pete was frantic. How can I get rid of this guy? he wondered. He hasn't paid his dues in this business, and he landed a part like this. He'll definitely ruin the show. Pete had to talk to Bubbles again.

In one quick motion Pilot Pete did a U-turn. "You know, James," he announced, "I'd like to go back to the hotel."

James shrugged. "I thought you wanted to go to an out-of-the-way place," he said in his soft voice.

"I don't feel well. I want to get back."

"That's okay." James yawned. "I'm a little tired anyway. It's important to be well rested this week, don't you think?"

"Sure."

"I think I'll order room service."

They went back to the hotel. Inside, James waved good-bye to Pete. "See you in the morning," he said cheerily as he headed for the staircase.

Pete stared after him for a minute and then headed for the bar. Bubbles and the Irish twins were finishing up their burgers.

"Mind if I join you?" he asked.

Bubbles looked up, surprised and relieved to see him. "You're back! I thought you were having a drink with James."

"I was, but I came home early."

"I'll say."

"We came up with some new ideas for the show," Noel explained. "Neil and I are going to head upstairs and work on the script."

"I'm ready," Neil declared as he got up from the chair. He patted Pete on the shoulder. "We'll write you a few good lines."

"Thanks, pal. Write a few less for James, would you?"

"I'll call you later for a progress report," Bubbles informed her writers.

When the brothers were out of earshot, Pete turned to her. "I have to talk to you about James."

Bubbles's eyes widened. "Petey, we've already been through this."

"No, I mean really. I'm not talking about killing him. But there's something strange about the whole situation. Did you know he's hardly done any acting?"

"Yes."

Pete grabbed her arm again. "Why did you cast him?"

"Roscoe had the final say over who got the job."

"But were you at all the auditions?"

"Yes."

"Wasn't there any actor in Los Angeles who could have done a better job with that part?"

"There were plenty of actors who could have done a much better job. But Roscoe took a liking to James. And to Loretta, for that matter. I don't think there are any Academy Awards in her future, either."

"Yes, but at least she's acted before. All this guy has done is studied with someone named Darby Woodsloe who gives a class on the beach." Pete's voice raised. "He is going to ruin the show!"

"Ssshhh," Bubbles instructed.

"We have to get him fired."

"How?"

"I don't know."

Bubbles's cell phone rang. She looked at the number on the caller ID. It was Roscoe calling.

"Hello, Parky," she answered quickly.

"How's the show going?"

"We're working on it."

Pete was frantically making faces at her. "Ask if we can meet with him," he whispered. "Tell him we need to talk."

Bubbles shook her head.

Pete nodded vigorously, hoping to change her mind.

"Bubbles, I'm calling to invite your group to my house for a dinner party tomorrow night. We'll have all the folks from the reality show as well. I always say a little friendly competition can put a spark in your tank."

"Is that what you always say?" Bubbles echoed.

"That's what I always say."

Finally, Bubbles found the nerve to bring up James. "Competition is wonderful, Roscoe. But I'm afraid we're having real problems with one of our actors. It turns out James really isn't very experienced. We don't know how the show can succeed with him. To tell you the truth, he's dreadful. Pete and I were just discussing this. I don't know how we can make it work without, well, firing him and getting someone else."

"Firing him!" Roscoe bellowed. "I laid out the conditions for you. Do you think Danny Madley is having an easy time with that reality show of his? Of course not! Some of his contestants are real dillies. But he has to make it look good, put together a great package with what he has. That's part of this competition. Creativity. Inventiveness. See if you can get blood out of a turnip. See you tomorrow night at seven! And one more thing: remind Pilot Pete they don't call him Pilot Pete for nothing." Roscoe hung up.

Bubbles put her cell phone down on the table. "James's job couldn't be more secure if his grandmother produced the show." She laughed slightly. "And he said you're not called Pilot Pete for nothing."

Pete slammed the table. "Now that gets me mad."

Bubbles looked into his eyes and decided that she could let him in on the plan. Pete was terribly upset and truly wanted their show to succeed. He needed a hit. They were both in the same boat. Maybe he could come up with some good ideas. Bubbles's sympathetic side temporarily got the best of her. "Pete, I don't feel comfortable talking here. I think I know how we can win this competition. Come up to my suite. There's something I want to tell you. I think you'll feel better."

"How?" he demanded.

"I told you I don't want to talk here. I have a plan. Let's go."

They got up and walked past a red-haired woman in a sequined jacket who was eating by herself at the next table.

Regan Reilly watched the two of them walk out together. Just what is her plan? Regan wondered.

32

A few minutes later, Regan signaled for the check. She couldn't believe the conversation she heard. She jotted down a few notes on the pad she kept in her purse. Bubbles and Pete were upset about one of the actors Roscoe had cast. And Bubbles has a plan she wanted to discuss privately with Pete. Did it have anything to do with Danny's reality show? What did she want to do?

Regan paid the check and quickly walked out of the bar. Her cell phone rang. It was Danny.

"Regan, are you at the 7's Hotel?"

"Yes."

Regan stood there in the small bar as Danny related everything that had happened since she left the Madleys. She couldn't believe it. Just what Danny needs right now. Come to think of it, Mrs. Madley did seem a little more high-strung than Regan remembered.

"Would you report the missing mail sack to security?" Danny asked.

"Yes. It gives me a good excuse to talk to hotel personnel. I can't believe your parents are staying here."

"Me, either. Call me when you're through."

"Sure thing." She hung up and walked over to the front desk. "May I see someone from security, please?" she asked the clerk.

"Can I tell him what this is regarding?" Skepticism was written all over his face.

"Yes. A mailbag was stolen from my friend's room."

The clerk picked up a walkie-talkie. "Security to the front, please. Security to the front desk."

A few minutes later a big bear of a guy appeared from around the corner, his walkie-talkie crackling. "What's going on?" he asked the clerk.

The clerk pointed at Regan.

"Yes, miss?" the bear inquired.

"My name is Regan Reilly. I'm a private investigator." She flashed him her ID. "Friends of mine are staying here. They just checked in at around six P.M., dropped their bags in their room, and came downstairs for a drink. When they returned to their room less than an hour later, a bag of mail they were to deliver was gone."

The bear didn't look too impressed. "What room?"

"Three twenty-three."

"Where are they now?"

"They were so upset they ran out to tell the people whose mail was missing."

"Let's go take a look at the room."

All was quiet on the third floor. The guard tried to push open the door to 323. It was securely locked.

"There doesn't seem to be a problem with the lock." He took out his passkey. A second later the door was open. Two suitcases were on the bed, open and neatly packed. The room was in order.

Regan leaned down, picked up a Cherry Chap Stick from the floor, and placed it on the dresser. "Who else has a passkey?" Regan asked.

"The usual people—the maids, other security people, the manager. I don't know who would want a sack of mail, though. Whose mail was it?"

"Have you heard of Aunt Agony and Uncle Heartburn?"

"Who?"

"Aunt Agony and Uncle Heartburn. They're advice columnists."

"You mean for the lovesick kind of people?"

"Among others," Regan said.

"I think I've seen their column in the paper. I don't read it, though."

"You don't need any advice, huh?"

He laughed. "I'm getting by. My girlfriend gives me a hard time sometimes, but we get along."

"That's good," Regan said. "Has anything unusual happened in the hotel lately?"

He shook his head. "No. Just the same old stuff. People get locked out of their rooms. People come in a little drunk after a night of gambling. This is a small hotel. We don't have many problems. We keep an eye on the parking lot. That's about it."

"I know you have a group from a sitcom staying here."

"Yeah, they have ten rooms on the third and fourth floors."

"Nice people?" Regan asked lightly.

"No problems. They haven't been here for very long."

"Do you have any security cameras in the halls?" Regan asked.

"No. I keep telling the manager we should put them in. But we haven't had any trouble, so they don't want to spend the money. We have no cameras in the hotel at all. I think that's dumb."

"It is dumb," Regan agreed. "I just can't understand why someone would steal the sack of mail and leave the suitcases un-touched. That's very strange. Could we take a little walk around the hotel?"

"Sure." They walked up and down the halls, peeked in all the storage closets, went down to the basement and laundry room for a quick look, and then went out behind the hotel where it was dark. But in Vegas at night, it's never too dark. Colorful neon lights flashed in the distance.

The bear shined his flashlight in a sweep-ing motion around the backyard of the ho-tel. The pool looked quiet and still. He then lifted the top of the Dumpster that was not far from the back exit. "Smells bad," he said as he illuminated the garbage with his flash-light.

"That it does."

"Doesn't look as if there's any mailbag in there," he said as he dropped the lid. It crashed back down with a sound that would wake the dead. "I guess a lot of peo-ple are going to be disappointed if their let-ters are lost, huh?"

"Sure. Agony and Heartburn can't answer all of them. But the letters are confidential. If that sack gets into the wrong hands, it could embarrass a lot of people. Agony and Heartburn act as shrinks for their readers. People write things that they wouldn't tell their best friend."

The guard laughed. "Some of those let-ters must be pretty funny."

I don't think they were meant to be. But he's right, Regan realized. I hope no one is sitting somewhere with a drink in one hand and the letters in the other, having a good laugh. But if Danny's mother couldn't resist the temptation, then why should whoever stole the letters respect anyone's privacy?

Regan gave the bear her card with her cell phone number on it. "Would you give me a call if anything turns up? Or if you get any ideas?"

"Sure. And next time I have a problem with my girlfriend, I'll write those guys a letter. I just hope it doesn't get lost."

Regan nodded as she walked to the front and waved down a taxi. Off for more fun, she thought as she pulled off her wig, glasses, and Las Vegas–style jacket, and stuffed everything in her bag.

Regan couldn't get Bubbles's conversation out of her mind. She couldn't help but wonder. Bubbles had the motive, but did she have the opportunity to steal that sack of mail? She was definitely one to keep an eye on.

◆

33

"Here we are!" Aunt Agony called as she banged on Danny's door. "Ready for our big night out in Vegas!"

Danny got up from his seat and looked at his parents forlornly. "That other thing you want to discuss with me is going to have to wait."

"Yes, dear," Maddy said nervously.

"How's my favorite aunt and uncle?" Danny joked when he answered the door. "Come in, come in. I don't think you've met my parents."

"Ohhhh—you can tell a lot about a person by his parents," Agony observed. She extended her arm. "Nice to meet you. Nice to meet you!"

Maddy and Agony shook hands while

Heartburn and Shep made each other's acquaintance.

"How's everything going?" Maddy inquired politely as they all sat down.

"Oh, we're having such fun," Agony declared. "These couples, I tell you. They are all so anxious to win the money. Can you blame them?"

"No, you can't," Shep answered. "After all, a million dollars."

"I think they all really love each other," Heartburn offered. "They have that certain something. We just have to decide who has the best chance of sticking it out through thick and thin, till death do them part. We all know that can be a challenge, don't we?"

"You said it," Shep agreed quickly. "Through thick and thin is the challenge."

"Danny is doing a wonderful job," Agony exclaimed and clapped her hands. "We're all going to celebrate when this show is picked over that boring sitcom. Right?"

"Right," Danny answered lamely.

"There's nothing like reality television. It's so unpredictable."

"That's for sure," Danny agreed with a loud sigh. "Which brings us to this moment."

"Are we on television now?" Heartburn joked.

"No!" Danny turned to his mother. Then he turned back to his guests. "In a nutshell," he said, speaking quickly, "my parents ate at your cafe on the way here today."

"How wonderful!" Agony exulted.

"Your waitress gave them a sack of mail to bring to you."

"Goody," Agony exclaimed. "I love my mail."

"It was stolen from their hotel room."

"Stolen?" Agony shrieked. "That's our livelihood."

"We were just trying to be helpful," Maddy cried.

"There are important letters in every delivery!" Agony yelped.

"Calm down, Agony. Calm down," Heartburn said. "We'll put a notice in our column that letters are missing, so if people want to write again—"

"We saved one of the letters," Maddy noted enthusiastically.

Agony, knowing human nature the way she did, was immediately suspicious. "What do you mean, saved one letter?"

"Well, it fell out of the bag in the backseat

of the car. I found it, so I just stuck it in my purse."

"Where is it?" Agony demanded.

Maddy pulled out the wine-stained letter from her little clutch.

"You were reading our mail!" Heartburn bellowed.

"It gets worse," Shep assured them.

Heartburn grabbed it and turned gray. "It's from a lawyer, dear."

"What does it say?"

Heartburn paused.

"What does it say?" Agony demanded.

"My ex-wife is threatening to talk to the tabloids if I don't pay the back alimony I owe her."

"Oh, my God!" Agony cried. "Haven't you paid her?"

"Not lately. Those taxes piled up when I wasn't looking."

"Oh, my God! When is the deadline and how much?"

"Tomorrow. Forty thousand dollars."

"Tomorrow! We don't have that kind of money! The column doesn't pay much yet. We need this show to get us going!"

Danny sat there, stunned. Not only had his mother caused trouble, but Heartburn was a real risk to the show. "If I'd known you had these problems . . ." he began.

"Don't start that, Sonny boy," Agony countered, no longer the sweet old lady. "Your mother can be arrested for tampering with our mail."

"God knows what else was in that sack," Shep commented.

"Can you pay your ex-wife off tomorrow?" Danny asked. "Because if you can't and she goes to the newspaper, there goes our show. You haven't paid alimony in how long?"

"A year," Heartburn said meekly. "And no, we don't have the money."

Danny turned to his parents. "Mom, Dad."

It was Shep's turn to go gray.

"We're all in this together. Dad, can you call your banker tomorrow?"

"To think we tried to save money by staying in a crappy hotel," Maddy whined.

"Security's obviously bad if they stole my mail." Agony harrumphed and crossed her legs. "That'll teach you a lesson."

Shep put his hand to his forehead. "Yes, I can make a phone call tomorrow."

"Thank God. We all have a vested interest in this show's getting on the air. Once

Agony and Heartburn get some on-air exposure, they will have the potential to make lots of money with future appearances and lectures." He turned and looked Agony directly in the eye. "Then you will pay my parents back, right?"

"We will."

"Even though my mother read the mail."

"That's right. As we say in the advice business, everybody has secrets. That's one we'll keep. You keep ours, we'll keep yours."

Danny sighed and got up. "We still have to go for our night on the town."

"There's one more thing," Maddy reminded him.

"Yes, Mom." Danny sat back down.

Maddy decided to relate this last tidbit in front of Agony and Heartburn. They might be helpful. "Missy is downstairs."

"Who's Missy?"

"I mean Honey."

"Honey, what is she doing here?"

"She wants to do makeovers on your contestants at the end of the week. You know, before the big ceremony in the balloon."

"I don't want her doing any makeovers!" Danny protested.

"It might not be a bad idea," Agony chimed in. "Our couples could use a little help in that department, if you ask me. Glam up the show."

Danny stared at Maddy in disbelief. "I thought you couldn't stand her."

"She's a lovely girl," Maddy insisted. "Just so lovely."

"So lovely you couldn't remember her name. Mom, you're not fooling me. Tell me what's going on."

"I can't," she protested. "I'll get in more trouble."

Shep still hadn't removed his hand from his forehead. Maddy looked to him for comfort, but he was in a trance thinking about the $40,000 that was about to say bye-bye to his bank account.

"Mom, what's going on? Tell me."

"Her friend Lucille heard us talking about the mail," Maddy admitted, pointing at Agony and Heartburn. "She threatened to go to the press if you didn't give Honey a chance to work on your show."

Agony clapped her hands. "Is this an old girlfriend?"

"Yes," Danny acknowledged with yet another sigh.

"What an unusual way to try to get a guy back. Next she'll be stalking you."

"She is persistent," Danny agreed.

"Oh, but she must love you," Agony noted, resuming her role as advice giver. "She must want you back very, very much."

Maddy was about to get sick. It galled her to have this floozy back in her son's life. But seeing her own name in the paper as part of a scandal would be worse. "Please, give her a chance."

"It seems I have no choice. I never liked that friend of hers, Lucille. Let's get out of here. We have a lot of people waiting for us."

"Danny, please be nice to Lucille," Maddy pleaded. "If she suspects anything . . ."

"I know," Danny relented as they walked out of the suite.

Maddy turned to Shep. "Dear, what do you want to do tonight?"

"Hit the casino. I'm down $40,000."

34

Honey and Lucille were sitting in the lobby for what felt like an eternity.

"Let's go," Honey suggested for the tenth time. "Danny must be putting up a stink with his mother."

"We're not leaving," Lucille insisted. "This is your only shot."

Honey's lip started to tremble.

"Don't! If it doesn't work, then you and Danny weren't meant to be."

"But we are meant to be!"

"That's what the next to last finalist on *The Bachelor* thought. The whole country watched her get dumped by the man of her dreams and then get whisked back to the limo. If it were me, I'd have told them I'd call a cab."

"Lucille!"

"It's true. Bing, bang, boom. Move on. I've seen enough card games in this city where the guy loses everything. He leaves the table broke. But he ends up back, one way or another."

"How does he get back in the game?"

"Usually by going to a pawn shop and selling his watch."

"Well, I just think we've been waiting a long time now. I do have some pride, you know."

"Swallow your pride, Honey. Just for tonight. Then we'll see what happens. Danny's mother is in deep trouble. I'm sure Agony and Heartburn aren't too thrilled with her right now."

The elevator door opened.

"Oh, my God, here they come," Lucille said. "Now keep cool."

Maddy came right over. She looked somewhat bedraggled. "Danny is so thrilled to have you working on the show, Honey." She turned around. "Danny! Honey is waiting."

Honey melted when she saw him. He was wearing the pair of jeans that she'd sewn the little heart on. It was underneath his belt.

They'd joked that no one knew it was there except them. She had on the little red sleeveless dress that he'd always liked, with the matching high-heeled red sandals. Would it help? she wondered.

Danny walked over and kissed her on the cheek. He nodded at Lucille. "Honey, my mother told me your idea about makeovers for the contestants. It sounds great. The hairdresser and makeup artist will do it free?"

"As long as they get on TV and can promote themselves," Honey answered breathlessly.

"Of course," Danny agreed. "What else is new? Can you set everything up for Thursday? You know what we're doing, I guess."

"One lucky couple will renew their vows in a hot air balloon," Honey noted, her voice cracking.

Keep it together, Honey, Lucille thought. Keep it together.

"That's right." Danny nodded. "So the makeover works at that point in the show."

Honey stared at him. She wanted him to take her in his arms. She wanted him to kiss her and tell her he missed her and couldn't live without her. She wanted him to say he never wanted them to be apart again. "Thursday is fine," she said.

"I'll call you Wednesday to make the final arrangements."

"Wonderful," Honey uttered. At least it's a start, she thought.

Aunt Agony and Uncle Heartburn came over to say hello.

"Make those girls look sexy," Heartburn said to Honey. "Just like you."

"Thank you, Uncle Heartburn." Honey glanced over at Danny and was disappointed that he didn't seem to be paying attention to the conversation.

"All right, we're out of here," Danny instructed his entourage. "Lucille, good to see you. Honey, we'll be in touch."

The group disappeared out the door.

Lucille looked at Honey. "Well?"

"Lucille, you know how I'm a little psychic sometimes?"

"Sort of."

"All of a sudden I'm worried. Like something bad is going to happen to Danny. I just feel it in my bones."

"Come on," Lucille groaned. "Let's go somewhere for a drink. You've got to line up the hairdresser and makeup artist. Don't think about it."

Honey went running out the door.

Lucille ran after her. "Honey, are you nuts?"

Danny was getting into the driver's seat of a Balloon Channel van. The others were already inside. Lucille grabbed Honey outside the front door of the hotel. "What are you doing?" she demanded.

"I just want to warn him."

"About what?"

"To be careful."

"Honey, you're losing it."

"I have a bad feeling."

"Keep it to yourself. You've made progress with him. You're going to ruin it."

Honey shrugged her off. "All right."

Together they watched as the van started to pull out. Together they heard the knocking of a flat tire, two flat tires. The van stopped before any harm was done.

Honey turned to Lucille. "I could have gotten credit for warning him."

Lucille snorted. "I got you this far. You owe me a drink."

35

After a quiet dinner at the mansion, Erene, Leo, Kitty, and Roscoe were enjoying espresso and dessert in the large dining room. "So what have you found out about Regan Reilly?" Roscoe asked Erene and Leo. A portrait of an expensively dressed man holding a cigar and a glass of brandy hung on the wall, but it had been a long time since the man had enjoyed such pleasures. He was the one in the slammer.

"She showed up at the 7's Heaven Hotel with a red wig on," Erene reported.

"I told you that if you made too much trouble it would backfire," Kitty warned. "Danny called her in because of the problems. I just know it."

"We didn't do it all," Roscoe reminded

her. "We're just trying to make this a fun
contest. So, Leo, who's causing the rest of
the trouble?"

"I don't know."

"Find out!" Roscoe yelled.

"That's what Regan's doing," Kitty noted
practically. "I hear she's a good investigator.
She met her boyfriend when her father was
kidnapped. It was such a romantic story. I
remember reading about it in a magazine."

"How does Danny know her anyway?"
Leo asked.

"Beats me," Kitty said. She broke a
cookie in half and licked the chocolate from
the middle.

"We can't let her get too close to our
operation," Roscoe continued. "She'll ruin
things. What can we do to keep her quiet—
you know, that's not illegal?"

Erene was about to quote a study but
clamped her mouth shut. Then she started
to open it. "We could try throwing her off the
trail."

"How?"

"Maybe we should lay off Danny for a
couple of days."

"Yeah," Kitty said. "If all goes well, maybe
she'll go home before the end of the week."

"Having her around on Friday could be real trouble," Roscoe said darkly.

"Your big problem," Kitty told Roscoe as she bit the cookie, "would be if someone really ruins Danny's show. That's what you should be worried about."

Roscoe whacked his cowboy boots with his riding stick. "What would Merv Griffin do?"

"He'd have a good lawyer lined up," Kitty announced.

"I don't appreciate that comment, Kathleen," Roscoe growled.

Kitty raised her eyebrows. She couldn't wait for the week to be over.

"We'll keep an eye on Regan Reilly," Leo promised. "We'll keep an eye on everyone."

"I can't wait to have them all here under one roof," Roscoe said. "Batten down the hatches, as they say. The storm is coming! Yippee!"

"It's more like hide the silver," Kitty muttered under her breath.

"I'm feeling restless. Do we have any reservations tomorrow morning for ballooning?" Roscoe asked.

"Negative," Erene answered.

"Then Kitty and I will go up tomorrow morning."

"Ohhhh," Kitty sighed. "That means getting up so early. We have to be out there at six o'clock," she whined.

"I thought you liked ballooning," Roscoe countered. His feelings were obviously hurt.

"When we do it in the late afternoon. It's getting up when it's still dark that kills me."

"Balloonists have to be morning people. They have to like getting up before the sun. Coffee never tastes better than at that ungodly hour. Why, this week in Albuquerque, the roads are jammed before daylight. All those adventurous folks heading out to the field with their steaming coffee mugs in hand. All those balloons going up in the air at once. The mass ascension is so colorful, so exciting." Roscoe's eyes got misty. "I wish I could be there, but this show is more important. And the contest had to be done this week so that Danny could take advantage of the festival."

Leo suggested that Roscoe go down there with Danny's group early on Friday morning.

"Friday's going to be very busy for us."

"They'll be back before lunch."

"I don't know, Leo. I don't want to look as if I'm playing favorites by spending more time with them."

"See how you feel."

"All my friends are down there at the festival," Roscoe remarked wistfully. "I'm sure they'll miss having me there this week. I'm sure they'll miss the Balloon Channel balloon. All the camaraderie. All the fun we have. Balloonists are the greatest people. But wait till they see what I do for the sport. The Balloon Federation of America will want to honor me, no doubt. They'll write me up in *Ballooning Magazine.* They'll put up a plaque in honor of me at the National Balloon Museum. The possibilities are endless—"

"As long as Regan Reilly doesn't find out what you're up to and put the kibosh on things," Kitty stated as she examined the assortment of cookies that remained on the plate. "I'll have just one more," she murmured.

Roscoe whacked his cowboy boot again. "Erene, Leo, what are our priorities right now?" He started snapping his fingers before anyone could answer. "Come on, come on."

"It seems that our number one priority," Erene replied, taking charge, "is to watch Regan Reilly. Let her keep things in order in Danny's shop, so to speak, but keep her nose out of our operation."

"And all things must lead to a good show on Friday night!" Roscoe decreed as he stood up. He stared at the portrait on the wall. "I don't want to end up in a cell next to him!"

That's all I'd need, Kitty thought. I'd have to go looking for a new boyfriend again. I couldn't take it. She got up out of her chair. "Time for a good night's rest so we can sail above the treetops tomorrow morning."

"Now you're talking." Roscoe smiled at Kitty. "And tomorrow night at this time we'll be dining together with the troops! It's going to be an exciting day!"

"You'd go nuts in a jail cell," Kitty noted as they started to walk out.

"They should do a study on balloonists who end up in the clink," Erene suggested. "To see if they have a harder time adapting to confinement. I have to believe that—"

"Good night, Erene!" Roscoe said brusquely. "I am not going to end up in jail.

If I do, it's your fault and Leo's fault! Remember that!"

"Yes, sir." Erene closed her file and said good night.

"Good night, boss," Leo echoed. Turning to Erene he whispered, "I hope we haven't gotten ourselves in too deep on this one."

◆

36

"Where are you going to, lady?" the cab-driver asked Regan. He was an older man with hoop earrings and wisps of gray hair protruding from a black beret.

"I'm not sure yet," Regan answered. "I have to call a friend. Why don't you drive toward the Strip?"

The driver rolled his eyes. "Why not? You're paying me." He started to hum a song from *Les Misérables.*

Regan dialed Danny's number and put her hand over her left ear. Her chauffeur was obviously a frustrated entertainer. Regan had no doubt that it was only a matter of time before he ended up on a reality show.

Danny answered his cell phone on the third ring. He sounded out of breath.

"Danny, it's Regan. What's going on?"

Danny exhaled loudly. "We just had to change two tires on the van."

"You got two flats at once?"

"They were slashed."

"Oh, my God, Danny."

"The start of the dream date."

"Did you have Sam record the proceedings?"

"Of course. This is a reality show. We're always looking for surprises."

"It seems as though you've gotten more than enough of them. Where are you going now?"

"The fountains in front of the Bellagio. The most romantic spot in town."

"I'll meet you there." She hung up the phone and leaned forward. It took a moment to get the driver's attention. He was changing lanes and deeply engrossed in his humming. "Excuse me!"

He looked in the rearview mirror. "You finally know where you're going?"

"The Bellagio. Drop me off in front of the fountains, please."

He nodded. "Bee-you-ta-ful!"

Regan sat back and looked out the window. So now someone's going after the Balloon Channel vans. Unbelievable.

A few moments later they pulled up to the sidewalk in front of the hotel. Regan paid the fare, got out, and looked around. Suddenly what sounded like a sonic boom rocked the area. The fountains sprang to life with enormous jets of water whooshing upward from the lake. The theme song from the movie *Titanic* started to play over the loudspeakers as the gusts of water swayed to the music. It was a spectacular sight to behold once your nervous system had recovered from the initial roar.

The sidewalk was crowded with tourists, many of whom were taking pictures. Regan walked among them until she finally spotted the *Love Above Sea Level* group. The camera was trained on Vicky and Chip who were arm in arm, gazing at the fountains. They turned to each other to share a little kiss on the lips. Ain't love grand? Regan thought as she walked over to Danny.

"How's it going?" she whispered.

"Well, at least it's going."

When the song was over, Aunt Agony stepped forward. "How do you two feel?" she asked.

Vicky glowed. "I feel as if we're on our honeymoon. We went to Niagara Falls. And here we are again, getting sprayed by water. It's soooooo cool."

Chip smiled. "We'll have to take another trip to Niagara Falls, honey. We'll have to relive that special, special time."

Uncle Heartburn felt the need to participate. "Were either of you ever in love before you met each other?"

Chip and Vicky both looked pained, but then Vicky laughed. "Not unless you count a bout of puppy love when I was twelve."

"And as for me," Chip replied, "I never knew what love meant until I met Vicky."

These guys should be working on the sitcom, Regan decided.

Agony was truly in her element. "It certainly sounds as though you two have found the spark again," she told them.

"It's burning brighter than ever," Chip assured her.

"Cut!" Danny called. "Time to go to dinner."

They got into the van. Regan took a seat in the back. There was just enough room for everyone. Danny drove, and Sam sat up front with his camera. Victor, Agony, and

Heartburn were in the second row of seats, and Chip and Vicky shared the third row with Regan. Was Regan imagining it, or did the lovebirds seem less lovey-dovey when they weren't on camera? Chip didn't have his arm around Vicky—they weren't even holding hands. And to think they were just insisting it was like their honeymoon.

"There is a small Italian restaurant just down the road that has agreed to give us a private room for all three dream dates," Danny explained. "Agony, Heartburn, Chip, and Vicky will have dinner at a quiet candlelit table. After they're finished, we'll saunter through the casino at the Bellagio. Sam will be recording it all—right, Sam?"

Sam nodded. "Like *Candid Camera.*"

Regan was trying to figure who Sam reminded her of. He was good-looking, with a quick and easy laugh. His friendly, relaxed manner must help put his subjects at ease. It certainly couldn't hurt. He was such a contrast to Victor who was much more intense.

"The rest of us will have hot dogs," Victor teased.

"Not true!" Danny said. "Don't worry, Regan, they'll have food for us."

Regan laughed. "Whatever!" What I'd really like, she thought, is to go back to the hotel and get some sleep.

Chip turned to Regan, winked at her, and patted her leg. "We'll get you a doggy bag."

That was weird, Regan thought. This couple is definitely strange. Vicky all of a sudden had become so exaggerated in her responses as she rhapsodized about Niagara Falls. Chip came off as a nerd when he tried to be romantic with his wife. It seemed so unnatural. But I guess that's what pressure will do to you, Regan mused. All three couples could use the money. Who couldn't? A million minus taxes would make most people's day. So they all have to play up this romantic act until Friday. It will be interesting to see if anyone cracks under the strain.

They pulled into the parking lot of a restaurant called Carlotta's. A neon caricature of a showgirl holding up a plate of spaghetti with steam rising from it was displayed prominently in the front window. Some place for a dream date, Regan thought. Danny had told her there were budget considerations. He had to do this on a shoestring. How odd that Roscoe would limit the amount spent on the production it-self but dangle a million-dollar prize.

The maitre d' greeted Danny warmly. "Did you get a picture of our showgirl?"

"We'll get that on the way out," Danny promised.

"Wonderful. Come upstairs."

The restaurant was lively. It had dark wood paneling, red tablecloths, dim lights, and noisy customers. The piano in the cor-ner was silent, but a tip jar suggested that the pianist would be returning shortly. A nar-row staircase with dark swirly carpeting led to the second floor. Regan followed Victor up the steps into a long, narrow, dingy room with a slightly musty smell and red-flocked wallpaper. A table set for four had been placed in the middle of the room.

Le Cirque it ain't, Regan thought.

"My ladies?" The maitre d' extended his arm and motioned to the table.

Regan backed away as Aunt Agony stepped forward and sat in the seat pulled out for her. Vicky followed. The men sat themselves.

"My name is Gianni," the maitre d' contin-ued in a faux Italian accent. "We will take

good care of you this evening. *Grazie.*" He
turned to Danny. "*Grazie.*"

"Thank you," Danny said as Gianni bowed
and disappeared downstairs.

I wish I could sit down, Regan thought.
She leaned against the wall as Danny
started to explain his game plan: "Obviously, we're not going to have the camera
on during the whole meal. There will be
times when Agony or Heartburn will ask you
special questions, and we'll record those
conversations."

Regan wondered what they might ask. It
was like having your therapy sessions taped
for the world to see. The meal began pleasantly with drinks and light conversation.

Once the appetizers were served, Agony
leaned forward with a soulful look on her
face. "I'd like each of you to tell us about
your worst date ever."

"You mean with each other?" Vicky asked
practically.

Agony and Heartburn laughed. "No, no,
no," Agony replied. "With someone else. I
understand you didn't meet until you were
both in your twenties. There must have
been other dates along the way."

"Well," Chip began, looking very uncomfortable in his chair. "I went out with a girl once who couldn't stop talking about what a creep her ex-husband was. They had joint custody of the dog. Every time her ex came to pick up Fido for the weekend, she'd taken him on a long walk. It made me a little nervous about her. So I never called her again. I heard she said some pretty bad things about me after that. I certainly dodged that bullet."

"And my worst date," Vicky offered, "was with a guy who picked me up at my apartment, insisted on coming in for a drink, and started going through all the papers on the kitchen counter when I went into the bedroom to freshen up. I caught him reading my mail!"

Heartburn coughed up the water he had just sipped.

Agony seemed very impatient. She didn't inquire about her husband's well-being and barely looked his way. I wonder what that's all about? Regan mused.

"That's some nerve!" Agony cried. "That is despicable! I can't stand nosy people!"

You can't stand nosy people? Regan marveled. With your job?

"Okay!" Danny interrupted. "That's

enough for now. Enjoy your appetizers." He turned to Regan. "Would you come downstairs with me for a few minutes? We can have a quick drink and snack at the bar."

"Sure."

"We'll be right back," Danny told the others. "Victor, I'll tell Gianni to set up a little table in the corner of the room here for you and Sam."

"Good enough. No more taping now?"

"Not till we get back." As Danny and Regan went down the staircase, Danny whispered, "Regan, you're not going to believe this. . . ."

37

"What do you want to tell me?" Pilot Pete asked Bubbles. They were in the living room of her suite. He was sitting in the straight-backed chair that he'd pulled out from under the desk. Bubbles was pacing, but there wasn't a lot of space for that.

"You and I both want the sitcom to work." She tossed back her red hair and smiled flirtatiously. "We want Roscoe to choose our show."

"You're stating the obvious, Bubbles."

"Don't get smart with me," Bubbles warned.

Pete laughed. "But we all have job security. That's our problem."

"James is forever," Bubbles nodded in agreement. "For better or for worse."

"Till death do us part."

"Petey, I've got to tell you. When you say that, it makes me nervous."

"You think I'm going to off James?" Pete challenged, his voice rising. "That offends me."

"Well, when you mentioned it in the bar, I thought you were serious."

"I'll admit I often feel like killing him. But do you think I'd put my whole life on the line for this lousy sitcom?"

"Don't call it a lousy sitcom."

"I'm serious. I've done a ton of pilots that haven't aired. And those were for the networks. You think I'd kill somebody to save a sitcom on Roscoe's Balloon Channel? How many people are going to end up watching the show anyway? Everyone's at the casinos."

"You never know," Bubbles retorted. "You know how many small cable shows have been picked up by the big boys? Huh?"

"You know how many haven't? And the ones that are successful are usually made by teenage kids doing a show out of their basement. It appeals to their demographic, which is huge. All they talk about in Hollywood is the 'demographics.' Demographics this, demographics that. If I hear that word one more time, I'll choke."

Bubbles looked alarmed. "We don't have any teenagers on our show!"

"If the show is a hit, we can always write in kids."

"That doesn't always work."

"Bubbles," Pete said, "we're getting off the track here. What is your big plan?"

"I have a boyfriend," Bubbles began.

"So. Did you think I was hitting on you?"

"No! I have a boyfriend who works on the reality show."

"You do?"

"Yes."

"Oh, my God."

"I know."

"What does he do there?"

"I can't tell you."

"Why not?"

"I think it's better if I keep his identity a secret."

"Why?"

"Petey, just listen for a minute. He is there as a spy for me. Right now he's trying to get the goods on the contestants. He's trying to find a reason to disqualify one of the couples so the show can't go on. He set up a special website for people to report any gossip they have on the contestants."

Pete stared at her. "Why are you telling me this?"

"I thought you'd want to know that there might be another way to win."

"Is your friend doing anything else to cause trouble?"

Bubbles hesitated. Maybe it wasn't such a good idea to confide in Petey. She thought he would be thrilled. She thought he would be comforted and cheered. But the look on his face was not cheerful. It was scary. Like when he suggested they kill James. "No," she lied. "But somebody is. There have been a lot of mishaps on the set."

"Mishaps? Like what?"

Bubbles wanted to kick herself. She must have been delusional to think she could trust this guy. He was like a psycho the way his face kept changing. One minute he seems like Mr. Rogers, the next Jack the Ripper. "Well, someone stole a camera. Things like that."

Pete stood and pointed his finger at her. "You've made me an accessory to whatever your friend decides to do to ruin the reality show," he accused, his voice raised. "I have to tell you that I don't like that. I don't like that at all." He stormed toward the door.

"Pete!" Bubbles cried.

He turned to her, yelled "Gotcha!" and then started to laugh hysterically. "I had you going there, didn't I?"

I'm going to have a nervous breakdown, Bubbles thought.

38

"Regan, things are getting messier every minute," Danny complained as the bartender poured them each a glass of red wine.

"I know the mail was stolen. What else happened?"

Danny put his head down on the bar, shook it from side to side, and then raised it up again. He quickly filled Regan in on his mother reading the letter from Agony and Heartburn's lawyer.

"No wonder she freaked out about Vicky's date reading her mail," Regan commented. "Everybody's got their problems. Scratch the surface of almost anybody's life—"

"On top of everything else, my ex-girl-friend—who dumped me and now wants me back—will be doing makeovers on the show on Thursday."

"Why?"

"She and her best friend overheard my mother talking about the mail and made lightly veiled threats to go to the papers if I don't give Honey a chance to work on the show."

"Is she a beautician?"

"No, she's a showgirl. But believe me, she knows every facialist, hairdresser, and makeup artist in town."

Regan smiled. "It sounds as if you still like her."

Danny shrugged. "Fool me once, shame on you. Fool me twice, shame on me."

Regan realized once again how lucky she was to have Jack. Their relationship had been so easy from the beginning. If only they lived in the same city, it would be perfect. She brought her mind back to the problems at hand. "We can't let anyone find out about Heartburn's ex-wife. That would really bring down the show."

"I know. It's like taking advice about etiquette from Bart Simpson."

Regan smiled. "Where are your parents now?"

"My father's trying to win his money back in the casino. Can you believe my mother read that mail? Can you believe it?"

Regan had a vague memory of Mrs. Madley in the makeshift kitchen in their grammar school on hot dog day, which was Tuesdays. A few of the mothers would come in and boil hundreds of hot dogs in a vat, the proceeds going to whatever the current cause was in the parish. Mrs. Madley never missed a Tuesday. She was always in the middle of things and frequently showed up at school when no other parents were around. Poor Danny. His mother hadn't changed, and now it really was causing him grief.

"I live several hundred miles away from her," Danny continued. "And she still manages to meddle in my life."

"She means well," Regan offered feebly.

"I know, but if Heartburn is exposed, then he and Agony will go to the police about my mother, I just know it. Which makes me a joke."

"Does anyone else know?"

Danny shook his head. "No. No one except my parents, Agony and Heartburn, Honey and Lucille."

"Keep it that way," Regan advised him. "I wouldn't tell Victor or Sam."

"Victor is in on everything," Danny said.

"You told me you think someone is trying to sabotage you. The most likely suspects are Victor and Sam. The assistants seem to come and go, and they don't have the access that those two have."

"But who could have tampered with the tires of the van?" Danny asked. "I just don't see how Victor or Sam could have done that without being noticed."

"To tell you the truth," Regan confided, "I think there's something more complicated going on here."

"What do you mean?"

"For one thing, that Roscoe Parker seems a little strange. How did you meet him?"

"In a poker game at one of the casinos."

"Was he a good bluffer?"

"Not really. He never stopped talking."

"I'm anxious to go to his house tomorrow night. I have an uneasy feeling about him. Anyone who would blow that annoying whistle like he did this afternoon has to have other pranks up his sleeve. And that's what I feel you've been a victim of—a lot of pranks. But some of them could be dangerous. And I haven't even told you what I overheard at the 7's Hotel."

"What?"

"Bubbles and Pete were at a table in the bar talking about how bad one of their actors is. Bubbles said she had something important to tell Pete, and they left. Then you called me, and I contacted security about the missing sack of mail. The security guard and I looked in your parents' room, but it was undisturbed. It's interesting that your parents are staying at that hotel."

"Only my mother could find a hotel like that one. She got a coupon for it somewhere or other."

"You know, it's very similar to the Fuzzy Dice—different themes but the same quality and atmosphere. I wonder who owns the two hotels."

"I haven't a clue," Danny admitted.

The bartender served them a small pizza and two more glasses of wine.

"That looks great," Regan said. "I'm starved."

"We'd better eat this fast and get back upstairs." Danny pulled a slice onto his plate, catching a dangling string of cheese with his fingers. "I'm afraid to think of what might be going on."

Ten minutes later Danny paid the check, and he and Regan ascended the creaky staircase. Agony and Heartburn were locked in a passionate embrace. Vicky and Chip were staring at them in disbelief as the camera rolled.

39

"Maddy, I don't want to play any slot machines," Shep insisted.

They'd gone over to the Venetian Hotel to walk around and grab a bite to eat. It was truly a fascinating place. Las Vegas's version of Italy's most romantic city included a 1,200-foot-long mini-replica of Venice's Grand Canal, known as the Canalazzo, where visitors could enjoy a twelve-minute boat ride while being serenaded by singing gondoliers. The sixty-five-foot-high domed ceiling was adorned by beautiful reproductions of famous Italian frescoes, and to the even bigger delight of many, there were numerous fancy shops. The Canalazzo ran through a ninety-store mall.

The Venetian resort complex included

everything from recreations of St. Mark's Square, the Doge's Palace, and the Rialto Bridge to an imported Madame Tussaud's Wax Museum. The hotel itself had more hotel rooms than the entire island of Bermuda. Two historians were on retainer to ensure that the resort maintained a genuine Italian flair.

Maddy loved to walk around the Venetian and eat at any of the many fine restaurants or even at one of the more casual dining spots. She oohed and aahed at all the sights and was serenaded by the buzz in the huge casino. But tonight neither she nor Shep could enjoy themselves.

Shep played a few games of roulette and lost. They'd eaten dinner, and he was ready to go back to their depressing hotel. What he really wanted to do was go home and sleep in his own bed. Today had been trying.

"Maybe I should call Danny to see how he's doing," Maddy suggested.

"Don't you dare."

"All right," Maddy agreed sheepishly.

They took a cab back to the 7's Hotel where Maddy headed straight for the registration desk. She rapped twice on the bell with her palm. "Hello," she called loudly. "Anybody home?"

The clerk emerged from the door behind the desk. "Madam, I was attending to a fax."

"Well, maybe that's why some important mail was stolen from my room," Maddy cried. "No security in this lobby. None at all. Anyone can walk in off the street and take off on a crime spree."

"Our guests' security is always our utmost priority," the clerk answered peevishly.

"I'm just grateful that I survived unscathed from the burglary in our room," Maddy said as Shep stood to the side, rubbing his forehead.

"We're ever so grateful as well," the clerk noted in a flat tone.

"What I wanted to know," Maddy continued, "is if by any chance the sack of mail has been located."

"No. It hasn't been seen." His expression seemed to say, "And probably never will."

"Disgraceful," Maddy commented as she stalked off, waving her hands. Shep followed her to the elevator and up into their room. They turned on the light, and once again Maddy gasped.

"What?" Shep asked wearily.

"This Cherry Chap Stick," Maddy said, picking it up off the dresser, "was definitely not here when we checked in. Whoever stole that sack of mail has chapped lips! I hope they bleed!"

40

By the time Regan got back to her room at the Fuzzy Dice Hotel, she couldn't have been more relieved. Aunt Agony and Uncle Heartburn had spent the evening trying to show everyone how in love they were. It was as if they were competing for the million-dollar prize, though Regan assumed they were motivated by the threat of Uncle Heartburn's troubles being revealed to a public who might turn against them.

The dream date group had traipsed through the casino at the Bellagio. Agony and Heartburn, arm in arm, then called it a night. It had been a long day for everyone.

Regan undressed and stepped into the shower. The warm water hitting her shoulders and the back of her neck felt wonder-

ful. This will help me sleep, she thought. I
wish I could call Jack and give him the latest, but it's the middle of the night in New
York. Wait till he finds out that it's not nec-
essarily the contestants we have to worry
about, it's the judges. Knowing Jack, he
wouldn't be surprised.

What surprised Regan was that there was
turndown service at the Fuzzy Dice. Her
dicey bedspread had been removed, folded
up, and draped over the dicey chair at the
desk. A little chocolate mint had been
placed on her pillow. That was a concept
Regan never quite understood. Chocolate
contained caffeine, which kept most people
awake. Why not put a slice of turkey on the
pillow? There was a chemical in turkey that
put people to sleep, as anyone who's had a
big Thanksgiving meal surely knows. The
third Thursday afternoon in November,
snores resounded all across America. Oh,
well . . .

Regan stepped out of the shower, dried
off, and put on a pair of light cotton pajamas. She made sure the lock on the door
was bolted and placed her sneakers next to
the bed. She didn't know why, but in this
place she wanted to be able to run at a

moment's notice. I should probably sleep in my clothes, she thought wryly.

When she lay down on the bed and got under the sheets that were not exactly made of the finest materials, she sighed. What did I get myself into? she wondered. In her mind she went over everything that had happened that day: Danny received a threatening letter. Barney fell and ended up in the hospital. She tripped. Roscoe threw everyone out of the studios at five o'clock. Elsa won the big bucks. Danny's parents showed up. The mail was stolen. And, of course, the revelation of Uncle Heartburn's problems with his ex. All this capped off by the dream date at Carlotta's.

Forget the Balloon Channel. This should be on *60 Minutes.*

Regan reached over and shut off the light. She punched the pillow a couple of times and settled in. Even though she felt surrounded by craziness and was somewhat befuddled about what to do next, she quickly fell fast asleep.

Tuesday, October 7

41

Roscoe and Kitty drove to the grounds of the Balloon Channel complex when it was still dark. In between yawns, Kitty took little sips from her mug of coffee. Roscoe was eyeing the skyline with delight as it started to brighten.

"Yup. We'll be up, up, and away in just a little while." Roscoe pointed to the sun that was just starting to peek over the horizon.

"I'm going to need a nap before tonight," Kitty said with a yawn.

"But you'll have had a spiritual experience to begin your day."

"I had some kind of experience when the alarm clock went off."

"Kitty, did you know that hot air balloons were used in warfare?" Roscoe asked, not waiting for an answer. "Soldiers used to follow the movements of the advancing enemy from up in a balloon. Others escaped wartorn cities only because they got out by balloon. And the modern hot air balloon was really produced as a military tool nearly fifty years ago by a man named Ed Yost. But hot air ballooning ended up more as a sport than anything. And I'm so glad it did. Kitty?"

Kitty's eyes were closed. They felt glued together. With all her might, she opened them. "Yes, Roscoe."

"Did you hear what I said?"

"Something about balloons."

"Never mind."

They pulled into the parking lot of the Balloon Channel complex which was now very quiet. There were a few cars parked in the lot. Roscoe had ordered the night crew to leave by 3 A.M. He didn't want the folks working at the ballooning company running into them.

Roscoe parked the Jaguar, and they walked across the field to the little bungalow that housed the ballooning business. Inside the bungalow, Roscoe's pilot, Marty, and his crew were drinking coffee and eating doughnuts.

"The wind is light," Marty observed. "A perfect day for ballooning."

"Well, let's get going," Roscoe said enthusiastically.

They went back outside where the crew went about getting the balloon ready for flight, spreading out the balloon's envelope, which was its fabric, and moving the inflation fan into place. They attached the safety line to the chase truck and made sure the pilot handed over the keys. There was a nip in the air, and that wonderful, fresh, early morning smell was invigorating to all. Suddenly from the parking lot a couple came running toward them.

"Can we get a ride?" they called, waving their arms. "We tried to call earlier, but there was no answer. We just got married last night in the Graceland Wedding Chapel."

Roscoe looked at Kitty. "Is it all right with you? I thought we'd just go up ourselves with Marty."

"I'm not awake yet, so it doesn't matter to me."

"Come on over," Roscoe called back to them.

The couple seemed very youthful. The bride had a flower in her hair and a long granny dress. The groom had on a blue jacket and khaki pants. She had long dark hair, and he was blond. They looked madly in love.

"My name is Kimberly, and this is my husband," she said and paused. "Oh, I just love saying that! This is the first time I ever used that word! *Husband!*"

"Jake's my name," he said with a goofy grin. "Can we go inside and buy tickets?"

"This is my balloon. It's on me," Roscoe said magnanimously and proceeded to introduce himself, Kitty, and Marty to the young couple. When the balloon was inflated, they all climbed into the wicker basket while the ground crew held it in place. Marty squeezed the blast valve, and a column of fire shot up into the balloon. It sounded like the roar of a dragon. One by one, as ordered by Marty, the ground crew let go of the basket. They stepped back as the balloon started its gentle ascent into the early morning sky. Marty squeezed the valve again, and it shot another blue flame up into the balloon. They rose higher and higher. Everything below seemed to be shrinking. The ground crew quickly secured the launch equipment and jumped into the chase truck, determined to keep up with the balloon's progress.

"We're floating," Kimberly whispered dreamily.

"It's like being in the arms of God," Roscoe declared.

Kitty felt a little queasy but knew that she had to grin and bare it.

"So you got married in the Graceland Chapel?" Roscoe asked.

"By an Elvis impersonator. It was so cool," Jake answered.

"So totally, totally cool," Kimberly agreed. " 'Love Me Tender' is our song."

"Was it a spur-of-the-moment decision to get married?" Kitty asked, her brow furrowed.

"Kind of." Kimberly giggled. "We got the marriage license yesterday afternoon."

"Where are you from?" Roscoe asked.

"Los Angeles."

"And where did you meet?"

"At an audition."

"You're actors?"

"Yes. Neither one of us has had much luck yet, but we're trying super hard," Kimberly explained, "super, super hard. Right, Jake?"

"Oh, yeah. It's tough to get a break down

there, you know?" Jake laughed, pointing at the desert below. "But the two of us are going to make it together."

Inwardly, Kitty grimaced. I give this union a year. Two at the most, she reflected. She took a deep breath and didn't dare glance over the basket. Instead, she trained an adoring gaze on Roscoe.

Roscoe stroked his chin, then banged his ever present riding crop on the basket. "I just thought of a perfect wedding present for you two."

"A present?" Kimberly repeated. "It's a wonderful gift to just let us come up in the balloon for free."

"That's true," Roscoe agreed. "But I have an even better present. Some folks are putting together a sitcom for me. They're taping it this Friday. I'll tell them to write you both in."

Kimberly started jumping up and down but was quickly subdued.

"Stop it!" Marty ordered.

"I'm sorry! Oh, but thank you. Thank you so much!" Kimberly threw her arms around Roscoe.

"Thank you!" Jake echoed. "We'll have to find a place to stay."

"Don't you have a hotel room?" Roscoe inquired, freeing himself from Kimberly's grip.

"No. We drove here yesterday in my old car. We're lucky we didn't break down in the middle of the desert. I've heard of people that happened to who died of sunstroke and dehydration."

"Yeah," Kimberly finished the story. "They forgot to pack water—and a wide-brimmed hat."

"Well, stay with us," Roscoe offered enthusiastically. "Kitty and I live in a big old mansion outside of town. There's a swimming pool. We're having a party tonight."

"Thank you, thank you!" Kimberly cried again, now grasping Roscoe's hand. "You remind me so much of my grandpa."

Roscoe's face fell as Kitty tried to stifle a laugh.

"Are you two married?" Kimberly asked.

"Nope," Kitty answered.

"My grandpa has a girlfriend, too. My mother keeps saying, 'All she's after is his pension.' "

Roscoe chuckled, but Kitty felt like throwing her overboard as the balloon drifted through the early morning sky. And this little chippy is going to be at the house for the next three days, she thought with irritation. I just know Roscoe's whole scheme is going to boomerang on him and end up kicking him in the butt.

"Roscoe," Jake observed, "you are one cool dude."

"I try." Roscoe smiled broadly. "I try."

The group settled into a peaceful silence as Marty skillfully guided the balloon. Kimberly and Jake had their arms wrapped around each other, thinking about all their future plans, Roscoe surveyed the ground below, thinking how he would one day rule Vegas, and Kitty stood huddled in the middle, thinking about the fact that she was freezing.

Finally, Marty asked Roscoe, "You ready to return to earth?"

"I am," Kitty volunteered.

"I never want this to end," Kimberly cooed.

"Totally, totally awesome," Jake agreed, nodding his head.

These two are going to be the death of me, Kitty thought.

"I suppose we must rejoin the real world," Roscoe announced dramatically.

Marty shut off the pilot light in the fuel tanks. The balloon started to descend over a large open field.

"Bend your knees and hang on for the landing," Marty instructed. "Don't get out until I tell you to."

Seconds later, as the basket hit the ground, Marty pulled the vent line until the basket slowed to a stop.

"Whoa!" Kimberly cried as the basket bounced three times on the grass.

Roscoe's cowboy hat went flying.

The ground crew ran to grab the lines. One of them grabbed the crown line that was attached to the top of the balloon. This pulled the collapsing balloon on its side. They held the basket in place while the passengers and pilot disembarked, so to speak.

"Time for our cork ceremony," Marty pronounced.

"Cool," Kimberly cried when she stood on firm ground. "In our wildest dreams we couldn't have imagined that we'd go up in a balloon *and* end up with acting roles. And now we're going to have champagne! We have so much to celebrate!"

"Roscoe, you've totally made our day," Jake said.

Just you wait, Kitty thought. Let's see if that's the tune you're singing by the end of the week.

42

When Regan woke, it took her a second to realize where she was. But her body was facing the desk, and the sight of the dicey bedspread was the first thing that greeted her. "Ohhhh," she sighed, and closed her eyes again. "This isn't Kansas anymore, is it, Toto?"

A few moments later Regan got out of bed. She dressed in a pair of jeans and a sleeveless black top. It was still early, only 8:10, so she decided to go downstairs and get a cup of coffee to bring back to her room. The world of reality TV wasn't starting until 10 when Danny's group was meeting to drive over to the studio. But Regan planned to go to Danny's suite at 9, and she wanted to call Jack before then. Danny's parents were going to call their bank at 9 to transfer $40,000 to Heartburn's account.

I think I'll provide more moral support to Danny than anything else, Regan reflected as she was directed to the room where the cocktail party had been the night before. A continental breakfast was laid out on a buffet table against the wall. Little plastic tables were scattered around the empty room.

Regan filled a large paper cup with coffee, added skim milk, and turned to head back up to her room. Barney stood in the doorway. Tears were flowing down his face. Regan wasn't sure whether to ask him if anything was wrong, since this seemed to be his usual state. But her natural curiosity got the best of her.

"Barney, what's wrong?"

He dabbed at his eyes. "I feel so afraid."

"Why?"

"I don't know where Elsa is."

Regan's eyes widened. "Uhh," she hesitated. "Aren't you two sharing a room?"

"We're man and wife," Barney said indignantly. "We love each other very much and—"

"Okay, okay. You're not talking to Aunt

Agony here. Now when's the last time you saw her?"

"In bed last night. We went to sleep at about midnight with our arms wrapped tightly around each other. . . ."

Not tight enough, Regan thought.

"I woke at four A.M. and my arms were empty."

"What did you do?" Regan asked.

"I called out. I said, 'Elsa, are you in the bathroom, dear?' And there was no response. So I turned on the light, and she was just plain missing."

"Are her clothes gone?"

Barney nodded as he blew his nose with his handkerchief. "She hadn't hung up the outfit she had on yesterday because she was so tired. She left it on the floor. But it was gone. She got dressed and left."

"Did you ask the clerk at the front desk if anyone saw her?" Regan asked.

"Yes. They told me that no one saw anything."

"Does she have insomnia?"

"Huh?"

"Insomnia—you know, trouble sleeping?"

Barney's eyes brightened. "As a matter of

fact, she kept talking all night about being wound up because of winning that money."

"I'd be wound up if I won over $400,000," Regan noted. "Maybe she went out to try to win some more money. This town operates twenty-four hours a day. In the casinos they pump in oxygen and keep the lights on so you don't know whether it's day or night." As Regan explained this to Barney, she prayed that it was true. And then a disturbing thought occurred to her. Might Barney have done something to Elsa so he could keep the money himself?

"She could have gone to another casino," Barney agreed. "She did say that there probably wouldn't be any more big wins in this hotel's slot machines. Not for a while, anyway. But she knows we have to leave at ten. And why didn't she leave me a note? If she's not back soon, we definitely have trouble."

"Has she ever done anything like this before?" Regan inquired.

"No! She's so square. So controlled. I've always been the wild one. The fact that she could never let go and follow her impulses was part of our problem."

It looks as if that problem is solved,

Barney boy, Regan thought, but she just nodded. "Why don't you come with me to Danny's suite for a minute? We can let him know what's up. The police won't even file a missing person's report this soon. She is an adult and has the right to get up in the middle of the night and leave the hotel. Of course, we can call to see if there are any reports of accidents."

"I'd like to get a cup of coffee first," Barney said, sniffling.

"Certainly." Regan was anxious to talk to Jack, but now she'd have to wait.

Barney went over to the buffet table and fixed himself a bagel with a big mound of cream cheese, and a large cup of coffee. He placed them on a tray with a glass of orange juice and a banana, and turned to Regan cheerfully. "Which table would you like?"

Regan stared at him. "Your choice."

They sat down in two small plastic chairs, and Regan marveled at his ability to eat so heartily when Elsa was missing. It hadn't hurt his appetite a bit. If anything happened to Jack, the last thing on my mind would be eating. Regan sighed and decided she might as well get a bagel, too. She chose a plain bagel from the tray. It felt damp. She picked up a few packets of raspberry jam and returned to the table. Barney's bagel had disappeared. His tears stopped flowing when he was eating.

"I think I'll get some cereal for my banana," Barney announced. A minute later he returned with a bowl of brown flakes and proceeded to slice up the banana, frowning intensely as he did so. He sprinkled the bowl with sugar, poured in a container of milk, dug a tablespoon into the food, and crunched away happily.

"Ready?" Regan asked when the bowl was empty.

"Yes. I feel much better."

"That's good. We should really let Danny know what's going on. Who knows? Elsa might surprise us all and come back with even more money in her pockets."

"I hope so, Regan."

As they left the breakfast room, Barney started to hiccup uncontrollably. "I ate too fast," he complained.

What you need is a good scare, Regan thought. And it seems to me you should have already gotten one.

Let's see how you feel at ten o'clock if Elsa's still AWOL.

———◆———

43

Noel and Neil had worked until three in the morning on the script, then met again at eight in Neil's room to go over everything. They were both exhausted.

"I think we've got it, bro," Noel announced in a tired but triumphant voice.

"It's funny," Neil agreed. "I think it's James-proof."

They both laughed.

"That guy is pathetic." Noel put down his mug of tea and picked up the phone next to the bed. "I'll call Bubbles and tell her the script is ready." When she answered and he identified himself, the harangue that came from the other end caught him off guard.

"I can't take it anymore!" Bubbles screamed.

"Can't take what?"

"Roscoe!"

"Roscoe? It's not even nine in the morning. What happened?"

"I called him a few minutes ago to ask if we could use his balloon tomorrow morning for our opening scene, and he tells me he has a young couple he wants us to write into the script! *I can't breathe! I can't take it! This is totally unfair!*"

"What?" Noel demanded. He felt a tingling sensation run through his body.

"*You heard me!*"

"We were up until the middle of the night working on this. It's perfect the way it is!" Noel threw his pen across the room.

Neil sunk back into his chair. He picked up the knife he'd used to butter his blueberry muffin and held it up to his throat.

"Don't tell me it's perfect. Now I feel even worse!" Bubbles cried. "I'm convinced that Roscoe just likes to make trouble."

"Welcome to Hollywood. You think this is bad? Neil and I once worked on a script where they made us change a thirty-five-year-old heart surgeon into a twenty-year-old surfer dude with aspirations for medical school. And that was three days before filming."

"Well, you've got yourself another surfer dude! These kids are young!"

"Are they coming to the studio today?"

"Yes. Right now they're at Roscoe's enjoying their wedding breakfast."

"Wedding breakfast?"

"They got married last night at Graceland Wedding Chapel and went for a balloon ride this morning at sunrise with Roscoe. That's how he met them."

"Are they actors?"

"Supposedly."

"They can't be as bad as James. And I have to say, Neil and I are pretty proud of ourselves with what we did with the script. It's James-proof."

"James-one-hundred-proof," Neil muttered.

"Wait till Pete finds out. He's not going to be happy," Bubbles predicted.

"Whose lines should we cut to make room for this new couple?" Noel asked, running his fingers through his hair.

"Not mine! Take them away from Grandma and her boyfriend if you have to. And I don't think Pilot Pete will be happy if you cut back on his air time."

"Hmmm, okay. Neil and I will think about this. Are we still meeting downstairs at nine-thirty?"

"Yes." Click.

Noel held the phone out, frowned, then hung it up. "More rewrites. We have to add a young couple to the cast."

"What are we going to do with them?"

"Beats me. It depends on what Roscoe wants."

Neil waved his hand. "Let's give the kids one line and send them up in a balloon."

Noel laughed. "Maybe we should have them kidnap James. The others would love that."

"Yeah. We'll make them sinister characters. Spies from another ballooning company."

Neil grunted and fell over on his bed. "What is it that Mom says about us?"

"That we should go for career counseling. That there must be some other profession that would make us happy."

Neil laughed wearily. "She's probably right. Something tells me this situation is only going to get 'worser and worser.' "

44

"I want to call Danny on the house phone and let him know we're coming up. He's not expecting anyone until nine," Regan explained to Barney.

Barney nodded and put his hand over his mouth to stifle another hiccup.

The lobby was fairly quiet. Regan picked up the phone on a table near the registration desk and dialed Danny's extension. He answered after three rings.

"Danny, it's Regan. I'm down in the lobby with Barney. We need to talk to you before your parents and Agony and Heartburn gather in your room."

"Barney needs to talk to me?" Danny repeated. "Now?"

"Yes. Can we come up?"

"Regan, is it bad?"

"It could be better," she answered honestly.

"Come on up. Nothing like getting the day off to a great start."

Regan hung up the phone, feeling sorry for Danny. Why do I have to give him the first bad news of the day? she wondered as they headed for the elevator.

Danny had the door of the suite open. Regan knocked and called out to him. "We're here."

"Come on in. I'm on the phone."

Barney followed Regan into the living room. "This is nice. Too bad the contestants don't get a suite."

"Too bad," Regan agreed wryly. "Have a seat."

"Okay, Mom, I'll see you in a few minutes." Danny hung up the phone. "Good morning, you two. I have to admit I'm afraid to ask. What's going on?"

"Elsa is missing," Barney moaned, his lip quivering.

"Missing?" Danny's eyes widened. His blond hair was still wet from the shower, and the smell of the citrus soap permeated the room. It was an invigorating start-of-the-day kind of smell.

Regan quickly relayed the story and concluded, "She could just be out gambling. We'll know at ten o'clock. If she doesn't show up, then we have real cause for concern. I'm going to call the police right now. They wouldn't consider Elsa a missing person yet. But they can be on the lookout for her . . ." She didn't want to finish the thought in front of Barney.

Danny felt terrible. Terrible for himself, terrible for Barney. Mostly terrible for himself. He had six contestants, and one was missing. And it was only Tuesday. "She did win a lot of money last night," he repeated to Barney in an attempt to comfort. "Maybe she needed to get some air."

"Why didn't she wake me?" Barney moaned, the tears starting to fall. "We love to go on walks together."

"In the middle of the night?" Danny asked, his voice rising.

"Twenty-four/seven. We love each other more than words can express."

Regan stood. "Let me call the police." As Regan dialed the local precinct, Victor arrived. He looked as fresh as a daisy in his khaki shorts and bright green polo shirt. His hair was gelled, he smelled of cologne, and he had a clipboard under his arm.

"You look happy," Danny observed.

"I'm all set to get going. Nothing like a good night's sleep." He paused and looked at Barney who was alternating hiccups with sobs. "Is something wrong here?"

Morosely, Danny filled him in on Elsa's disappearance as Regan conversed with an officer at the police department. She hung up and told Barney, "They took her description and will let us know if they come up with anything."

"I think I'd better lie down," Barney said meekly. "Danny, what will we do if she's not here by ten o'clock?"

Danny shook his head as though he was trying to clear it. "I have to get over to the studio with the others. We'll start with the segments we have planned for today. When Elsa gets back," he continued optimistically, "we'll have someone come to get you. Regan, would you mind waiting here with Barney?"

"Not at all. Barney, go take a rest. Maybe Elsa will come back. I'll be here in Danny's room until it's time for everyone to go."

Barney hiccuped and walked toward the door. "These are the best of times, the worst of times," he recited as he exited.

Victor shook his head. "Dollars to dough-nuts Elsa is sitting at a slot machine some-where, losing money."

"Why do you say that?" Regan asked.

"I've been around this town for a long time. People like Elsa win big money, and they've got to have more. So they start playing like crazy. They keep losing, but they can't stop. They think they can win their money back. Before you know it, they've lost everything. This town was built on people losing money, not winning."

"But she won over $400,000," Regan said with genuine concern. "That's 1.6 million quarters. I doubt she's used that up in one night."

"Her arm would be pretty tired," Danny observed.

"They have five-dollar slot machines. Money can disappear pretty fast into those," Victor reminded them.

"Maybe Elsa's afraid to come back if she lost a lot of her money," Regan suggested.

"Talk about a true test of love!" Danny ex-claimed. "Wouldn't that be great for the show? Can Barney handle the fact that she squandered their recently won fortune?"

"Danny!" Regan cried.

"I know, I know. I'm just trying to look on the bright side of things."

"Your parents are going to be here in a few minutes," Regan prodded him.

"Right. Victor, I have some things to talk over with my parents. Why don't you get some breakfast and come back a few minutes before ten?"

Victor looked hurt. "Regan, do you want to have breakfast with me?" he asked.

"Thanks, but I have to talk to Danny's parents."

"It's a New Jersey kind of thing," Danny said awkwardly.

"Is there anything wrong?" Victor asked.

"There was a little incident that I didn't get to tell you about," Danny noted as Regan held her breath. "My parents were delivering a sack of mail to Agony and Heartburn; it was stolen from their room at the 7's Hotel last night."

"It must be someone from the sitcom!" Victor cried vehemently. "They're staying there, and I bet they're in on it!"

"You think?" Danny asked.

"Of course. Upset the major players on our show. Sure!"

Is Victor being real? Regan wondered. Or is this an act?

There was a knock at the door. Danny answered it and found Sam standing in the hall.

"Sam, come on in."

"Heyyyyy," Sam greeted everyone as he walked in. He seemed to be half asleep. He had on a fresh pair of shorts and a checked shirt, and the water in his blond hair was slowly evaporating.

Guys are so lucky, Regan reflected. They step out of the shower and are out the door in two minutes. Most women would look like hell if they didn't do a little bit of futzing with a hair dryer.

"I just saw Barney in the hallway. He looked a little upset and said you all were in here."

"Elsa got out of bed last night and disappeared," Danny said flatly.

"Bummer."

"It is a bummer," Danny agreed.

"She won all that dough. Maybe she went out to have a good time."

"That seems to be the consensus." Danny sighed. "One way or the other."

"What are you going to do if she doesn't come back?" Sam asked. "It would kind of kill the show."

"Either that or the competition between the two remaining couples would be cranked up a few notches," Victor said excitedly, his brow furrowed. "You know, boss, that could work, too."

"Guys," Regan chided them. "We have someone missing here. Let's just hope she's all right. That should be our first concern."

There was another knock at the door. This time it was Agony and Heartburn whom Danny escorted into the room.

When they saw Regan, Victor, and Sam, they both looked taken aback.

"Victor and Sam are just leaving," Danny explained.

"I am?" Sam countered. "Man, I just got here."

"We have some things to take care of," Danny told him.

"Hello Aunt and Uncle," Victor said as he got up from the couch. "I know when I'm not wanted."

"I guess I'm not wanted, either," Sam said dejectedly. "But I could use some eggs."

"That's right," Danny agreed. "See you guys in about an hour. We plan to leave here at ten o'clock, Elsa or no Elsa."

"What happened to Elsa?" Agony asked.

"She got out of bed in the middle of the night and never came back."

"She won all that money. And as is so often the case, money is the root of all evil," Agony declared solemnly.

"It helps to have money to pay the bills," Heartburn noted feebly.

"The two strongest motivating forces in our lives—love and money," Agony continued. "People have killed for them. Killed without a second thought."

Is Aunt Agony losing it? Regan wondered. Oh, well. She probably had a bad night's sleep. Her career as an advice columnist could be out the window if this story leaks.

Sam and Victor both shuffled out. It was hard to tell who was more reluctant to leave.

Aunt Agony looked at Regan questioningly.

"Regan knows everything that's going on," Danny explained quickly. "She is a private investigator I hired to help make sure things go smoothly. And she's my friend."

"So you're not planning a reality show?" Agony inquired.

Regan smiled. "Not anytime soon."

Aunt Agony put her fingers to her lips. "Don't tell a soul, Regan, about our problems. But I think I can trust you. It is my business to read people."

"Mine, too," Regan replied. She noticed Heartburn flinch. "And my lips are sealed," she continued reassuringly. "I really want Danny's show to work."

Heartburn sighed. "I never should have married that Evelyn. She was bad news from day one. It would ruin us if someone found out I owe back alimony."

"Sssssshhhhh!" Agony ordered. "Don't say that! Once you release words into the universe, they reverberate."

"I just want to get this over with," Heartburn declared.

"My parents will be here any minute," Danny promised. "Would you like some coffee?"

"No, we're jittery enough," Agony noted. "By the way, I had a magnificent idea in the middle of the night."

"What's that?"

"We can give the Rorschach test today."

"The Rorschach test?" Danny repeated, sounding very doubtful.

"Yes! You know, you pour ink on a piece of paper, fold it in half, and then ask people to interpret the design. You can tell a lot about a person from that test. Their emotions, their intelligence, whether they're compatible with their partner. You wouldn't believe how differently two people who are supposedly perfect for each other can interpret the same blob of black ink."

"It's the old 'you say tow-may-tow, I say ta-mah-tow,' " Heartburn added. Then he sang, "Let's call the whole thing off."

"I can't afford for any of the couples to call the whole thing off," Danny groaned. "We have to keep this operation together until Friday."

"Of course!" Agony said. "But it will be fun. Where one person sees a flower, another sees a weed."

Ten to one Elsa sees a slot machine and Barney sees a hankie, Regan thought.

A few minutes later Shep and Maddy arrived. Neither of them looked very well rested.

"Sorry we're late," Maddy apologized. "Oh, Regan, hello. Please don't tell anyone back in New Jersey about this."

"I already warned her," Agony chirped.

"Regan is here to help me out," Danny stated firmly.

"We're a little late because we called our financial adviser this morning," Maddy announced. "He is already transferring the money to your account."

Heartburn ran over and hugged Shep. "Thank you."

"You're welcome."

Agony and Maddy also hugged. "No sign of the mail, I suppose?" Agony inquired.

"No," Maddy admitted. "But we do have the $40,000 for you."

"I gathered that."

Regan watched the two couples with interest and realized that each couple had something hanging over the other's heads. They could easily ruin one another. Now there's an idea for a reality show.

"Let me call my lawyer and let him know everything is okay," Heartburn said.

"Did you explain to your lawyer where you were getting the money?" Maddy asked nervously.

Heartburn paused and looked at her. "I advised my counsel that my producer's parents were very understanding people who are giving me a loan."

Ten minutes later all the arrangements had been made. It's amazing how fast a lot of money can change hands, Regan marveled. From Shep and Maddy's account to Heartburn and Agony's account to the ex-wife's account. From the slot machine to Elsa to God knows where.

"Well, Danny," Maddy asked. "Are you going over to the studio this morning?"

"Yes, Mom. But one of our contestants is missing."

Shep looked as if he was about to cry. I'll never get my money back, he worried. This show is never going to make it to the air.

45

Nora and Luke were in the air on the way to Santa Fe, three hours into the flight, the time when passengers often start to get itchy. Nora was reading a novel. Luke had dozed for a bit, then opened his eyes and reached for the in-flight magazine in the seat pocket in front of him. Flipping through it, he came across an article on the Albuquerque Hot Air Balloon Fiesta.

"Look at this." Luke leaned closer to Nora, the magazine wide open in his hands.

Nora peered over her glasses. "What's that?"

"It's a picture of the special shapes balloons at last year's balloon festival."

Nora smiled. "It reminds me of the Macy's Thanksgiving Day parade."

"Yes. Except Macy's doesn't have Hamlet."

"Hamlet?" Nora asked. "The Shakespearean character?"

"No." Luke pointed to the picture. "A flying pink pig."

Chuckling, Nora glanced at the array of unusual balloons on the double-page spread. "Let's see. A beer can, Noah's ark, a soccer ball, Mr. Potato Head, an octopus, a hot dog, a hamburger, a witch, and a castle."

"Among others." Luke laughed. He turned the page and proceeded to read the article about the Albuquerque Balloon Fiesta. It was the biggest balloon fiesta in the country with over 750 balloons registered. A number of years ago the festival had become even more popular when they added an evening event called the Balloon Glow, or "Glowdeo." The balloons are tethered to the ground and the pilots fire up their burners, causing the balloons to glow like huge lanterns. Spectators have a great time walking around the field and chatting with the pilots. Numerous vendors are on hand to provide refreshments. The evening is capped off with a spectacular fireworks show.

Not bad, Luke thought. And you don't have to get up before dawn. He turned the page again, and his eyes widened at the headline DEBUT FLIGHT OF WEDDING CAKE BALLOON. Luke read the article about a couple who had custom ordered a special-shaped wedding cake balloon. At 300,000 cubic feet, it was the largest special-shaped balloon ever built. The husband and wife were both balloon pilots and were starting a new business. They planned to travel across the country with the balloon and be hired out for weddings—either to bring a wedding party up in the air for the actual ceremony or have a bride and groom leave their reception in the balloon.

"Nora, look at this."

"Yes, dear." Nora looked up again. She was used to these interruptions. Luke got restless on airplanes, and even though they were sitting in first class, his six-foot-five frame never seemed to settle in.

"Here's a story about the couple who own the wedding cake balloon. It's making its debut in Albuquerque. And it's the largest special-shaped balloon ever built."

"It is?" Nora asked with alarm in her voice.

"Yes."

"I don't like the idea of Regan going up in a balloon that is brand new and so big."

"I'm surprised it doesn't mention anything about Danny's show," Luke remarked.

"These articles have long lead times. I have the idea that Danny's show wasn't conceived until very recently." Nora leaned over and looked at the picture of the smiling couple. Her lips moved as she read, " 'Randy Jupiter and Alice Mars Jupiter met at a society for people named after planets. They both have a special affinity for the universe at large and decided to pursue the sport of hot air ballooning. Together they became pilots, and they go ballooning whenever possible. When Alice's elderly aunt, Venus Mars, passed over to the great beyond and left her niece a tidy inheritance, Randy and Alice asked themselves what they wanted to do with the rest of their lives. Their passion for balloons guided them. They decided to quit their jobs and spend their time up, up, and away. The Jupiters had the wedding cake balloon specially designed and are looking forward to attending balloon festivals and weddings all over the country. Flying the balloon in Hawaii is one of their dreams, as they're sure plenty of newlyweds honeymooning on the lush islands would love to ride in the balloon and take home pictures of themselves in an eight-story wedding cake.' " Nora looked up at Luke. "Aunt Venus must have left them a lot of money."

"Must have."

"I still don't like the idea of Regan going up in that balloon."

Luke patted her shoulder. "We'll call her when we land. I'm sure everything will be just fine."

"I don't know. Danny's show has been having so much trouble . . ." She hesitated. The plane started to experience turbulence.

A flight attendant's voice came over the sound system. "The captain has advised us that we're hitting a bumpy patch, so please make sure your seat belts are fastened."

"A bumpy patch," Nora muttered. "It reminds me of a balloon landing."

"Don't worry, dear. Regan will be fine. This couple sounds interesting. I'm anxious to meet them."

"As long as the meeting takes place on the ground," Nora insisted, "on planet Earth."

———◆———

46

"We'll leave you be, dear," Maddy told Danny. "We're going to lie out by the pool at our hotel. It's not the most luxurious pool, but it'll do."

"Be careful, would you? It's hot out there today," Danny warned.

"I'll do my best to see that we have a quiet day," Shep assured his son.

"I'll call you later," Maddy announced as they walked toward the door. "Regan, it's so good to see you. How are your parents?"

"They're fine. Thanks."

"Are they in New Jersey now?"

"No, they're actually on their way to Santa Fe."

"Really?"

"Yes. We may see them at the balloon fiesta in Albuquerque on Friday morning."

"Shep, we should go to that!"

"Come on, Maddy," Shep snapped.

"Bye, all," Maddy called as she disappeared.

Aunt Agony looked at Danny with sympathy. "Are you an only child?"

"I have a sister in Maine."

"God is good," Agony whispered.

"Agony, I need to get some breakfast," Heartburn stated impatiently.

"So do I. Don't you think my stomach is growling? I've been too worried to eat. Now that things are settled, I'd like to have a nutritious breakfast. We have a lot to cover with those contestants today." Agony started for the door. "See you folks downstairs at ten."

When the door shut behind them, Danny flopped onto the couch. "I'm worn out, and we haven't even turned on the camera yet."

"Well, Danny, you dodged a big bullet. Now let's just hope Elsa finds her way home."

"Why does everything keep going wrong?" Danny whined.

Regan looked thoughtful. "Danny, there's

something fishy going on. I'm glad we're going to Roscoe's tonight. I'm anxious to get the lay of the land, so to speak. I also want to get a load of those sitcom people."

"Bubbles is a trip," Danny noted. "She's as competitive as they get."

Regan looked at her watch. "I'm going to my room to make a phone call."

"Are you calling Mr. Reilly?" Danny teased.

"As a matter of fact, yes. I didn't get to talk to him this morning. Once I ran into Barney, that was it. Jack was going to see what he could find out about Roscoe, if anything."

"Okay. I'll be down in the lobby."

Regan went back to her room. Naturally, the maid was in there making the bed. I'll never be able to make this call, Regan despaired. It feels as though I'll never get a chance to talk to Jack.

"Hello," the maid greeted Regan in a heavily accented voice as she pulled the spread up under the pillows.

"Hello." Regan could see that the maid hadn't cleaned the bathroom yet. "Do you think you could come back in a little while? I have to make a phone call."

The maid stared at her blankly.

Regan pantomimed making a phone call.

"Okay." The maid pulled a Cherry Chap Stick out of her pocket and applied it to her lips. "I come back." She walked out as she ran the Chap Stick around her lips one more time.

Regan remembered the Cherry Chap Stick on the floor of Maddy and Shep's room. Well, it's dry out here, Regan reasoned. Everyone gets chapped lips. Regan sat on the bed and reached for the receiver, but something stopped her. I'll use my cell phone, she decided. Even though the reception would be better on the land line, she chose to use her cell. She dialed Jack's number quickly.

"Regan!" he answered, picking up immediately. "How are you?"

"Oh, Jack, you wouldn't believe it."

"I'm sure I won't." He laughed. "Don't tell me. You won big money, and you're running off with someone else."

Regan giggled. "No, I didn't win any money but the contestant who hit the jackpot is on the loose." Regan filled him in on that story and the mail saga.

"It sounds like you're earning your pay.

Are you sure you're going to be free by Friday night?"

"Definitely," Regan insisted. "Friday night I'm with you."

"I'm certainly glad to hear that."

"Did you find anything out about the contestants?" Regan asked him.

"Without Social Security numbers, it's tough. But that Roscoe is some character."

"Do tell."

"He's been married three times. He owned a coal mine, a bar, and a dry cleaning chain, and has been involved in various business ventures along the way. Nothing illegal. He's smart and rich, but he's a loose cannon. He reinvents himself and enjoys his reputation for being outrageous. He's very fond of gambling and has businesses in several cities with casinos. First he rented out catamarans at a marina near Atlantic City. Then he bought a ski rental place in Lake Tahoe. He moved to Las Vegas and got into the balloon business. He started the cable TV station and bought all that land for his cable headquarters. Supposedly he really wants to make a name for himself with his television channel."

"How did you find this out?"

"One of my guys here has a contact out in Las Vegas."

"Well, I definitely think Roscoe is pushing the envelope this week. We're having dinner at his house tonight. It should be interesting."

"Regan. I don't like spending so much time away from you."

"I don't like it, either, Jack," Regan said softly.

"Last night I had two slices of pizza and went to sleep."

"I had pizza, too. At the bar at Carlotta's, a second-rate Italian restaurant, while two of the contestants were having their dream date upstairs."

"I think we need a few dream dates." Jack chuckled.

"Not at Carlotta's," Regan assured him.

"I'll think something up for this weekend."

When Regan hung up, she smiled and sighed. Three thousand miles is too far apart to live, she thought. She got up, brushed her teeth, and freshened her makeup. It was almost ten o'clock. She hurried downstairs where most of the group had gathered. Barney was seated on a

couch in the lobby. The others were standing around him.

"I couldn't be alone," he told Regan.

Sam was there, recording the contestants' movements. His camera was focused
on Barney, sitting forlornly on the couch.
Victor and Danny were on the side, going
over the notes on Victor's clipboard. Chip
and Vicky and Bill and Suzette were whis-
pering among themselves about the missing Elsa, while doing their best to look
very much in love. Agony and Heartburn
stepped off the elevator a few minutes later,
hand in hand.

"It looks as if we're ready to go," Danny
instructed the group. "Barney, I'm sorry.
We'll be in touch with you. Let's hope Elsa
returns soon."

Barney nodded grimly. He looked like so
many of the saddened contestants on the
reality shows, contestants who had gotten
the boot. "I'm going to wait here till Elsa
gets back," he announced stoically.

You may be waiting until the cows come
home, Regan thought.

Suddenly the front door to the hotel flung
open. A dazed and bedraggled Elsa entered
the lobby, hundred-dollar bills sticking out

of her pockets. Barney jumped up and ran to her, his arms outstretched. It was a reunion that made lost Lassie's homecoming with his master, Timmy, seem positively coldhearted.

"You're back!" Barney cried. "I can't believe you're safe!"

"I don't know what happened," Elsa confessed, looking confused. "All I knew was that I had to get back here. Back to you. Back by ten o'clock."

Sam was taping the whole scene.

Suzette looked as if she wanted to throw a punch at someone. "I'm sick of this!" she growled under her breath to Bill. "This is unfair! We don't have a chance! Those two are doing everything they can to get attention!"

I agree, Regan thought. I totally agree.

47

The *Take Me Higher* group gathered around the conference table in their office at the Balloon Channel. Back to the scene of the crime, Bubbles reflected. She'd called her boyfriend this morning to complain about the latest additions to the cast.

"Cheer up," he advised. "Danny's going crazy. One of the contestants is missing."

That news had made Bubbles's day. "Then there's a chance we'll win by default!" she'd replied excitedly.

"I wouldn't go that far. Danny is already thinking of ways to proceed if she's gone to that great casino in the sky."

"Sweetie!" Bubbles had cried.

"I'm just kidding. I'm sure this woman is

fine. She won big money last night and is probably out on a bender."

"I just hope she stays away long enough to ruin the show."

Bubbles's cell phone vibrated in her pocket when she was riding in the van from the hotel. She checked the caller ID but didn't answer. When they all piled out at the Balloon Channel, she read the text message on her phone.

It read: The contestant hath returned.

Now she was in a really bad mood.

"Here we are," James announced cheerfully as everyone took the seats they had occupied the day before. "I woke up this morning, and I thought to myself: I can't believe how lucky I am. I am going to work as an actor today, and I'm actually getting paid for it."

"It is amazing," Pilot Pete agreed. "Absolutely amazing."

"Remarkable," Loretta added. "And from now on I'd like you all to call me by my character's name, Grandma. I want to play the role perfectly so that I'll really feel like Grandma on Friday.

Grandma's boyfriend, Hal, frowned. "I

don't want to call you Grandma. That
doesn't sound very romantic to me."

"You can call me Loretta. But only you."

"I'm really glad you're all getting into your
parts," Bubbles interrupted. "But there's
one thing you should all know. Roscoe
called me this morning. He has a couple of
actors he wants to add to the show."

Pilot Pete turned bright red. "What?"

Bubbles stared at him. This is why I
waited to tell him until now, she thought.
Safety in numbers. The guy was scary. She
tried to remain calm. There was no use let-
ting them know how upset she was. "Yes. A
young couple from Los Angeles who came
to Las Vegas to get married. Noel and Neil
are working on ways to squeeze them in
with just a couple of lines."

"Make them extras!" Grandma cried.
"That's all they deserve!"

"Noel and I are working to preserve the in-
tegrity of all your roles," Neil assured her.

"We want Roscoe to be happy with us,"
Bubbles reminded everyone. "So let's all
put on a cheerful front and do the best we
can." She started passing around copies of
the revised script. "This will obviously be
changed again, but let's do a read through.

Roscoe told me he was going to bring the new actors over here this morning to meet us."

"I certainly hope they can act," James said, looking from one to the other for approval.

"Yeah." Pete stared back at him. "There's nothing worse than having to work with a bad actor."

James threw his hands into the air. "I totally agree."

"Let's start, shall we?" Bubbles asked through clenched teeth. *If Pete doesn't kill James by the end of the week, then I just might.*

Up in his office, Roscoe stared at the televisions on his wall, a huge grin on his face. "I knew adding this couple to the mix would drive them crazy," he exclaimed to Erene and Leo who were sitting across the desk from him. Kitty was back at the house in the Jacuzzi, still trying to get warm.

"I'm glad you believe in equal opportunity crazy-making," Leo noted. "You've certainly done enough to Danny."

"As I've told you a hundred times before, when life throws you lemons, make lemonade. Competition is what brings out the best in us. And, besides, not all of Danny's troubles have been my fault. Did you get the torches for tonight?"

"Yes," Erene replied. "The backyard will have that reality show feeling."

"Good. I love that. And we'll roast marshmallows."

"We'll roast marshmallows."

"Erene, are Kimberly and Jake downstairs?"

"Yes. They're in the greenroom downstairs waiting for you to take them to meet Bubbles and the gang."

The station had a greenroom that had yet to see the likes of any real stars. Roscoe's shows were just getting off the ground, and his viewership was small. But he believed they would prevail. It was only a matter of time before Oscar-winning actors and directors would be rubbing shoulders in there, "fighting over the cheese and crackers," as he put it.

"I'll see you folks tonight," Roscoe announced. "After I make these introductions, I'm going home to rest up for the party."

Erene and Leo were both relieved. "We'll be here," Leo told his boss. "See you later."

Roscoe found Kimberly stretched out on

the couch in the greenroom, fast asleep.
Jake was in the chair next to her, lightly tapping a pen against the coffee table.

"Hi, Roscoe," Jake whispered.

"Look at that sleeping beauty."

"She is a beauty, isn't she?" Jake said
reverentially.

"She's a knockout."

Jake gently woke Kimberly, and the three-
some walked over to the *Take Me Higher*
offices. Roscoe knocked on the door of
the conference room. Bubbles answered
quickly. When she got a look at Kimberly,
she wanted to scream. I'm supposed to be
the babe on this show! she thought furiously. It was all she could do not to slam the
door in her flawless face.

48

It didn't take Regan long to realize that Elsa was more than a little bit tipsy. Her words were slurred, and she was unsteady on her feet. Her hair was uncombed, and her clothes were rumpled, even allowing for the fact that she'd left them in a pile on the floor the night before. When Danny ordered Sam to stop shooting, he addressed the group. "Chip, Vicky, Suzette, and Bill, why don't you all get into the van with Agony and Heartburn? Sam and Victor will bring you over to the studio. Regan and I will wait here with Barney until Elsa is ready to leave."

Who knows how long that could take? Regan wondered.

"What happened to you anyway?"

Suzette blurted out. The others all waited, frozen in place, for Elsa's answer.

Elsa looked at Suzette and blinked her bloodshot eyes several times. "I had a terrible nightmare last night."

Barney looked appalled. "You did, my sweetness?"

Elsa nodded. "I dreamt someone took all the money that I won."

"But I thought they hadn't even given it to you yet," Suzette challenged.

This is getting to be like *Survivor,* Regan thought. Suzette is clearly not a happy camper and wants to send Elsa packing.

"You know how dreams are! In my mind, I already had all that money, Barney and I were going to retire on that money, and suddenly it was gone. I woke up in a sweat and wanted to talk to Barney, but he had taken a pain pill for his arm and was fast asleep." Elsa pretended to snore, which clearly annoyed Barney. After three fake snores she continued. "Usually Barney is there for me when I have a nightmare, but last night he was out like a light. Zonk City. I didn't want to disturb him."

"My arm was very sore when I went to

bed," Barney explained a tad defensively. "I'm very sensitive to medication."

The doctor gave him pain pills for that slight sprain? Regan wondered.

"I was lying there and I felt so restless," Elsa said with a slight slur. "The thrill of winning that money was still pulsing through my veins. It was a brilliant feeling. I was wide awake and wanted to win more for my Barney, so he'd never have to work another day in his life."

Hmmm, Regan thought. A lot of women would go nuts having their husbands retire at such a young age. What was that old saying? I married you for better or for worse, but not for lunch. Or, as Regan's grandmother always joked, "Having a retired husband is like having a piano in the kitchen."

"But work is good for the soul," Agony said passionately. "We must remember that. Idle hands are the devil's tools."

Her hands weren't idle, Regan reflected. That was the problem. She headed straight for the slot machines. Regan noticed that Danny had asked Sam to turn the camera back on.

"I wanted to double our money!" Elsa cried.

"Did you?" Barney asked quickly.

Sadly, Elsa shook her head and pulled several hundred-dollar bills out of her pants pockets. "I got some credit, I think."

Oh, boy, Regan thought. Welcome to Las Vegas.

"Where did you go?" Suzette continued.

Elsa took a deep breath. "I think I took a cab up to the Strip. I went to the first casino I saw and played the slot machines. A nice waitress gave me sweet drinks. I told her I liked Shirley Temples, and she said she had something I'd like even better. Boy, did they taste good. I told her I'd won a lot of money yesterday."

Bad move, Regan thought.

"Then I started walking around and playing some game where the marble goes around and around and around until it goes "pop" in the slot. They gave me more drinks there. I played until the marble made me dizzy and I almost fell down. Then somebody gave me a coupon for a free buffet breakfast. So I went to the coffee shop and had blueberry pancakes, and I think I dozed off in the booth. The waitress woke me up and asked me to leave. And here I am!"

"They took advantage of you!" Barney cried. "They liquored you up so they could get your money. Bait and trap, that's what it was. Bait and trap!"

"What casino did you go to?" Regan asked her.

Elsa scrunched up her face. "One of the smaller ones. I forget the name. But I think I walked through the Bellagio. And I kept saying to myself, ten o'clock, ten o'clock. I have to be back by ten o'clock. I made it, didn't I?"

"Yes, you did, my love." Barney choked out the words.

Agony walked over to Elsa and Barney and grabbed their hands. "It's not how we act as a couple, it's how we react. I'm glad to see Barney so concerned about his wife's welfare. He is a most understanding spouse. Other men might have gotten angry that Elsa took off in the middle of the night, without even having the consideration to leave a scribbled note. This shows your love is strong and good and can weather many storms."

"I have a headache and feel a wee bit sick," Elsa moaned.

"Cut!" Danny cried.

Sam shut off the camera.

"Come on, folks," Victor instructed the group. "The van's right outside."

Agony was still clenching Barney and Elsa's hands. "Elsa, take a long shower, get some breakfast, and we'll see you at the studio. We're doing Rorschach tests today. You'll love them."

"Rorschach tests?" Barney repeated.

"Yes. You look at smeared ink on a page and tell us what you see, and then Elsa comes out of a soundproof booth and tells us what she sees."

"You have a soundproof booth?" Barney asked.

"No. But Elsa will wait in the next room."

"Sounds brilliant," Elsa said, taking an unsteady step forward. "I can't wait to compare what we see, right, Barn?"

"Right."

"Agony," Victor interrupted, "the others are waiting."

"Coming! Coming!" she trilled.

"We'll walk upstairs with you," Danny told Elsa and Barney.

"You don't have to. I can take care of my wife."

"I have to go upstairs anyway," Danny said.

"And I want to stop in my room," Regan added.

Together they took the elevator to the third floor. Danny headed left toward his suite. Regan, Barney, and Elsa turned right. Barney had his arm around Elsa, guiding her along. They approached their room and stopped. Regan stopped with them. Her room was three doors past theirs.

"Drink a lot of water," Regan instructed Elsa. "And take a couple of aspirin."

"I'll take good care of her," Barney assured Regan, standing in place.

"Okay. I'll see you in a bit." Regan started toward her room. She could hear Barney turning the key in the door. Suddenly Regan turned and started back toward the elevator. She wanted to go downstairs and grab another cup of coffee. Barney turned to Regan in a panic as she was about to pass their room and pulled the door closed again. But not before Regan saw a cot set up next to their bed.

"It's such a mess in there," Barney said quickly.

"Mostly my fault," Elsa admitted as she leaned against Barney.

"The rooms are small," Regan said sympathetically. "And, of course, there are two of you. See you in a bit." As Regan pressed the elevator button, she couldn't help but wonder. If those two are so much in love, what is a cot doing in their room? Barney said he was holding Elsa in his arms last night when they went to sleep. Those two are frauds, she thought. They're not in love anymore. Suzette is right. They're doing whatever they can to attract attention and win the million dollars. Then they'll split the money and go their separate ways.

Or is someone else staying in their room? But who?

I have to find out more about those two, she decided.

49

Honey and Lucille had quite a night. Honey was so excited about working with Danny that she could hardly contain herself.

"It's a dream come true," she said to Lucille more than once.

"Yeah, yeah," Lucille said. "If you miss this bus, you'll catch the next one."

"I don't want another bus," Honey insisted.

They'd gone to Caesar's Palace for a drink, caught the late show, and then met up with some friends who had just gotten off work. They casino-hopped, and then the whole group went to breakfast. It had been a long night, but Honey hadn't felt so energetic in months.

Honey got home as the sun was rising.

She slept for a few hours and woke up at ten, which was early for her. Her brain was buzzing too much to slumber for long. She made her tea and then got on the phone. Thursday was only two days away, and she wanted to make all the arrangements. She called her hairdresser friend, Alex. He had his own little salon, Snippy Clips, located in a mini-mall in town. He did a decent enough business but was facing stiff competition from the big hotels with their fancy spas and beauty parlors. Alex always wore black leather pants and a disgusted expression. His black hair was cut in a long shag.

"Alex!" Honey said to him when he answered his cell phone. "This is Honey."

"Hi, doll," he answered. "What's up? I just did your hair. Don't tell me you don't like it. I'll have to scream."

Honey could hear the whir of hair dryers in the background. "I love it! I'm calling because I have the most fabulous opportunity for you!" she cried.

"What's that?" Alex usually sounded vaguely bored.

"How would you like to do makeovers on reality show contestants—on television?"

"What television?"

"The Balloon Channel."

"Forget it!"

"This could be very big," Honey screeched. "They're giving a million-dollar prize to the couple who wins the contest."

"That's Roscoe Parker's station, right?"

"Yes."

"I cut his hair once. He's cheap. The tip he gave me was insulting."

"You could get a lot of publicity for your salon from this."

"How much are they paying?"

"Well," Honey hesitated. "They're not paying."

"Is this the show that Danny is producing?"

"Yes."

At the other end of the phone, Alex rolled his eyes. My clients and their romances, he thought. I should get paid as a therapist. "When are you talking about?"

"Thursday." Honey could tell he was interested. "I was thinking we could ask Ellen Kaiden to do the makeup," she suggested. Ellen worked in the salon with Alex and could do wonders on anyone's face. She turned many a mouse into a roaring lion for a night on the town in Vegas.

"I suppose you want her to work for free as well," Alex said with a sigh.

"Yes. But it will be great exposure for both of you."

"When will the show air?" he asked.

"Probably Friday night."

"Probably?"

"They're in competition with a sitcom for the air time. Roscoe's going to pick one show or the other."

"You mean we might not even be on TV? Honey, puh-leeze! Spare me this aggravation!"

"Danny's show is really good. All it needs is your expert touch. Please, Alex, please. Someday I'll repay you. I'm always telling people how good you are and that they should make an appointment with you."

"Whatever happened to your dear friend Lucille? I did her hair once and never saw her again."

"She likes to cut it herself."

"*Aaaagh!* I'm going to be ill."

"Her grandfather was a barber and taught her a few tricks."

"Don't mention it to me again," Alex scolded. "Stories like that raise my stress levels. What time on Thursday?"

"Noon. At the Balloon Channel."

"How many people?"

"Three men and three women."

Alex sighed again. "All right, Honey. But if you ever switch hairdressers, I'm going to hunt you down."

"If I move to Alaska," Honey replied dramatically, "I will always come back to you to get my hair cut."

"And highlighted."

"And highlighted."

"Will Roscoe Parker be there?"

"I don't know."

"I'll try not to be too rude if I see him."

"I appreciate that."

Honey hung up and sighed. Two more days. She prayed silently that nothing would happen to halt production of Danny's show before she could get there. She kept getting bad feelings about *Love Above Sea Level.* Honey and her grandmother were both a little psychic, and right now Honey had the feeling that Danny could be in danger. Let him be safe, she prayed. Let him come back to me. And let that sitcom be a real stinker. Thank you, God. Amen. Honey picked up the phone and called her grandmother.

"Mimi, it's me." Honey updated her grandmother on her troubles. "What do you think?"

"I see clouds around Danny," Mimi replied. "A lot of clouds."

"He's going up in a hot air balloon on Friday."

"That could be it. But these are dark clouds. You're not supposed to go up in those balloons when there are dark clouds in the sky. Am I right, Honey, baby?"

"You're right, Mimi," Honey said in despair. "You're absolutely right."

50

Maddy and Shep were lying out by the pool of the 7's Hotel. Shep would really have preferred to be back home with his financial statements. His heart was beating rapidly over the $40,000 withdrawal he had made this morning.

Next to him, Maddy smelled like a coconut. She had slathered special lotion all over herself and was reclining with her eyes closed. There was no one else out by the pool, as is often the case with these third-rate hotels. Nobody ever seems to use the pool. It's there because if they don't have one, people don't want to make a reservation. They just want to be able to say, "And the hotel has a pool."

Shep watched one of the maids come out

the back door for a smoke. She placed a large box on the ground, lit a cigarette, turned on her cell phone, and made a call. A few moments later a dark sedan pulled into the driveway, and the maid handed over the package to the driver. That seems odd, Shep thought. He squinted but couldn't see what the driver looked like. The car had Nevada license plates. Shep got up and walked to the far end of the pool very casually so he could get a closer look at the car. He noted the license plate number as the sedan drove off.

Shep decided to call Regan. The incident might be nothing, but it did look suspicious to him. He hurried back to his chair.

"Maddy. Do you have a pen?"

"Huh?"

"I need a pen." He kept repeating the license number to himself.

Maddy sat up and quickly retrieved a 7's Hotel pen from her beach bag. Shep wrote the number in the margin of the newspaper he was reading.

"What are you doing?" Maddy asked.

"It's just a hunch. But you should always report suspicious behavior, right, dear?"

"Around this joint especially!" Maddy nodded emphatically. "They've already stolen the mail. What next?"

"Sssshhhh," Shep warned. "Let's go up to the room and call Danny and Regan."

"Now you're talking!" Maddy paused. "But why?"

"I want to see if Regan Reilly can trace a license plate number."

"She's a smart girl. I'm sure she can make a few phone calls. If only she didn't have that boyfriend. . . ."

But Shep was already hurrying toward the back door to the hotel. Maddy slipped into her flip-flops and raced to keep up with him.

51

Coffee in hand, Regan went to her room and called the police to tell them Elsa had returned. She chatted for a few minutes with the desk sergeant and told him she was a private investigator working on Danny's show.

"You're doing security for a reality show?" he asked. "I've watched a few of those on TV. Some of those contestants are real nuts. If you need any help, give us a call," he offered.

"Thanks." Regan went back to Danny's room and told him about the cot in Barney and Elsa's room.

Danny couldn't help but laugh. "Those two have a cot in their room?"

"A cot."

"That is definitely weird."

"That's what I thought. Barney specifically told me that he was holding Elsa tight last night and that she must have slipped out of his arms. But I don't believe him. I think they're faking their love for each other."

"A cot," Danny repeated.

"A cot. My friend Bernadette Castro will be sorry it wasn't one of her pull-out couches."

Danny chuckled. "Regan, all I have to do is make it through Friday. You know how many of those reality show couples break up after ten minutes? The guy picks the girl or the girl picks the guy, and they're supposed to get married and live happily ever after. It rarely happens! If Barney and Elsa are chosen to renew their vows and then go their separate ways, well, so what? I just want Roscoe to choose our show, and I want to make it a good show. If one of the contestants wants to sleep on a cot, then so be it."

"I'm telling you, Danny, there's something more going on here. If he hadn't told me about holding her tight, I would just have thought it was certainly weird they had a cot, but I could have accepted it."

"Lucy and Ricky Ricardo slept in twin beds," Danny reminded her.

Regan smiled. "Back then you weren't allowed to show a couple on television in the same bed. And there had to be a rug on the floor between them."

"Times have changed."

"No kidding."

"I just wish I knew their Social Security numbers."

"Forget it, Regan. Roscoe won't let us ask for any more information. These are my contestants, and I have to work with them. And, please, I don't want to tell Agony or Heartburn about the cot situation. If for some reason I lose them this week, I don't want them blabbing about Barney and Elsa."

"Lose them?"

"I just hope Heartburn's ex is out spending my parents' money right now and keeps her mouth shut about Heartburn's delinquency with the alimony payments."

Regan sat down on the couch. "I wonder how long it's going to take Elsa to sober up."

Danny looked at his watch. "She can nap at the studio. But we've got to leave soon."

The phone rang. Danny picked it up. "Hello. . . . Oh, hi, Dad. . . . What? Are you sure? I don't want to make any waves. . . . Okay, here's Regan." Danny handed her the phone. "My father has a license plate number he wants you to check out."

Regan held the phone to her ear. "Hi, Mr. Madley. . . . Oh, okay, Shep. . . . Sure. . . . Uh huh. . . ." Regan reached for the pad and pen next to the phone. "I'll call it in. Thanks. We'll let you know. Bye."

"Can you believe it?" Danny asked when Regan hung up. "My parents can't help themselves! They just can't stay out of other people's business!"

"Danny, this might be important." Regan called her new friend at the police station and asked him to run the plate.

"Sure. I'll call you back with that."

A few minutes later the phone rang again. The sergeant told Regan that the car was registered to the Parker Organization.

Regan's eyes widened. "The Parker Organization? Would that be Roscoe Parker's organization?"

"It would. He owns a number of small businesses around the city."

"Would he own the 7's Heaven Hotel by any chance?"

"I believe he does. I think he owns the 7's Hotel and the Fuzzy Dice. That's where you are, right?"

"Right."

"He likes to give his businesses memorable names. Hot Air Cable. Fuzzy Dice Hotel. If something has an unusual name, Roscoe probably owns it."

"Thanks, sergeant. You've been very helpful." Regan hung up.

"Well?" Danny asked.

"He owns this hotel and the 7's."

Danny shrugged. "That's not so unusual. He's having us stay in these places because he gives himself a good rate."

Regan smiled. "But he never told you he owned this hotel."

"No. Maybe he was embarrassed. This isn't exactly the Ritz."

Regan's cell phone rang. She looked at the caller ID. "Now it's my mother calling. . . . Hi, Mom."

"We're in the car with Harry and Linda and are headed to their house. Is everything all right?"

"Yes." Regan decided she couldn't go into detail with her mother right now.

"Well, your father found an article in the in-flight magazine about the couple who own the wedding cake balloon."

"Oh, really?"

"Yes. Did you know it's their debut flight on Friday morning?"

"No, I didn't."

"Well, it is. I don't like the idea of your going up in it."

"It's okay, Mom. We'll be careful," Regan promised. "Hold on a second." She quickly told Danny about the article.

"I don't know them," Danny admitted.

"How did you find out about the balloon?"

"When I suggested the winning couple renew their vows in a balloon, Roscoe said he knew of a couple who had a new wedding cake balloon. He arranged for us to go up with them. I don't even know their names."

"Mom, what are their names?" Regan asked.

"Oh, wait till you get a load of this." Nora laughed. "Randy Jupiter and Alice Mars Jupiter."

"You're kidding."

"No. Well, dear, I just wanted to check in. You're breaking up. We'll talk again soon."

"Okay. Bye, Mom." Regan hung up. "That's interesting. Both of our parents checking in and all roads lead to Roscoe."

There was a knock at the door. Danny got up, crossed the living room, and answered it. Barney and Elsa were standing there, smiling. Elsa was clinging to a water bottle.

"Elsa feels much better now," Barney stated.

"I feel much better."

Regan thought she looked much better, relatively speaking. She had obviously washed her hair, and the clothes she was wearing looked as if she'd actually gotten them off a hanger.

"Well, then, let's go. We have a lot to do at the studio and then we have to get ready for dinner at Roscoe's tonight," Danny reminded them.

"I can't wait." Elsa giggled.

Me, either, Regan thought.

———◆———

52

Erene sat at her desk, feeling paralyzed. How could she have made such a stupid mistake? Even though her office with its majestic view of the mountains was climate controlled, Erene was sweating under her khaki-colored linen business suit. Her heart was beating rapidly, and her mind was racing. She felt things were out of her control, a feeling that she detested.

How had she gotten into this mess? Working for Roscoe doesn't suit my personality, she tried to convince herself. Las Vegas does not suit my personality. Leo does not suit my personality. There's nothing I can do, she thought with despair. Nothing. Well, maybe something. I can update my resume. Erene opened her personal file on the computer.

She sighed deeply and assessed her situation. I need to be in a place where people value forms and surveys and conduct their affairs in a businesslike manner. A place where research is taken seriously. I don't want to be criticized for quoting surveys.

Erene looked around her office and realized there was a lot she liked about working for Roscoe. I like my corner office with the beige carpeting and southwestern art and soothing sand-colored furniture. I like the private plane and flexible hours and dinners at the mansion. I don't want to leave. But Roscoe's going to have a fit when he finds out I messed up. It wouldn't do any good to tell him now. Who knows? she pondered. Maybe in some crazy way things will work out for the best.

"Am I interrupting you?" Leo sauntered into her office without waiting for an answer. His Hawaiian shirt looked so cheerful and his drawstring pants so casual. For the life of her, Erene couldn't imagine going to work dressed like that. The only clothes she owned that could be considered free and easy were her pajamas.

Erene started gnawing on her finger. "Not at all. What's up?"

"What if this whole plan falls on its face?" Leo asked her.

"What do you mean?" she asked, nearly removing the tip of her index finger.

"You know what I mean. Do you think this is all going to work out the way we hoped?"

Erene shrugged. She felt terribly alone.

"Maybe we all got too ambitious." Leo ran his fingers through his hair. "And Roscoe is going to blame us if everything falls apart. I'm thinking of updating my resume. Have you given any thought to that?"

"Leo," Erene began as her stomach dropped to the level of her sensible business pumps. "We committed ourselves to this venture with Roscoe. Let's do our best to make it work. Next week we can decide whether it's worth sticking around."

"If he still wants us."

"If he still wants us. Who knows?" she added lightly. "Maybe by next week we'll be famous."

"Let's hope for the right reasons," Leo posited. "I'm afraid the publicity we get won't be very good."

"Reporters keep calling," Erene acknowledged, trying to sound upbeat. "They all want to interview Roscoe about this competition. He certainly has the local media interested."

"But he doesn't want to talk to any reporters whatsoever until Friday when he makes his announcement."

"A newspaper guy even called my house late last night," Erene complained.

"That's annoying. Why didn't you screen the call?"

"I was on the phone with my best friend. The call waiting beeped, and I figured it had to be Roscoe, so I answered it." She laughed lightly. "I got rid of him fast."

"That's good. Because by Friday night, press will be swarming this place."

"That's what I'm afraid of," Erene admitted quietly.

53

Tuesday was quite a day for the dueling shows.

Roscoe had insisted that the *Take Me Higher* writers give juicy parts to "these nice young folks." The cast had taken several breaks while Noel and Neil, with the help of Bubbles, worked to fit two more people into the script. Grandma, her boyfriend Hal, James, and Pilot Pete spent most of the day sitting outside in lawn chairs sipping iced tea. Pete kept checking his messages in Los Angeles, praying there were new auditions on the horizon. The rest of the time the costume designer had the cast trying on various outfits, including the heavy eighteenth-century clothing they'd wear for the opening scene in the farmer's field.

Kimberly and Jake, still in their wedding clothes, roamed the grounds of the Balloon Channel complex with great interest. They quickly learned that many of the buildings were off limits.

"You're not allowed near there," James warned as they headed toward the *Love Above Sea Level* building. "That's enemy territory."

"You call it enemy territory?" Kimberly asked with surprise.

"That's what it is," Pete said. "It's them against us."

"Do you know much about their show?" Jake asked.

"Reality TV," James sniffed. "Something about couples renewing their wedding vows."

"Wow!" Jake cried. "Maybe we could be on that show, too!"

"We could renew our vows, like, within a couple of days of getting married," Kimberly giggled. "How cool is that?" She and Jake gave each other a little kiss.

Pilot Pete and James stared at them.

"Just kidding," Kimberly assured them. "We're actors. We know firsthand how unhappy actors are about all these reality shows. We don't want any part of them."

Give me a break, Pilot Pete thought. These two were so young. They had plenty more auditions in their future. If this didn't work out, so what? They'd get in their car and drive back to Los Angeles with a good story to tell.

Meanwhile, inside the *Love Above Sea Level* studio, the Rorschach tests were proving disastrous from the standpoint of future harmony.

Where Suzette saw pom-poms, Bill saw scraggly bushes.

Where Chip saw an oriental rug, Vicky saw a bedspread.

Where Elsa saw a roulette wheel, Barney saw a pizza pie.

Regan had gone into a private room to call Danny's parents to tell them about the mysterious car's registration.

"Roscoe Parker owns the hotel?" Shep exclaimed, unable to hide his surprise.

"Roscoe owns the hotel?" Maddy echoed. She was leaning in to listen while Shep held the phone. "Sounds strange to me."

"Yes," Regan agreed. "He owns the hotel we're staying at as well."

"I'm telling you, Regan," Shep insisted, "the way that maid handed over the box, she was being very secretive. She didn't want anybody to see what was going on."

Regan thought of the maid in her room, the short blond woman with the Chap Stick. "What did the maid look like?"

"She had on a maid's uniform. I think it was gray."

"Uh-huh," Regan murmured, hoping for more information.

"I think she was stocky with blond hair. I was kind of far away."

Sounds like my maid Regan reflected. Could the maid have arranged for someone to come to pick up the box? she wondered. Is that what happened to Agony's sack of mail? The maid worked for Roscoe Parker. Regan thought of something else. The camera and the sack of mail were both stolen on the premises of establishments owned by Roscoe.

"Regan," Maddy cried excitedly. "This maid is probably guilty, huh?"

"I didn't say that, Maddy. And, anyway, guilty of what?"

"But you asked what she looked like."

"That's because I was thinking of the maid in my room today. She was stocky with blond hair, although she's definitely not a natural blond. It's silly, but she was using a Cherry Chap Stick, and there was a Cherry Chap Stick on the floor of your room when the security guard and I took a peek in there last night."

"That Chap Stick wasn't there when we checked in!" Maddy declared. "I know it wasn't. Whoever took the sack of Agony's mail was using that Cherry Chap Stick!"

"Are you sure the Chap Stick wasn't there when you first got there?" Regan asked.

"Positive. I've stayed in a lot of hotels, and I always inspect the room the minute I walk in to make sure it's good and clean. Ever since the time I accidentally stepped on a pile of someone's toenail clippings next to the bed. It was gross, let me tell you. I was in my bare feet. After that happened, I became a little phobic about the whole thing. I would have noticed that Chap Stick!"

Thank you for sharing, Regan thought.

Shep grunted. He'd heard that toenail

story at least a thousand times. "Maddy, please," was all he could say.

"I just wanted Regan to know why I'm so sure the Chap Stick wasn't there when we arrived."

"I believe you," Regan assured Maddy. She could just picture Maddy on a witness stand telling this tale.

"We'll keep our eyes open," Maddy declared emphatically. "We'll call you if anything else seems suspicious."

"Please do." Regan hung up the phone and reflected on the fishy goings-on. What did it all mean? A cot in a couple's room, a mysterious Cherry Chap Stick, a maid making a drop-off, and a missing sack of mail. Not to mention the stolen camera and the threatening letter.

Regan sighed and went back into the studio where a mini-kitchen was set up. The smell of sautéing onions filled the air. Heartburn was teaching the couples how to make his famous chili.

"A couple that cooks together usually eats together," he proclaimed.

One would think, Regan mused.

"And a couple that eats together has the opportunity to communicate," Heartburn continued as he sprinkled spices into the sizzling pan, looking very relaxed. He was clearly in his element. Much more so than when he was trying to give advice, Regan noticed. What a surprise.

"Sometimes Barney likes to watch the telly when we eat dinner. Is that okay?" Elsa asked.

The telly? Regan wondered. She's still a little tipsy.

"As long as it's a program you both enjoy, that's fine. Now after you sauté the onions, you brown the meat. . . ."

Regan looked at her watch impatiently and realized they had a few more hours before the whistle blew and they could go back to the hotel to freshen up for Roscoe's dinner party. She couldn't wait to talk to Roscoe Parker. Up close and personal. And, for that matter, everyone else involved in this competition.

54

"Everything looks perfect," Kitty assured Roscoe.

"You think so, baby?"

"I do."

They were sitting in the gazebo sipping cocktails. The yard was positively festive. Torches were ready to be lit. The large grill was waiting for the hot dogs and hamburgers to be tossed over the coals. Tables were decorated with red-and-white-checked tablecloths and set with colorful dishes. A bartender was busy at his post preparing pitchers of piña coladas. A campfire had been set up on one side of the yard, surrounded by a wide circle of rocks. Roscoe planned to end the night around the campfire with everyone roasting marshmallows and enjoying a storytelling session that he planned to lead.

Roscoe sipped his single malt scotch and looked around at the grounds admiringly. He felt like the king of Las Vegas. He was dressed in his best blue jeans with a string tie and his favorite cowboy hat. The cologne he was wearing came from an expensive bottle with a picture of a cowboy and a carved silver top. Roscoe lit a Cuban cigar and took an appreciative puff. There was nothing he liked better than the feeling of power. Tonight he had tremendous power over everyone who was convening at his home. They all wanted to please him. All except that Regan Reilly.

Kitty had rested most of the morning, and read, and then primped for hours. She was now fully made up, with her long curly hair stylishly full and exotic. She was wearing a bright flowered long skirt and a white ruffled blouse. "This is my favorite time of day," she told Roscoe.

"My favorite time of day is the crack of dawn when I can fly in my balloon."

Crack of dawn, Kitty thought. An expression she'd come to hate.

Roscoe's cell phone rang. "Roscoe

Parker," he answered importantly. "Erene, where are you? . . . Well, I'm glad to hear you're on your way. . . . What's that? . . . I know the press is after me. They'll hear from me Friday night. . . . Nothing's going to leak out. See you. Bye." He snapped his phone closed. "Erene is such a worrywart." He laughed.

Kimberly and Jake had come out of the house and were standing near the gazebo, looking around in awe and sipping piña coladas.

"Sit down with us," Roscoe insisted. "Tell us about your rehearsal today."

"Surrrrre," Jake answered as they took seats at the large round table. He looked freshly scrubbed. He had big brown eyes and laughed easily.

"Do your parents know yet that you two went and got hitched?" Roscoe asked.

Kimberly and Jake quickly looked at each other.

"No," they answered in unison. "Not yet!" Kimberly giggled.

Roscoe pushed his cell phone toward them, then pulled the cigar out of his mouth. "Why don't you call them right now? I'd love to hear you tell them about your wedding and your acting job. That would make me very happy."

Kimberly made a funny face. "Oh, I don't know. I'm a little scared to call my parents right now. We were thinking that we would tell them in person."

"Where do they live?" Roscoe asked.

"Iowa."

"When do you plan to tell them?"

"They're coming out for Thanksgiving, I think."

"So you plan to wait a while. What about you, Jake? Are you afraid to call your parents, too?"

"My dad would tell me I'm too young. And today's my Mom's birthday. I don't want to ruin it for her."

"So call and say happy birthday."

"Oh, thanks, Roscoe, but actually they went away for my mom's birthday."

"Where did they go?"

"It's a surprise. My dad wouldn't tell anyone."

"Where do they live?"

"Baltimore."

"Good crab cakes there. Hard to get around here."

"Totally," Jake agreed, quickly changing

the subject. "I think Noel and Neil are really trying to write us good parts."

"They'd better," Roscoe exclaimed.

"Bubbles is sooooo driven," Kimberly said, her eyes widening. "This is some competition, huh?"

Roscoe smiled. "It's the survival of the fittest."

"Just like the show *Survivor,* huh?" Jake remarked.

Roscoe took a swig of his scotch. "Something like that."

55

After they got back to the Fuzzy Dice Hotel, Regan went up to her room to get ready for the evening. She had about an hour and a half free and decided to take a bath. The tub was a good place to relax and think.

The hotel bathtub was nothing to brag about, but at least it held enough comforting warm water for Regan to enjoy a good soak. She turned on the faucets, filled the tub as high as she dared, and then gingerly stepped in. It was just the right temperature. Resting her head back against a scrunched-up towel, Regan closed her eyes. It felt a little like she was floating. Like in a hot air balloon, she thought.

Reviewing the events of the day, Regan

was grateful that there had been no thefts, threatening letters, or people falling on the floor. She was also grateful that Elsa came back safely. Maddy and Shep's report of mysterious goings-on at the 7's Hotel was the new glitch.

Regan thought about the three couples on Danny's show. She didn't trust any of them. Barney and Elsa were certainly getting the lion's share of the attention. Were they for real? The dramatic way Elsa straggled back today and the condition she was in. Barney seeming so ecstatic to see her. And why did she use the word "telly"? That was a British word. There was something else she said today. What was it? Regan couldn't remember.

Chip and Vicky looked more like brother and sister than husband and wife. They were both tall and dark-haired, and their faces were similar. He was a character, though—an outdoorsman. Today when they doled out bowls of Heartburn's famous chili, Chip took his serving and walked over to a quiet corner of the studio. He was about to take a seat on the floor, but one dirty look from Vicky and he straightened up. I guess he can't help himself, Regan thought. He'd rather be camping.

And then there were Suzette and Bill. Suzette seemed a little crazed today, clearly unhappy with her fellow contestants Barney and Elsa. When the group came outside the studio to ride back to the hotel, Suzette ran into the field to do a few cartwheels. "It's the way I relieve stress," she explained. "There are few things that excite me as much as the sight of acres of grass. It's like a big gymnasium to me." Skinny Bill tried to look happy as his wife proceeded to do three back flips in a row. "Can you imagine how lucky I am," he sputtered, "to have a wife in her forties who can throw her body around like a teenager?"

Sam recorded it all.

Maybe Suzette and Chip would be better suited to each other, Regan thought. The ground beckons them both.

Next, Regan considered Aunt Agony and Uncle Heartburn. They had spent the day smiling and cajoling the contestants. Would anyone try to bribe them? Regan wondered. She thought it was unlikely. Agony and Heartburn have enough to hide. The last thing they need is for the world to learn they took a bribe from contestants on the show.

The contestants on *Love Above Sea Level* are all vying for the same prize, and naturally it's causing a lot of stress. Tonight we meet the big competition—the sitcom crowd. I wonder how that will play out. Roscoe must love this, Regan realized.

The phone in the bedroom rang. Regan groaned. Nothing worse than getting out of the tub before you're psychologically prepared. It figures that this hotel wouldn't have phones in the bathroom. She stood up and grabbed a towel, wrapped it around herself, hurried into the bedroom, and grabbed the phone. "Hello."

"Regan, it's your Aunt Agony."

My Aunt Agony, Regan thought. That's a good one. "Hi, there," she replied as she dripped on the floor.

"I have some bad news," Agony announced solemnly. "Heartburn and I are going to have to quit the show."

"What are you talking about?"

"Someone slipped a threatening note under our door."

Here we go, Regan thought.

"It said that if we go on with this show, there will be trouble in our future."

"What kind of trouble?"

"It doesn't say."

"It doesn't mention Heartburn's problems?"

"No."

"Agony, there's going to be trouble in your future if you don't go through with the show."

"Why?"

"Because you'll create more suspicion by suddenly dropping out. Because you've made a commitment to Danny. Because the media exposure is supposed to help you and Heartburn book more public appearances that will enable you to pay back Danny's parents. Let me ask you something."

"What?"

"Would you stop writing your column if someone said you'd have trouble if you continued giving advice?"

"Lord, no."

"This is no different. You can't back out. This is very important to Danny. He didn't want to say anything, but yesterday he received a threatening note. Someone

doesn't want *Love Above Sea Level* to succeed. And whoever it is is trying to scare
people."

"Danny got a threatening note, too?"
Agony asked.

"Yes."

"Oh, good. That makes me feel so much
better."

This from an advice columnist, Regan
thought. "I'll stop by and pick up the note in
a few minutes. I'd like to compare it to the
one Danny received," Regan explained.
"Have you talked to him?"

"His line is busy."

"I'll let him know."

"Thank you, Regan. You give such good
advice. Maybe we should have you help us
pick the winning couple."

"That's okay. We'll leave that to you two.
After all, you're the experts." Regan's voice
croaked out those last few words.

When she hung up the phone, Regan
stood in place for a minute. Who is sending
these notes? she wondered. Instinct told
her it wasn't Roscoe. He wouldn't do anything to make one of the shows collapse en-
tirely.

Could it be the trusty adviser Victor or

surfer Sam? She intended to keep a close eye on them both tonight. And on the sitcom crew. Who knew what they could be plotting?

56

Bubbles checked her image in the mirror. I look pretty good, she thought. She was dressed in black leather pants and a rust top that looked terrific with her red hair. The tough, acerbic demeanor she portrayed on-stage came through a little too much in real life, and she did her best to try to soften it. These days it wasn't easy. She'd just gotten off the phone with her boyfriend. He'd left another note.

"I don't know whether it'll do any good," he cautioned.

"I just wish you knew why they had that meeting this morning in Danny's room."

"I told you. They kicked us out. I have no idea."

As Bubbles left her room to join the others

in the lobby, James was coming down the hall, looking especially chipper. His clothes were still of the drab and depressing variety, but there was something about his expression.

"You look happy," Bubbles remarked.

"I love parties."

"Me, too," Bubbles muttered.

Downstairs, the *Take Me Higher* group gathered.

"This is getting to feel like a tour group," Pilot Pete remarked. "I went on one of those group vacations once and absolutely hated it."

"You're an actor," Grandma scolded. "You should have used the opportunity to observe human nature."

"I've had enough of human nature," Pete told her. "And I've won plenty of acting awards. I know my craft."

"You've won awards?" James asked with awe. "Which ones?"

"They were back when I was in college," Pete replied curtly. "Have you won any acting awards?" he asked dismissively.

"No, I haven't," James replied. "But I have my fingers crossed." He held up his hand with, sure enough, two fingers wrapped around each other. "My teacher told me I have what it takes."

"Let's not quibble, please," Bubbles requested. "Let's put on a united front for Roscoe. We have to show him that we're the ones who will put on a good program, week in and week out. He has to recognize that we're easy to work with."

Grandma waved her hand. "I've worked with some of the biggest jerks in Hollywood. It gets on your nerves. This group seems as if it'd be pretty good as a unit, all things considered."

"Thanks, Grandma," Bubbles said wryly. "Now let's get going." As the group walked out to the van, Pete leaned over and whispered in Bubbles's ear. "When we get there, are you going to tell me which guy is your boyfriend?"

Bubbles shuddered. Pete's breath was hot, and the tone of his voice was positively creepy. She looked up at him. He was grinning down at her like a maniac.

"He's not going to be there," she lied.

"I don't believe you," Pete countered. Then he started laughing that horror movie laugh. *"Wha ha ha ha ha.* I don't believe you for one minute. *Wha ha ha."*

If this show doesn't work out, I'm quitting the business, Bubbles promised herself. Either that or I'll lose my mind.

"Wha ha ha ha," Pete continued as he took his seat in the van.

"What's so funny?" Grandma demanded.

"Bubbles. She cracks me up."

"You sound like you're cracking up," Grandma observed.

Not before Friday, Bubbles prayed. Please. Not before Friday.

57

Regan rang the bell of Danny's suite. As soon as he answered, Danny could tell by the expression on Regan's face that all was not well.

"What now?" he asked.

"You look like you're the young Hollywood producer ready for lunch at Spago's," Regan replied, ignoring his question and noticing his khaki pants and blue blazer.

"I'll be lucky if I can afford to eat at the hot dog stand on the corner when this is all through," Danny answered. "Tell me what's wrong."

"Heartburn and Agony got a threatening note under their door."

Danny threw up his hands. "What?!"

"Agony threatened to quit the show, but I

talked her into staying." She pulled the note out of her purse.

"I knew there was a reason I hired you, Regan," Danny said appreciatively as he took the note from her and unfolded it. "It's different handwriting from the last one."

"I know, but it's similar. They're both on plain white paper. This one is big black lettering. The last one was big red lettering. They both have a lot of exclamation points."

Danny read aloud:

Dear Agony and Heartburn,
There will be trouble in your future
if you continue with *Love Above Sea*
***Level!!!* Quit now!!!**

"Well," Danny noted. "It gets to the point."

"I've got to tell you something, Danny. I have my suspicions that this is the work of either Victor or Sam."

"Why?"

"You called me because you thought there was someone working for you who was trying to sabotage the show. Those two have the most access. Neither one of them wanted to leave today when your parents and Agony and Heartburn were in the room.

They both knew something was up. Whoever wrote the note probably thought it was
a safe bet to target Agony and Heartburn.
They also knew which room they were in."

"Roscoe does own this hotel," Danny reminded Regan.

"I don't think he'd try to completely ruin
your show. If Agony and Heartburn quit,
what would you do? The show couldn't
go on."

"So what do we do?"

"Just be careful. We'll go to Roscoe's and
mingle and watch everybody."

"Well, at least there's nothing new from
my mother this afternoon," Danny remarked
as he folded up the letter and handed it
back to Regan.

"She has the whole evening ahead of her."

Danny laughed. "Thanks, Regan. Something else for me to worry about."

58

The two Balloon Channel vans pulled up, one behind the other, in Roscoe's driveway. The driver of the first vehicle, which held Bubbles and the gang, pressed in a code, and the gates swung open. The vehicles continued to the end of a long driveway and came to a halt.

Both groups got out and looked at one another warily.

Bubbles and Danny, the only two who knew one another, walked toward each other to shake hands.

"Hello, Bubbles." Danny put out his hand.

"Hello, Danny."

No other introductions were made. Everyone meandered to the backyard where country music was playing softly from several speakers. The two groups stayed far apart, just like the Hatfields and McCoys.

"Greetings," Roscoe cried as he jumped up from his seat in the gazebo and ran over to join his guests. "Team A and Team B are here together!"

"Who's Team A and who's Team B?" Bubbles asked.

"I haven't decided yet," he said jovially. "But I want you all to meet one another. We need to break the ice. Grab a drink and come sit around the campfire. I'd like everyone to introduce themselves."

Danny got Regan a glass of wine, and they walked together to the "campsite." They sat down on the rocks, and Regan looked around at all the others. Chip looked absolutely thrilled. He was sitting on the ground, and it was actually encouraged. He should apply for a job with Roscoe after this competition, Regan thought.

It was a beautiful desert evening. The sky was streaked with color, and the air was crisp and clear. If it weren't for the circumstances, this could be a great party, Regan thought. She wished Jack were there. For a lot of reasons. He could certainly help her scope things out.

"Now," Roscoe began, standing in the center of the group near the unlit campfire. "We're going to go around the circle and introduce ourselves, first names only, and then tell everyone what the heck you're doing here." He laughed. "I am Roscoe, and I'm looking forward to a great show on Friday night."

"I'm Kitty, and I'm a friend of Roscoe's."

"I'm Kimberly, and me and my brand-new husband, Jake, met Roscoe and Kitty this morning on the balloon, and he invited us to be on his sitcom. It's so amazing!"

"And I'm Jake."

New additions to the sitcom, Regan observed. Interesting.

"I'm Erene, and I work for Roscoe."

"I'm Leo, and I work for Roscoe."

This is like a bad group therapy session, Regan thought. No one's offering much information. When it was Regan's turn to introduce herself she offered, "I'm Regan, and I'm a friend of Danny's."

"A friend?" Roscoe repeated questioningly, his eyebrows raised.

"Yes. A friend."

"It's good to have friends," Roscoe commented.

Regan took particular interest as those who worked on the sitcom introduced themselves. Bubbles and Pete were the two she had seen the other night at the bar. What was her plan? Regan wondered. Could Bubbles possibly be in cahoots with someone from our group? Like Victor or Sam?

When the introductions were finished, Roscoe cleared his throat and looked around at everyone. "Well, that was easy. I just wanted to get you started. Now enjoy the party." He turned toward Regan and Danny. "Why don't you come and sit with me and Kitty for a few minutes?"

"Sure," Danny said, accepting the invitation.

They went over to the gazebo, and the new young couple joined them. "Are we invited?" Kimberly asked.

"Take a load off," Roscoe said.

"You two got lucky, huh?" Regan commented.

"Yes."

"Where do you live?"

"Los Angeles," Jake answered quickly.

"Can you believe these two are only twenty-one?" Roscoe asked.

No, Regan thought. They look older than that. I know actors lie about their age, but these two are mid-twenties at the very least. Maybe from a distance they look twenty-one.

"They just got married last night at the Graceland Wedding Chapel."

"You did?" Regan asked. "Congratulations."

"Thank you," they both murmured.

"And now you have an acting job."

"Yes."

"Married life is getting off to a good start."

"It is," Kimberly agreed. "What do you do, Regan?"

There is just something about the way she said that, Regan observed. It didn't sound quite as casual as she might have intended.

"I've done a lot of different kinds of work," she answered honestly. "Now I'm really interested in the whole reality show business."

"She's helping me out," Danny piped up.

"Roscoe, you certainly have a lot going on," Regan commented.

"I'm interested in a lot of different things. Problem is, I get bored easily. So I'm always onto something new."

"What kind of things are you interested in?"

"You name it."

Regan realized that he was not about to open up.

Roscoe turned to Kitty. "I think we'd better say hello to some of our other guests."

"Yes, let's mingle," Kitty agreed.

They got up and left. Just like that. They walked over to Erene and Leo who were standing together.

"How's your show going?" Jake asked Danny.

"Just fine."

"We hear you're picking a couple to renew their vows. That's so great."

Regan wanted to get a look inside the house. "If you'll excuse me, I'll be right back."

"Sure, Regan."

Regan asked one of the caterers where the ladies' room was and wandered into the large kitchen and down a hallway. She passed a wood-paneled den with red leather furniture that had a lot of pictures hanging on the wall. She paused and stepped inside. It was quiet and dimly lit. Gazing up, Regan saw Roscoe posing with a host of celebrities: Liberace, Merv Griffin, Wayne Newton, Alan Funt, Desi Arnaz, Dean Martin, Chevy Chase, Rita Rudner, Jerry Seinfeld, Céline Dion. As a matter of fact, the only pictures of Roscoe not posing with a celebrity were ones of him waving from a balloon.

"Do you like my photo collection?" a voice behind Regan asked.

Regan spun around. Roscoe was standing in the doorway. "They're fun. You certainly get around."

"And you're a curious girl. I can tell."

Regan smiled. "Like you, I'm interested in a lot of different things."

"A good way to be."

"I think so." Regan nodded in agreement.

"I love surprises," Roscoe said.

"Surprises?"

"Yes." Roscoe sipped his scotch. "I love it when I surprise people. I hate for things to get boring."

"Right." Regan nodded again.

"I hear you needed to use the ladies' room."

"Yes, I do."

"It's right down the hall and around the corner here."

"Thank you."

Roscoe remained in the doorway.

He's trying to psyche me out. And I'm not going to let him. "Thank you so much for having us here tonight. Could I get by, please?" Regan asked sweetly.

"Of course. See you outside." He turned and left.

Regan sighed. She walked out of the room toward the bathroom. The wallpaper in the hallway was gold striped with ornate sconces every few feet. It felt a tad overdone. When she rounded the corner, Victor was standing there.

"Hi, Regan," he said.

"Hi. You waiting for the bathroom?"

"Yes. I think there are a lot more of them around here, but this is the one the bartender told me to use."

The bathroom door opened, and out came Bubbles. "Hello," she said quickly to Regan as she passed. Victor went into the bathroom and shut the door. Regan leaned against the wall, and two seconds later Sam appeared. Very interesting, Regan thought. Victor and Sam and Bubbles.

"This place is something, isn't it?" Sam asked.

"It sure is." Regan glanced over at the bookshelf hanging on the wall outside the bathroom. On it were six books. They were all written by her mother. A chill ran through Regan's body.

Outside, the hot dogs and hamburgers were sizzling on the grill.

"Come and get it," Roscoe cried.

Salad trimmings were spread out on a large buffet table. Everyone helped themselves and found places at smaller tables on the patio. Not surprisingly, there wasn't a lot of mingling between Team A and Team B. But Danny and Regan sat with Erene and Leo and Bubbles and James.

"This is such fun, isn't it?" Bubbles said when she sat down with her plate.

Now there's an actress for you, Regan thought. Nobody here is having a good time. Erene, for one, seemed extremely nervous to Regan. What was her problem? Questioning her and Leo about Roscoe and their work proved absolutely fruitless. They refused to talk about Hot Air Cable.

When the dinner was finished, Roscoe handed out carved sticks to everyone.

"These are for your marshmallows," he explained. Once again he invited everyone to gather around the campfire, which still hadn't been lit. First there was a speech to hear from Roscoe. James rushed out from the house. "Wait for me," he yelled, looking for an empty place.

"Sit over there," Roscoe ordered. "Between Suzette and Elsa."

"Okay." James squeezed into the small space between the two women. "Excuse me," he said as his arm brushed Suzette. "Pardon." He almost fell into Elsa's lap.

"I love ballooning," Roscoe began. "I like the freedom—I hate to be confined—and the adventure. I wanted both teams here to use ballooning in their shows so you could share that freedom and adventure with our viewers. And I want to say that I know you've both been very creative in the way you've done it." He raised his glass. "To both teams."

They all raised their glasses. "Hear! Hear!"

"And no matter how it all turns out," Roscoe continued, "I hope you all will look back on this week with pure pleasure."

Yeah, right, Regan thought. Too many of these people's lives are going to be greatly

affected by the outcome this Friday. This is
not all fun and games. You might be onto
me, Roscoe Parker, but I'm onto you, too. I
just need a little more information.

Luke and Nora were enjoying cocktails with Harry and Linda on their spacious deck facing the snow-covered mountains. The home, decorated in pastel tones with over-stuffed couches and chairs, had a real southwestern feel. The large floor-to-ceiling windows brought the desert and mountains inside. It was where Linda had lived until she met Harry ten years ago. Now they spent most of their time in New York but came to Santa Fe as often as possible.

"This is so wonderful," Nora said, sighing.

Linda was a petite blond in her late forties. "I love to paint here," she said as she cut a piece of cheese, placed it on a cracker, and handed it to Nora. "It's so peaceful."

Harry had salt-and-pepper hair and was

in his mid-fifties. "It's a great place to read manuscripts."

"Regan and Jack should visit Santa Fe, don't you think, Luke?" Nora asked.

Luke laughed. "Nora, you think Regan and Jack should go everywhere."

"Well, they should. They're perfect together. She's met enough Mr. Wrongs along the way. She's finally found the right one."

"When Harry and I met, I'd reached the point where I was sure I'd be single forever," Linda said.

"You're so lucky," Harry said with a smile as he reached over and helped himself to a piece of cheese.

Linda shook her head and laughed. "So are you, pal."

"I know that."

"Nora would love to plan a wedding," Luke said.

"Luke!"

"It's true, isn't it? I'm telling you. If Regan marries Jack, Nora will invite my two kidnappers and make them guests of honor."

"Aren't they still in jail?" Harry asked.

"We'll get them a dispensation for the day," Luke said and laughed.

Nora smiled. "Very funny. All I want is for Regan to be happy and safe."

"I hope we get to see her on Friday," Linda said.

"Well, that's the plan. They'll be here Friday morning."

"Ballooning with Mars and Jupiter," Luke drawled.

"I can't wait to see that balloon," Linda said enthusiastically. "I'm telling you, it's quite a spectacle when all the special shape balloons ascend into the morning sky. People bring their kids. The place is a madhouse. It's a lot of fun." She jumped up. "May I refresh your drinks?"

Harry looked at his watch. "We should probably get going. Our dinner reservation is at eight, and the restaurants are pretty crowded this week with the writer's conference and the balloon festival."

They drove into town to Linda and Harry's favorite Italian restaurant. The restaurant was simple yet elegant with white stucco walls, votive candles on the tables, and gleaming wood floors. It was crowded but not too noisy. A corner table was reserved for them.

As they sat down, the always observant

Nora turned to Luke and whispered, "Are those the Jupiters?"

"What?"

"The hot air balloon couple in the magazine. At the next table."

Luke turned and looked at the middle-aged couple. "I think it is."

Alice Jupiter glanced back at them.

"We read about you today in the airline magazine," Nora called over. "Our daughter is going up in your balloon on Friday morning with the reality show."

"Ohhhhh," they both said, smiling and nodding. "Is she one of the contestants?" Randy Jupiter asked.

Nora almost passed out at the thought. "No. She's working with the producer."

"Roscoe Parker?"

"No. Danny Madley."

"That's good. Because that Roscoe Parker is a very unstable man," Alice said, waving her hand.

"Unstable?" Nora repeated with dismay.

"He wanted us to try to scare the passengers."

"Scare the passengers?"

"Yes. He asked us to pretend the balloon was out of control. A video camera will be recording everything, and he wanted to catch the passengers' reactions on tape."

"Oh, dear God." Nora put her hand on Luke's arm.

"Oh, but don't worry," Alice Mars Jupiter said brightly. "We told him 'no way.' My husband and I are both very responsible pilots. We'll both be up in the balloon to make sure everything goes smoothly."

"Thank you." Nora sank into her chair. Suddenly she didn't feel like eating.

"We'll be at the balloon field Friday morning," Linda told Alice.

"Great. Come by when we're setting up. We're going to be smack in the middle of the field. The fiesta organizers think our balloon is going to get a load of attention."

That's what I'm afraid of, Nora realized. That is just what I'm afraid of.

60

"Good night, all," Roscoe yelled as he and Kitty waved at the departing vans. "See you tomorrow." They turned and headed back into the house, his arm around Kitty's shoulder. It was like a heartwarming scene from an old movie.

The vans pulled out onto the dark, lonely road and headed back to the bright lights of town.

Regan was sitting in the second row of seats, next to Agony and Heartburn.

"Everyone there seemed pretty normal," Agony commented.

Regan looked at her. "You think so?"

Agony shrugged. "What's normal these days? It actually covers a broad range."

"That's for sure," Regan agreed. She

looked out the window, feeling frustrated. She was sure Roscoe had something planned. How could she find out what it was? He said he loves to surprise people. I'll bet. She knew that the collection of her mother's books on that shelf was no coincidence. And something about that young couple who just got married didn't ring true. Running into both Sam and Victor by the bathroom at the exact time Bubbles was using the facilities made her wonder. Could one of them have written the threatening note today?

A thought occurred to Regan. Had anyone checked the website today? She'd be curious to see if there was anything new written about the show. She'd have to ask Danny about that first thing in the morning. He looked tired and worried, and she didn't want to bother him now. She'd let him get a good night's sleep.

The main thing was to keep the production of *Love Above Sea Level* glued together until Friday. Help Danny put on an entertaining show and then go home, Regan thought. But in the meantime, I don't intend to let anyone ruin *Love Above Sea Level.* No matter how hard they try.

Wednesday, October 8

———◆———

61

Early Wednesday morning, Regan went to Danny's suite with a cup of coffee in hand. He had his computer on. They pulled up the Blowing the Lid Off website and found a brief description of the competition between the two shows and pictures of the reality show contestants. They checked the message board to see the comments that people had written in.

"One of those contestants is going to blow. Just you watch."
"Never heard of any of them."
"Elsa needs a new haircut."
"They're all strange."
"I saw Chip and Vicky at a shopping

mall once. They were having a big fight."

"I was on the same cheerleading squad as Suzette in grammar school. She has strong legs!"

"I hope the show makes it to the air. I'd give anything to see Bill lose. He dumped me for Suzette. I'm not surprised his marriage was on the rocks."

"Chip and Vicky were my neighbors when they first got married. He was always sitting in his backyard communing with nature. Weird!"

"Barney looks like a goof. So does Elsa."

Regan read the last message. "Charming comments."

Danny laughed. "I know. Can you imagine? At least there's nothing here that's too bad for our purposes."

"Just that one of the contestants will probably blow," Regan pointed out.

Danny looked weary. "What can we do?" he asked. "Some people have nothing better to do than write nasty messages. They sit at their computer hundreds of miles away, safe in their anonymity."

"I hope you're right, Danny. But I have something else to tell you."

Danny closed his eyes. "What?"

"I talked to my mother this morning."

"And?"

"My parents ran into the couple who own the wedding cake balloon. They said Roscoe wanted them to deliberately scare us when we go up in the balloon on Friday. He asked them to pretend the balloon was out of control. He knew that it would all be on tape."

"Are you kidding?" Danny asked incredulously.

"Nope. I wish I was."

Danny sighed. "I think Roscoe is full of hot air himself. He's nothing but a blowhard. He's like a big dopey kid."

Regan nodded.

"Well, time to get started on day three of *Love Above Sea Level*," Danny noted with obviously more optimism than he felt.

Danny and Regan met the others and set off to Hoover Dam, that marvel of modern engineering that kept the lights of Las Vegas blinking. It was thirty miles away. A picnic lunch had been packed. They walked around in the bright sunshine, went into the visitors center, and ate lunch in a parking lot overlooking the massive curved wall that was the dam. It was an impressive sight. The dam held up to 9.2 trillion gallons of water in Lake Mead, a reservoir created when the dam was constructed in the 1930s. The three couples walked hand in hand across the road that crosses the dam at the top. Sam photographed everyone as they crossed the border into Arizona and stood under a big clock that displayed Arizona time, an hour ahead of Nevada.

"It's important to enjoy nature together," Aunt Agony opined as she grabbed Heartburn's hand and breathed in the clear fresh air.

After a couple of hours they returned to the studio for another round of questions that the spouses answered separately. Today's topic centered on the always controversial topic: money.

"What would you do with the million dollars if you won it?" Agony asked sweetly.

Each contestant seemed to be taken by surprise with the question.

Suzette said start a cheerleading camp; Bill said retire.

Chip said buy a big spread of land; Vicky

said she'd seen some nice new condos that she'd love to own.

Elsa said buy a new house for her mother; Barney said splurge for a few months and then figure it out.

When Agony called the couples back together, her eyes were glistening. "I'm very disappointed," she scolded. "None of you mentioned giving any money to friends in need. After all, a friend in need is a friend indeed. Don't you people have any friends?"

Regan almost laughed out loud at the looks on all their faces. She was sure that all three couples would be spending their private time tonight pondering all the possible questions Agony might ask them tomorrow. Like the finalists in a beauty pageant the couples would be prepared with a statement about doing good for others—no matter what the question.

Regan was relieved when Suzette's and Bill's names were drawn from the hat for the evening's dream date. Suzette wouldn't have been happy if she and Bill had to wait another night. Back to Carlotta's they went. Suzette seemed to be basking in the undivided attention she and Bill were finally receiving from Agony and Heartburn.

"When Bill and I first got together," she said lovingly over shrimp cocktails, "it was at a high school dance. The band was playing 'Bridge Over Troubled Water,' and Bill came over and asked me to dance. I was so nervous. It was a slow dance. But the minute Bill put his arms around me, I felt safe. That has always been our song." Suzette closed her eyes. "And I've felt safe ever since."

Bill was buttering a piece of bread, nodding his head in agreement.

"Whenever we have trouble, we play that song and dance in our living room. It brings us back to that magical night," Suzette continued, her eyes now open and brimming with tears.

"Do you feel that?" Agony asked Bill.

Bill's mouth was stuffed with the warm, delicious Italian bread.

"Absolutely," he tried to say.

Suzette winced. "Dear," she reprimanded lightly. "Don't talk with your mouth full."

"That's healthy," Agony said, nodding her head in approval. "That you can correct your spouse in front of other people and he doesn't freak out. When Heartburn and I first met, I always had to tell him to stop talking with his mouth full. Problem was, he was always in the kitchen cooking, constantly testing the food." She laughed. "So his mouth was always full. Right, dear?"

Sitting on the sidelines, Regan thought longingly of PBS.

62

The sitcom group had filmed their opening bit in the balloon at dawn, with the rooster, sheep, and lamb. They had only one take to get it right. Bubbles, Pete, and James were in the balloon that landed in the field. Grandma, Hal, Kimberly, and Jake, reenacting the terror of the farmers in France two hundred years ago, came running out with their pitchforks to stop the aliens from invading their farm.

Much to Bubbles's relief, the shoot went well. The rooster never shut up, which made the piece very funny. It would be a great opener for the show. She and her crew returned to the studio to rehearse the final script. Kimberly and Jake were playing a young couple, recently married, who stopped by the family ballooning company to sign up for a sunset ride. After much gnashing of teeth, Noel and Neil had come up with this concept.

"Truth is stranger than fiction," Noel said to Neil. "We may as well use it."

"You're right, man."

James was still a terrible actor, but there was a glimmer of humor coming through in his line readings. One line he delivered was actually funny. Give him fifty years, and he could actually learn to act, Bubbles thought. She went to bed Wednesday night feeling better than she had in at least a week.

Maddy and Shep spent the day hanging around the 7's Hotel, waiting for something to happen. To Maddy's dismay, all was quiet. No secret dropoffs, no burglaries, nothing. Finally she and Shep went up to the Strip for a little excitement. They had dinner, walked around, and came back.

"Do you think we can go home tomorrow?" Shep implored Maddy.

"No. Danny needs us."

♦ ♦ ♦

Honey had a show to do Wednesday night. She'd spent most of the day at Alex's salon.

"For the hundredth time, I have everything," Alex assured her. "Don't worry."

When Honey got home from work at 1 A.M., she set her alarm and tried to sleep. They had to be at the studio at noon. But she had a restless night.

She had a terrible premonition that something was going to go wrong.

Thursday, October 9

63

At 11:45 A.M. on Thursday, Danny made an announcement to his group. They were in the studio. "We're going to be doing something special this afternoon."

"What's that?" Vicky asked excitedly.

"Makeovers."

"Makeovers?" they all murmured.

"You think we need makeovers?" Elsa was clearly insulted.

"Well," Danny said, struggling for the right words. "Not exactly makeovers. We have a hairdresser and a makeup artist who are going to style your hair and apply your makeup. They'll give you tips on how to do it yourself—if you'd like, of course."

"I'm not shaving my mustache," Barney grumbled.

"That's okay. You can do what you want."

Regan stepped in for Danny. "We thought this would be fun. You're all going to be getting dressed up before we get on the plane to Albuquerque tomorrow morning. If you've never had a makeover, you'll find it a treat. Most women like to have their hair styled."

"Not me," Elsa declared vehemently. "No one is touching my hair."

You've got to be kidding, Regan thought.

"Barney loves my hair this way. Right, Barney?"

"I love it!"

"That's fine, Elsa. You can have your makeup done if you like."

"All right."

"I think this sounds great," Vicky said. "I think my hair can use a trim."

"Good," Regan answered. "They'll be arriving in a few minutes."

"There's not much you can do with my hair," Bill complained, touching his red wisps. "I haven't got much left. And I've never worn makeup, and I never will."

"Maybe the hairdresser can give you a little trim as well then," Regan suggested, trying not to sound exasperated.

"Relax for a few minutes, everybody," Danny urged. "We'll work it out when they get here."

Victor appeared in the doorway. "They're here."

"Here goes nothing," Danny said quietly to Regan. They walked out to greet the beauty crew in the reception area.

"Honey," Danny said stiffly, walking toward his former girlfriend.

"Hi, Danny," she said in a little voice as he kissed her cheek. She had on a pair of tight pants, a sleeveless top, and high heels. Her hair and makeup were perfect. When Honey saw Regan, she looked crestfallen.

"I'm Regan Reilly," Regan said quickly, extending her hand to Honey. "I'm working on the show with Danny."

Honey looked somewhat relieved. "Danny and Regan, this is Alex, the best hairdresser in Vegas, and Ellen, our favorite makeup artist."

Alex looked like an aging punk rocker, and Ellen appeared to be in her early twenties. She wore no makeup and was moving her body to music only she could hear. Headphones clung to her skull. She pulled them off. "Hello."

"Where are our victims?" Alex asked.

"We'll bring you to them," Danny replied nervously.

Regan noticed that Danny couldn't take his eyes off Honey as they helped gather up the several black cases of makeup and beauty-making paraphernalia. He still has a thing for her, she thought. They all walked in silence back down the hallway into the studio.

Honey took one look at Elsa, and her face lit up. "Hi!" she said warmly. "I remember you! You were in the casino the other night!"

Barney rushed over to Honey. "Please," he said to Honey quietly. "That was a very bad night for my wife. Just don't mention it."

"Okay, okay." Honey glanced nervously at Danny. She looked as if she was going to cry. "I didn't mean to upset her."

"Honey," Regan interrupted. "Let me show you the dressing room where you can set up. There are big mirrors and lots of counter space."

"Faboo," Alex said.

Honey walked next to Regan. "I didn't mean anything."

"It's all right. Where did you see her?"

"At the Bellagio the other night. It was about three in the morning. She was sitting in the lobby reading a book and underlining stuff."

"She was? Are you sure?"

"I'm positive. My friend Lucille and I passed through there a couple of times. We thought it was strange that someone was sitting in a lobby in Vegas at that hour reading—with a big highlighting marker, no less. And how can you forget that hairdo of hers?"

"That's very interesting, Honey," Regan said.

"I thought so."

For the next few hours the cameras recorded the transformation of the contestants. Suzette and Vicky both had their hair cut and then swept up into elegant chignons. Ellen deftly applied makeup that made both women look sophisticated and infinitely more attractive.

"I'll just take a little rouge," Elsa insisted, closing her eyes and wincing. She wouldn't let Alex touch her hair.

The men had their hair trimmed, which took about three minutes each.

When they were finished, Agony exclaimed, "This is wonderful. Our contestants all look their absolute best. How are we to choose, Heartburn?" she asked dramatically. "These three couples all deserve to renew their vows and win a million dollars."

"It will be a tough, tough decision," Heartburn agreed.

"Cut!" Danny yelled. "Thanks so much, Alex, Ellen, and Honey. I think this is a great addition to *Love Above Sea Level.*"

"You'll be sure to mention my salon?" Alex asked.

"More than once," Danny promised.

Regan noticed that Honey looked bereft as she prepared to leave. She pulled Danny aside. "Why don't you invite them to the screening tomorrow afternoon?"

Danny looked at Regan and didn't say anything.

"Sometimes having too much pride can be foolish, Danny. She's crazy about you."

"All right, all right," he muttered. He went back to the group who were packing up the endless brushes and combs, and cans and tubes and bottles. "If you people want to come to the screening tomorrow afternoon, it should be kind of fun. That's when Roscoe will decide if our show or the sitcom will air."

"I'd love to," Honey replied quickly. "What time?"

"Five o'clock at the Balloon Channel. I hope you all can make it." Danny waved good-bye and walked out of the room.

"Mission accomplished, darling." Alex air-kissed Honey as she burst into tears.

64

"I feel pretty . . ." Suzette sang, twirling around the studio.

"Sweetheart, please don't do a cartwheel," Bill requested. "Your hair looks great that way."

"I'm tempted, but I won't."

"You all look gorgeous," Agony proclaimed yet again.

"Three fine-looking couples," Heartburn agreed.

Danny came back into the room.

"The makeovers were a wonderful idea, Danny," Agony observed. "It's given us all a little lift."

"That's great. I'm so glad." Danny looked at his watch. "It's three o'clock now. I think we're going to call it a day. I have to meet with the editors who will be getting the show ready tonight. When we get back from Albuquerque tomorrow, they'll splice in the final scene from the balloon fiesta."

Regan could feel almost a collective inhalation of breaths.

"Hard to believe, isn't it?" Danny asked no one in particular.

Yes, Regan thought.

"Tonight we have Elsa and Barney's dream date. The rest of you are free until three A.M. when we meet in the lobby for the flight to Albuquerque."

"Three A.M.?" Heartburn repeated with a frown.

"Three A.M.," Danny confirmed. "We'll drive over to the studio complex to board Roscoe's plane. It's about an hour's flight. We have a stretch limo to take us from the airport in Albuquerque out to the balloon field. We want to be there before the sun rises."

"Maybe we won't go to bed," Vicky said. "I don't want to ruin my hair and makeup."

"You look so beautiful, we should go dancing. Dance the night away until it's time to fly away," Chip said tenderly.

I'm going to gag, Regan thought.

"Do whatever you want," Danny told them. "Just be in the lobby at three A.M., dressed in whatever you think is appropriate for renewing your vows."

"Except," Regan chimed in, "the women should not wear long dresses. When the balloon lands, we'll all be tumbling out of the basket."

"And the winners will have a million-dollar check in their hands!" Agony cried.

Suzette ran to do a cartwheel but stopped herself. "I almost lost my head." She laughed.

It's getting to be that otherworldly time, Regan thought. The time when these six realize how drastically their lives could change within the next twenty-four hours. When imaginations start going wild at the thought of having a million dollars minus taxes in hand. Who will be the lucky two? she wondered.

65

They made it an early dinner with Elsa and Barney. Everyone wanted to get back early because the wake-up calls were going to be coming in at an ungodly hour. At Carlotta's the maitre d' was once again thrilled to see Danny and his compatriots.

"I have a special table for you," he joked as he led them to the private room upstairs.

Elsa seemed very interested in Agony and Heartburn's life as advice columnists. "That must make you feel so good," she said. "To know that you're helping people."

"Oh, yes," Agony exclaimed. "It's a wonderful feeling."

"Is your column on the Internet?" Elsa asked.

"Yes, it is," Heartburn answered as he sniffed his red wine.

"I'll have to look for it there."

Why not look in the newspaper? Regan wondered. Agony and Heartburn had a ways to go to build their reputation, but they were certainly known in this area. She thought that Elsa and Barney lived in Nevada.

When they got back to the hotel, it was ten o'clock. Regan went directly to her room and was so happy to peel off her clothes and put on a T-shirt. She washed her face, brushed her teeth, and fell back onto the bed. She then reached for the phone and ordered a wake-up call. An automated voice confirmed that Regan would be called at 2 A.M.

The voice doesn't even sound surprised, Regan chuckled to herself. Now what else before I turn out the light? Charge the cell phone. At that second it began to ring. She leaned over, grabbed her purse from the dresser, and fumbled for her phone. Finally she felt it and pulled it out.

"Hello."

"So you're not out rolling dice?" Jack teased.

Regan smiled contentedly and lay back down on the bed. "One more day! Hey, it's late in New York. You're still up."

"I couldn't sleep. And I was thinking about how much better tomorrow night will be than tonight. As long as you don't fall in love with Uncle Heartburn or one of the contestants before then."

Regan laughed. "I don't think there's much chance of that. To think, though, that by tomorrow night I'll have been to Albuquerque and back, and then on to Los Angeles."

The teasing note left Jack's voice. "Hey, what time are you going to Albuquerque?"

"We're meeting in the lobby at three A.M."

"Three?"

"Three."

"In that case I'll let you get some sleep. I don't want you to be totally zonked tomorrow night."

"Something tells me I won't be."

"Something tells me you won't be, either." Jack laughed. "At least I hope not."

Friday, October 10

———◆———

66

When the phone rang, Regan was stunned out of her slumber. In a complete fog she picked up the receiver.

"Hello," the same automated voice from the night before said. "This is your wake-up call. Good morning. It is now two o'clock. The temperature outside is—"

Regan dropped the phone back in its cradle. This is worse than I imagined it would be. Bleary-eyed, she got out of bed and hurried to turn on the shower. It was the only way to get her body moving. The shower didn't make Regan feel as good as it did at, say, 7 or 8 A.M., but it certainly helped. Regan washed her hair, stepped out, dried off, and turned on the hair dryer. She was sure it was going to wake the dead. Why do hair dryers sound so much louder in the middle of the night? she wondered.

Regan knew it was cold out there on these October ballooning mornings. Or at least she heard it was. When she looked at what she had to wear, she decided on a pair of jeans, a lavender polo shirt, and a long-sleeved sweater. She'd carry a quilted cotton jacket. Layering was big with balloonists, or so she'd been told. She wasn't going to be on camera, so she didn't have to dress for the occasion.

When she saw the couples assembled in the lobby, they all looked as if they were going to a wedding. The three women had on cocktail dresses, and their husbands were wearing suits and ties. Despite their attempt to look festive, no one seemed happy. The tension among the couples was palpable.

"I didn't wash my makeup off last night," Suzette told Regan. "It looked so great, I thought it would last through the balloon ride."

"Me, too," Elsa said, grabbing Suzette's hand a little too hard.

But you had only "a little rouge," Regan remembered. She then looked over at Vicky.

It was obvious that her face also hadn't been near running water since before the makeovers.

Victor, Sam, and Danny were all sporting blue jeans. Good, Regan thought. I'm not underdressed for the Big Day.

Victor had arranged for a large pot of coffee to be available to them in the lobby. There were even little mini-doughnuts.

"You're a prince," Regan told him fervently as she poured herself a large cup of java.

Victor turned to her and smiled a genuine smile. "Thank you, Regan. It's going to be a long day. We may as well get the caffeine going."

A few minutes later the group piled into the van and drove down the Strip. The neon lights were still blinking, and people were walking around as if it were midday.

That's Vegas, Regan thought. It really is 24/7. She suddenly thought of what Honey had said about Elsa sitting at the Bellagio and reading a book at three in the morning. Could Honey have been mistaken? Regan glanced over at Elsa who was staring straight ahead.

They rode in silence, eventually passing

the main entrance of the Balloon Channel complex on their way to a private road that led to the airstrip. The parking lot of the complex was dark, but there were a number of cars parked there. I wonder what's going on, Regan thought.

They boarded Roscoe's plane, which seated twenty people. Regan sat with Danny toward the front. The pilot closed the door, locked it, and they took off into the night. It felt as if they were off on some secret mission.

Agony and Heartburn had taken seats together in the back. Regan wondered if they'd made up their minds yet about who would win.

When they landed, a white stretch limousine met them on the tarmac. Reminds me of prom night, Regan thought as the three couples in their dressy clothes got in. The others followed. It was still dark as the limo drove out of the airport and onto the highway. When the driver took the exit for the balloon field, the traffic started to get heavy. Their limo had a special pass that gave them access to the parking lot closest to the balloon field. When they were dropped off next to one of the entrance gates, the sun was just appearing on the horizon, and the air was calm but nippy.

"Look at all this!" Elsa cried.

The massive field was filled with people spreading out their balloons' envelopes, preparing them for inflation. Danny took out a small piece of paper from his pocket and checked it. He pointed. "They're supposed to be over this way."

The *Love Above Sea Level* group followed, taking in the sights as Sam recorded everything. All the special-shaped balloons would soon be springing to life. On the ground was everything from colorful cartoon characters to monsters to witches.

The Jupiters were in the field, as excited as can be. Reporters from the local news stations were already there with television cameras, anxious for an interview with Danny and Aunt Agony and Uncle Heartburn. The "wedding cake" was laid out on the ground, ready for inflation.

"We hear you're doing a reality show," the newscasters said to Danny.

"Yes." Danny smiled, pleased that this might actually be a reality. As Danny answered the reporters' questions, Regan looked around. Her parents and Harry and

Linda were making their way over. She hurried to them, excited to see familiar faces.

"Regan!" Nora cried. "There you are!"

"Hi, Mom, Dad." Regan hugged her parents. "Harry, Linda, it's so good to see you."

"We wouldn't miss this."

"But we're not going to get to see you for long," Nora said with a sigh.

"I know. I wish we could stay after the balloon ride. But we have to get back to Vegas so they can edit the footage from the fiesta. And something tells me that once the winners are announced, the other contestants aren't going to be too interested in sticking around."

"Do you have any idea who's going to win?" Harry asked.

Regan rolled her eyes. "I haven't a clue."

"Regan, you look tired," Nora said with concern.

"Getting up at two in the morning will do that to you. But I'll be fine," Regan insisted.

A few minutes later Danny came over. "Remember me?" he asked Luke and Nora jokingly as he was introduced to Harry and Linda.

"I remember you," Nora said fondly. "How are your parents?"

"The same," Danny answered with a smile.

Luke shook his hand. "Give them our best."

Victor called over to Danny. "We're getting started. They want us to go up first."

"Okay."

"Regan, be careful," Nora urged as Danny's group moved closer to the balloon. The fan was on, and a powerful stream of air was being pumped into the wedding cake. It was incredible to watch the balloon begin to take shape and slowly come to life. The crew members were in their positions, holding ropes on either side of the envelope to help spread it out evenly while inflating. Finally, Randy used the blast valve on the burner, and a column of flame shot twenty feet in the air and into the balloon. Fully inflated, the wedding cake stood eight stories high. The balloon was covered with roses, and a formal bride and groom stood on top. It was ready for action.

One by one the passengers were helped into the basket. The three female contestants now had on sneakers with their cocktail dresses. Sam was getting a shot of their feet. Once inside the basket, Regan looked over at Nora, who was trying to smile but had that worried look on her face. As ordered by Randy, one by one the crew let go of the basket, and the cake started to rise. It seemed as though all eyes at the fiesta were on them.

This really is a kick, Regan marveled as she looked down. Throngs of people were waving up at them and smiling. Some were taking pictures. Other balloons were getting ready to lift off. Within seconds the people below looked smaller and smaller as the balloon floated higher and higher into the air.

Moving like a cloud, they were all silent. For most of them, this was their first time in a balloon. There was no question it was a magical feeling they were all experiencing. Even if there was a lot of tension in the group.

"Here we are," Agony said as they drifted along. Regan was standing next to her. Sam was focusing the camera on Agony.

"That's right," Danny chimed in. "Here we are. And I think it's about that time."

Agony looked at Heartburn for dramatic effect. She pulled a check out of the pocket of her old-fashioned granny dress. The check was folded in half. She held it up.

Regan glanced at the three couples, all of whom couldn't take their eyes off the check. "Heartburn and I had a very rough decision to make," Agony continued. "All three couples here have worked very hard to rekindle the spark they once felt. Sometimes life can get a little boring, and when it does, we may think our mate is boring. That's a mistake—most of the time, I hope." She laughed lightly. "We have to work to keep the spark burning, just like our pilot here has to know when to spark the flames to keep this balloon going—"

"Agony, this is only a half hour show," Danny joked.

Everyone laughed nervously as they climbed higher and higher.

Regan looked down and was startled to see how far away the ground looked.

"Okay, okay. Well, Heartburn and I have decided that the couple who has not only worked hard to make their marriage work but who has seemed destined to stay together no matter what happens to them are none other than"—she opened the check, paused, looked at them all, made sure she was looking straight at the camera, and then dramatically announced—"Barney and Elsa Schmidt."

Regan turned to look at Barney and Elsa to congratulate them. The next few moments went by in a blur. Suzette's body stiffened, and she charged toward Agony with a fire in her eyes that looked like it was from one of the bulls running in Pamplona.

"No!" Suzette screamed. In an instant she lifted Agony up in the air by her ankles, as if she were giving a boost to a fellow cheerleader, and started to throw her into a back flip over the side of the balloon basket. Agony howled as her tiny body went flying backward. Regan lunged forward and caught Agony's knees before she went completely overboard. Dangling out of the basket, Agony screamed bloody murder as Regan struggled to get a good grip and hang onto her.

"*Aaaaghhhhhhh,*" Agony cried, her arms flailing. The check fluttered from her hand and drifted earthward. Danny and Heartburn wrestled Suzette to the floor as Regan used all her strength to hold onto Agony's skinny legs. Suzette was still struggling violently, still trying to get to Agony. Bill was in shock, unable to move. Victor and Chip surged forward, and the balloon tilted on its side. Victor positioned himself behind Regan, who was hanging over the basket. Regan felt as if she were straining every muscle in her body. Victor reached over the basket and managed to grab one of Agony's arms. Together, he and Regan pulled her to safety as they fell back into the basket. As they did so, Agony's left elbow socked Regan squarely in the eye.

"Back to your places!" Randy screamed. "If this burner gets lopsided, it'll burn a hole in the mouth of the balloon."

"I knew you were going to pick them!" Suzette screamed. *"We never had a chance!"*

"Emergency landing! Emergency landing!" Alice Jupiter radioed to the chase crew. "Notify the police."

"Are you crazy?" Bill suddenly started screaming at Suzette, whose arms were being held behind her back by Danny and Victor.

Agony dissolved into Regan's arms and was shivering violently. She wouldn't let go of Regan, even to be held by Heartburn. Regan thought she felt like a little bird.

"You saved my life, Regan." Agony's breath came in short, harsh gasps.

"You're okay now," Regan assured her. She blinked and could feel her eye closing from the impact of the blow. Regan's heart was beating rapidly.

Randy started to bring the balloon down as Suzette sceamed uncontrollably.

Everyone was in absolute shock as they clung to the sides of the basket.

"Bend your knees everyone," Randy ordered. "And hang on while we land."

Danny and Victor had to let go of Suzette. When the basket hit the ground and tumbled on its side, not far downfield from where they took off, Suzette hurriedly crawled out and took off. Regan crawled out, ran after her, and tackled her to the ground.

Screaming like a madwoman, Suzette pushed Regan off and started to get up. Regan lunged for her and managed to tackle her again, then dug her knees into Suzette's back. With all her might, Regan struggled to keep the crazy cheerleader down on the ground.

A police car pulled onto the field, sirens blaring and lights flashing. The officers jumped out and cuffed Suzette as Danny ran to help Regan to her feet.

As Regan tried to catch her breath, she put her hand up over her eye, which was throbbing. "I think we now know which contestant has the violent tendencies," she deadpanned.

"I think it's a safe bet." Danny's voice was shaky.

Nora and Luke and Harry and Linda came running toward them.

"Regan!" Nora cried.

"Mom, I'm okay."

"I had a bad feeling about this . . ." Nora hugged Regan tightly. "Then when I saw that basket tipping like that . . ."

Bill was crying, talking to one of the officers, as Suzette was ushered into the back of the police car. "She didn't mean to hurt anyone. She's just very competitive. It dates back to her first cheerleading competition."

"At least Agony and Heartburn didn't pick those two. That definitely would have been the wrong choice," Regan said, still struggling to catch her breath. "But I bet dollars to doughnuts they turn up on another reality show."

"Regan. Your father and I are going back

to Vegas with you," Nora said emphatically. "We'll fly home from there tonight or tomorrow. Right now I can't let you out of my sight."

"Sure," Regan agreed, happy to have the company. She laughed wryly. "And two seats just opened up on the plane."

67

On the plane ride back to Vegas, Regan held an ice pack to her eye, which was slowly starting to bruise. Aunt Agony kept coming over to fuss. She wanted to sit next to Regan, but Nora wasn't about to give up that spot. Nora was staying close to her only child. The image of that tilting balloon and a figure hanging out of it was still too fresh in her mind. Luke was across the aisle, watching his wife and daughter with concern.

Suzette's meltdown was all anyone was talking about.

"I'm just grateful we didn't give her the million bucks," Agony said. "We might never have known what a nut she is."

"Now we know," Regan replied. "And at

least she's safely behind bars before she really hurts somebody. People with violent tempers explode eventually," she muttered as she adjusted the ice pack.

"Like the website warned us," Danny commented.

Danny had phoned ahead to inform Roscoe what happened. The story had already made the local morning news in Albuquerque and would probably be on the national broadcasts by the time the evening news rolled around.

Roscoe had expressed his concern even though it secretly delighted him. He could just smell the ratings.

"Regan's parents are with us," Danny told Roscoe. "They're coming to the screening today. I'd like to invite my parents as well."

"The more the merrier," Roscoe insisted.

"By the way," Danny said. "You'll have to cancel the check and issue a new one. It floated away when Agony did her back flip."

"No problem," Roscoe insisted. When he hung up the phone, he was practically salivating.

Chip and Vicky were not as disappointed as they would have been if things had gone as planned in the wedding cake balloon.

They had spoken to their parents and checked their messages at home. An agent had already left his name and number and asked them to call him back about a book deal.

Barney and Elsa were, of course, in ecstasy. Their arms were wrapped around each other the whole flight.

When they arrived in Vegas, Danny went straight to the editing room. Luke and Nora went with Regan to the Fuzzy Dice Hotel.

"Let's go someplace else for lunch," Nora pleaded as soon as she got a look at the place.

"Fine with me," Regan agreed.

68

At five o'clock sharp all the interested parties gathered in the screening room of the Balloon Channel complex. Everyone from the sitcom and the reality show was there as well as several of Roscoe's employees whom Regan had never seen before. Nora and Luke were sitting with Danny's parents. Regan was sitting in the front row with Danny. She noticed Honey sitting by herself in the back and invited her to sit with them. Danny sat between the two women. Also in the front row were Bubbles, Pilot Pete, James, Kitty, and Roscoe.

Roscoe walked onto the stage and welcomed everyone. For the grand finale of the competition he had chosen to wear his custom-made burgundy leather jacket, silver-buckled belt, polished butter-soft leather boots, and one of his favorite string ties. "This has been an interesting week. We are all anxious to view both shows, so let's not waste any more time. We'll start with *Take Me Higher.*" He signaled to the technician in the control booth who lowered the lights as he took his seat next to Kitty.

Soft music filled the room. Onto the screen flashed the words *Take Me Higher.* A voice-over began: "Hot air ballooning has been around for years, but it hasn't always been safe in the air or on the ground. As a matter of fact, whenever you land, there's a very good chance you're trespassing. . . ." The screen showed a montage of the actors in the balloon, dressed in period clothing, landing in a field and offering champagne to farmers who were about to attack them with pitchforks.

"Suzette would have been perfect as one of the farmers," Regan whispered to Danny. And come to think of it, what happened to our champagne this morning? she wondered. If anyone deserved champagne, it was *moi.*

The montage was amusing, and so was the sitcom. But James was positively dreadful. People tried to laugh at his jokes out of politeness, but his presence in a scene was disastrous. He was stiff and spoke in a monotone. Regan glanced over at Bubbles. Her face was tense, and she was gripping the arms of her chair. Pilot Pete was wringing his hands. The screen faded to black, and the audience applauded.

Next up was *Love Above Sea Level.*

Danny's voice boomed out of the sound system as the show opened with a shot of the faux hot air balloon outside the Paris Hotel. "Welcome to *Love Above Sea Level,* where three couples compete to renew their vows in a hot air balloon, on a ride that's sure to be unforgettable. . . ."

Danny leaned over to Regan. "That part was taped before this morning's adventures," he whispered.

Regan smiled. The show was actually good. It captured the fun parts of the week and included the incredible scene on the balloon. Sam, being the consummate professional he was, never put the camera down to help. He recorded every last detail, which made for great drama. Elsa and Barney had done a wrap-up in the studio with Danny, expressing how happy they were to be the winning couple. "All our good luck this week," Elsa gushed. "First winning at the slot machine and then winning the reality show contest. But what makes me luckiest is being married to Barney."

Danny wrapped up the segment with a joke about the check being in the mail, and the program ended with a scene from the special shapes parade—brightly colored balloons of all shapes and sizes floated across the screen.

The audience clapped, and Barney whistled while the lights went up.

Roscoe took the stage again. He paused and smiled. "Could we have that winning couple up here, please?"

Barney and Elsa walked hand in hand up to the stage, beaming.

Roscoe cleared his throat. "You know, everyone, I wanted this contest to be fun. Reality shows are the craze these days, and it's hard to make a new show, reality or sitcom, any different from what has already been on the air. 'What's the twist?' everyone asks. I know you're all waiting for me to announce which show will air tonight and wondering why I'm digressing. Well, I'm digressing because the answer to which show will air tonight is . . ."

Everyone waited.

Roscoe looked around the room, enjoying the drama. "The show I choose is . . . neither!"

A collective gasp went up in the room. *"Neither!"* everyone began to shout at once.

"Wait," Roscoe yelled above the clamor. "You see, all week I've been making my own reality show about your shows competing with each other."

"What?" Bubbles shrieked.

"Yes!" Roscoe cried. "We had hidden cameras in the studios and the public rooms of your hotels. We planned many of the mishaps and recorded your reactions to everything—the mail getting stolen, the camera getting stolen, Elsa winning at the slot machine, and lots more. Wait till you see it. It's a scream. My staff here did a great job working all night, every night, reviewing all the hours and hours of tapes that we had recorded."

"Elsa didn't really win the money at the slot machine?" Danny asked.

"No! We brought in a slot machine that had been used on a movie set. It has nothing but cherries on the reels. We hired someone to sit at it until you got back from the studio. She was a great little actress, wasn't she?" Roscoe asked. "I think she's just joined us."

Little, Regan thought. She turned and saw the woman in the back of the theater. A broad smile on her face, she got up to take a bow.

"But do Elsa and Barney still win the million dollars?" Danny asked heatedly.

"Well, that's something else I want to tell you. James, would you please stand up?"

James obeyed.

"The twist here is . . . Barney, Elsa, and James are not who they appear to be. They are all Shakespearean actors from Stratford, England. Aren't they the best? Elsa and James are actually man and wife. Say hello to Sir Linsley and Lady Lotus."

A melee broke out in the screening room. Pilot Pete leaped from his seat. His arms reached for James's throat. Aunt Agony started screaming about her stolen mail and how she and Heartburn would become a laughingstock for choosing a couple who weren't even married. She ran to the stage and started beating on Roscoe with her little fists. But Pilot Pete was the real danger. He had knocked James to the ground. His fingers were wrapped around James's neck, and he was choking the life out of him.

"Stop it!" Bubbles screamed. "Stop it!"

Regan and Danny both were trying to grab Pilot Pete. Elsa jumped off the stage to tackle Pete. Her wig came off to reveal a short, stylish cut that gave her a whole new look.

Honey was trying to calm Aunt Agony who she thought was going to have a heart attack. Poor Heartburn was still in his seat, stunned and barely able to breathe. The whole day had been too much for him.

"Pete, are you nuts?" Bubbles shrieked as Regan and Danny pulled him away from James who was caressing his well-wrung neck.

"*Am I nuts?*" he screamed, his face beet red and the veins in his temple bulging out. "What about you? You and your boyfriend writing threatening notes to the other team! Here!" he pulled an envelope out of his pocket. You dropped this the other day. You can give it to Sam now!"

"Sam!" Danny repeated in disbelief.

Sam put down the camera and ran out of the building.

Regan noticed that Jake was taking lots of pictures while Kimberly was scribbling notes. They must be reporters, Regan realized. What a surprise.

"Everyone, please!" Roscoe pleaded. "This was supposed to be fun! You'll all still be on the air!"

"You're a fraud, Roscoe!" Danny yelled out to him.

"No, I'm not. I just wanted to create a reality show that people would remember. I thought *Imus in the Morning* might want to have me on his show to talk about it."

"You can talk to Imus from behind bars. Stealing mail is a federal offense. And I'm sure a lot of your other hijinks are illegal, too," Danny snapped.

"I just wanted my show to be a little bit *Candid Camera,* a little bit *Fear Factor,* and a little bit of a mystery. I even thought up clues like creating suspicion with Chap Sticks. All I've ever wanted was to be like Merv Griffin. He's created such great shows!"

"Merv Griffin hates reality shows where

people lie, cheat, and steal to get ahead," Regan informed Roscoe.

"How do you know that?"

"I read his book. I wish you had."

"Lawsuit! Lawsuit!" people started to scream.

Kimberly whipped out her cell phone, no longer playing the part of an ingenue. "I've got a front-page story! Hold the presses!"

Erene slumped in her chair. Kimberly was a reporter. Erene had been afraid of that from the moment Roscoe told her that a young couple showed up at the balloon field the morning after Erene answered her phone with "Roscoe, I told you. The balloon pilot will be ready to take you up tomorrow morning." She was afraid that it had been a reporter on the other end. Oh, well, maybe she'd write a good story. But everyone was screaming about lawsuits. Erene ran over to Roscoe and whispered in his ear.

"Attention," Roscoe cried. "My trusted adviser, Erene, has made a wonderful suggestion. If you all promise to forgive me and not do anything silly like press charges, I will give all of you who worked on the shows from the very beginning and now feel cheated $100,000 each for your pain and suffering. Honestly, I just wanted to create a fun show. I only wanted to make people laugh. . . ."

Suddenly the room was silent.

"I'll take it," Pilot Pete shouted.

"I'll take it."

"I'll take it."

And around the room they went.

Pete, Grandma, her boyfriend, Noel, Neil, Aunt Agony, Uncle Heartburn, Vicky, Chip, and Danny all said they'd take the money.

"I'll take it," Bubbles cried.

"You and Sam tried to ruin our show!" Danny challenged.

"We only wrote a few letters. That was it. Besides, Sam did a great job for you."

"What about the oil on the floor? And the platform collapsing?"

"The platform wasn't anyone's fault," Leo admitted. "It was old. We should have gotten rid of it a long time ago."

"Sam did put the oil on the floor. But then he wiped it up!" Bubbles insisted.

"He didn't do a very thorough job," Regan chimed in. "Because I slipped on it a couple of hours after Barney did."

Barney jumped up. "I saw oil on the floor, so I staged that fall."

"Good job, Barney," Roscoe applauded. "Honest, everyone. I just thought you'd be happy to be involved with a reality show that would end up with a lot of publicity. I still might make you famous. Heck, I was outsmarted by that little couple Jake and Kimberly. I thought they were newlyweds. It turns out they're reporters. You'll be reading about this whole thing very soon."

"Next week's edition of *Worldly Wickedness,*" Kimberly stated proudly. "It hits the stands on Monday."

"It's clear that the actors and crews will accept your offer," Danny told Roscoe. "But Regan should get the money, too."

"Regan Reilly saved my life!" Agony cried. "If I had been killed, Heartburn would have sued you for hundreds of millions."

Heartburn nodded vehemently.

Regan started to protest. "Danny—"

"Regan Reilly gets a hundred thousand, too," Roscoe announced. "And I hope her mother will agree to have lunch with my dear Kitty. Kitty loves your books."

"I'd be happy to," Nora called out.

"Will you take the money, Regan?" Roscoe asked.

"If you insist."

"I do. Good. Now we're bringing in food and drinks and at eight o'clock we can watch my show as it is broadcast over Hot Air Cable. That's about an hour and a half from now. I'm telling you, it's really good. I think you'll all be pleasantly surprised."

There was a spontaneous round of applause. Roscoe looked thrilled.

Regan felt a tap on her shoulder. She turned around and was amazed to see Jack. He looked better than ever.

"That's some shiner you've got there." He tenderly touched the skin around her eye.

"Well, you're certainly a sight for sore eyes," Regan teased. "There's been a lot of excitement today."

"I heard."

"I was about to leave to meet you in Los Angeles," Regan said softly.

"When I found out about the balloon mishap this morning, I flew straight here. I wanted to get to you before anything else happened."

"How did you know?"

"I have my ways. Will you come outside with me for a minute?"

"Sure."

Jack waved a quick hello to a beaming

Luke and Nora as Regan followed him out the door. "We'll be back soon," he promised.

Jack grabbed Regan's hand and started running with her toward the field. "We have to hurry before it gets too dark."

"Where are we going?" In the distance Regan could see the Balloon Channel balloon inflated and ready to fly. "Jack!"

"We won't be gone long."

"I think that one balloon ride this morning filled my quota for today very nicely."

"This time it will be different, I promise. Just you, me, and the pilot."

The ground crew helped Regan and Jack into the basket. Moments later they were floating in the air. The pilot seemed very busy, concentrating on his tasks.

The sky was gorgeous, streaked with red and orange and gold.

Jack and Regan were standing with their arms around each other, staring out at the beauty before them. Jack turned to Regan. "Miss Reilly."

"Yes, Mr. Reilly."

"You take me out of this world."

Regan smiled. "You do the same for me."

"That's why I thought that this would be

an appropriate place to ask you a certain question."

Regan waited. Her heart skipped a beat.

"Regan, will you marry me?"

Tears stung Regan's eyes. "Yes, yes, I will marry you."

Jack reached into his pocket, pulled out a brilliant diamond ring, and slipped it on her finger. "I love you, Regan Reilly. I want to be with you all my life."

"I love you, too."

Jack leaned down and kissed her as the balloon floated gently across the sky.

Down below, Nora and Luke were staring up. This time Nora had a huge smile on her face. "I bet he's popped the question by now," she said.

"Maybe they can have a quickie wedding right here in Vegas," Luke suggested wryly.

"Bite your tongue." Nora laughed. "Regan and I are going to have a grand time planning this wedding."

"The world had better watch out," Luke drawled, "for the two Mrs. Reillys."

When Regan and Jack stepped back inside the auditorium, everyone was holding a glass of champagne. Nora and Luke walked over and handed glasses to them.

"We're so happy." Nora kissed Regan and hugged Jack.

"Word travels fast," Regan commented.

"Jack called your father's cell phone this morning to ask for your hand," Nora explained.

"This morning?"

"Right after we left the balloon field. We told him what happened."

"Talk about timing." Regan laughed.

"That's when I decided to come straight to Vegas," Jack explained, his arm tightening around Regan. "Before I somehow lost you."

Roscoe jumped up on the stage. "A toast to Regan and Jake Reilly."

"Jack Reilly," Regan called out.

"Oh, that's right. Jake's the whippersnapper reporter." Roscoe held out his glass. "To Regan and Jack Reilly. Many years of happiness."

"Hear! Hear!" everyone toasted.

"Two minutes till showtime. Everyone find your seat," Roscoe instructed.

Danny and Honey hurried over to Regan and Jack. They looked like a couple again. Danny had his hand on Honey's back, and she was smiling from ear to ear.

They both congratulated Regan effusively.

As Danny shook Jack's hand, Honey turned to Regan. "Thank you, Regan," she whispered.

"For what?"

"I think you know."

Regan smiled. "I hope you and Danny will come to the wedding."

"Regan, I would love that."

"Sit down, everybody!" Roscoe cried.

The two couples took seats in the front row. Luke and Nora were sitting with Maddy and Shep one row behind them. Maddy was softening toward Honey. The makeovers had really improved Danny's show. The caring way Honey ran onstage to calm Agony made her think that maybe she wouldn't make such a bad daughter-in-law after all. And now that Regan Reilly was definitely out of the running, Maddy decided she'd better be nice to Honey. It was obvious Danny cared about her.

The lights went down, and everyone waited quietly. The screen lit up, and there was Roscoe's smiling face. "Welcome to *Roscoe's Reality Show* where nothing is as it seems."

That's for sure, Regan muttered.

For the next forty-five minutes they watched as the two groups struggled with their shows. Elsa didn't really win at the slots. It was a ruse. "James" had actually won a number of comedy awards. He said that playing the role of a bad actor was more difficult than he had imagined. Elsa had played several femmes fatales onstage in Britain. It was the first time Barney had used crying to define a character.

If Suzette only knew this was a ruse, Regan thought, she'd have pushed everyone out of the balloon. She's probably in a jail cell in Albuquerque right now, hanging off the bars.

In the end, Roscoe's show was funny and clever. The scenes of Bubbles almost losing it with James were priceless. Elsa rolling around on the floor with the slot machine woman had everyone laughing. Regan even laughed at the scene where she and Barney had breakfast together. The expressions on her face were priceless. When the lights went up and people applauded, Roscoe stood. "There's one more thing—we've decided that the Balloon Channel needs you. So Danny and Bubbles, I'm hiring you both to continue producing your shows. Come to my office at nine A.M. tomorrow to sign your contracts."

Pilot Pete jumped in the air. "The curse is broken," he cried. "I'm in a pilot that made it to the small screen!"

"James" stood. "Unfortunately you're going to have to replace me."

Pete slapped him on the back. "That's okay, Sir Linsley. Maybe you can do a guest shot when you come back to town."

"Jolly good."

Danny was beaming. So were his parents.

They were thrilled that he'd have a steady job.

"We'll be on television all the time," Agony joyfully proclaimed.

"You all seem so much happier than when I said I'd give you each a hundred thousand dollars. Does that mean I don't have to pay it?" Roscoe teased.

"No!" they all yelled and laughed. *"Pay up!"*

Roscoe laughed and waved his hands at them. He was having the time of his life. Maybe the television station would make him a big shot after all. "Well, I'm so glad I'll be working with you all. Regan"—he glanced down at her in the front row—"can we convince you and Jack to be part of our team?"

Regan smiled and shook her head. "Thank you, but we have other plans."